to
all the
boys
I've
loved
before

Also by Jenny Han

Shug

The Summer I Turned Pretty

It's Not Summer Without You

We'll Always Have Summer

Cowritten with Siobhan Vivian

Burn for Burn

Fire with Fire

to all the boys I've loved before

JENNY HAN

SIMON & SCHUSTER BFYR

New York   London   Toronto   Sydney   New Delhi

SIMON & SCHUSTER BFYR

An imprint of Simon & Schuster Children's Publishing Division

1230 Avenue of the Americas, New York, New York 10020

This book is a work of fiction. Any references to historical events, real
people, or real places are used fictitiously. Other names, characters, places, and
events are products of the author's imagination, and any resemblance to actual
events or places or persons, living or dead, is entirely coincidental.

SIMON & SCHUSTER BFYR is a trademark of Simon & Schuster, Inc.

For information about special discounts for bulk purchases, please contact Simon & Schuster
Special Sales at 1-866-506-1949 or business@simonandschuster.com.

The Simon & Schuster Speakers Bureau can bring authors to your live event. For
more information or to book an event, contact the Simon & Schuster Speakers Bureau
at 1-866-248-3049 or visit our website at www.simonspeakers.com.

Book design by Lucy Ruth Cummins

The text for this book is set in Bembo Std.

Manufactured in the United States of America

Library of Congress Cataloging-in-Publication Data

Han, Jenny.

To all the boys I've loved before / Jenny Han. — First edition.

pages cm

Summary: "Lara Jean writes love letters to all the boys she has loved and then hides them
in a hatbox until one day those letters are accidentally sent"—Provided by publisher.

ISBN 978-1-4424-2670-2 (hardback) — ISBN 978-1-4424-2672-6 (ebook)

[1. Love—Fiction. 2. Dating (Social customs)—Fiction. 3. Sisters—Fiction.] I. Title.

II. Title: To all the boys I have loved before.

PZ7.H18944To 2014

[Fic]—dc23

2013022311

ISBN 978-1-4814-3895-7 (proprietary hardcover edition)

For my sister, Susan—
Han girls forever

to
all the
boys
I've
loved
before

I like to save things. Not important things like whales or people or the environment. Silly things. Porcelain bells, the kind you get at souvenir shops. Cookie cutters you'll never use, because who needs a cookie in the shape of a foot? Ribbons for my hair. Love letters. Of all the things I save, I guess you could say my love letters are my most prized possession.

I keep my letters in a teal hatbox my mom bought me from a vintage store downtown. They aren't love letters that someone else wrote for me; I don't have any of those. These are ones I've written. There's one for every boy I've ever loved—five in all.

When I write, I hold nothing back. I write like he'll never read it. Because he never will. Every secret thought, every careful observation, everything I've saved up inside me, I put it all in the letter. When I'm done, I seal it, I address it, and then I put it in my teal hatbox.

They're not love letters in the strictest sense of the word. My letters are for when I don't want to be in love anymore. They're for good-bye. Because after I write my letter, I'm no longer consumed by my all-consuming love. I can eat my cereal and not wonder if he likes bananas over his Cheerios too; I can sing along to love songs and not be singing them to him. If love is like a possession, maybe my letters are like my exorcisms. My letters set me free. Or at least they're supposed to.

1

JOSH IS MARGOT'S BOYFRIEND, BUT I GUESS
you could say my whole family is a little in love with him.
It's hard to say who most of all. Before he was Margot's boyfriend, he was just Josh. He was always there. I say always, but
I guess that's not true. He moved next door five years ago
but it feels like always.

My dad loves Josh because he's a boy and my dad is surrounded by girls. I mean it: all day long he is surrounded
by females. My dad is an ob-gyn, and he also happens to be
the father of three daughters, so it's like girls, girls, girls all
day. He also likes Josh because Josh likes comics and he'll go
fishing with him. My dad tried to take us fishing once, and
I cried when my shoes got mud on them, and Margot cried
when her book got wet, and Kitty cried because Kitty was
still practically a baby.

Kitty loves Josh because he'll play cards with her and not
get bored. Or at least pretend to not get bored. They make
deals with each other—if I win this next hand, you have
to make me a toasted crunchy-peanut-butter-sandwich, no
crusts. That's Kitty. Inevitably there won't be crunchy peanut
butter and Josh will say too bad, pick something else. But
then Kitty will wear him down and he'll run out and buy
some, because that's Josh.

If I had to say why Margot loves him, I think maybe I would say it's because we all do.

We are in the living room, Kitty is pasting pictures of dogs to a giant piece of cardboard. There's paper and scraps all around her. Humming to herself, she says, "When Daddy asks me what I want for Christmas, I am just going to say, 'Pick any one of these breeds and we'll be good.'"

Margot and Josh are on the couch; I'm lying on the floor, watching TV. Josh popped a big bowl of popcorn, and I devote myself to it, handfuls and handfuls of it.

A commercial comes on for perfume: a girl is running around the streets of Paris in an orchid-colored halter dress that is thin as tissue paper. What I wouldn't give to be that girl in that tissue-paper dress running around Paris in springtime! I sit up so suddenly I choke on a kernel of popcorn. Between coughs I say, "Margot, let's meet in Paris for my spring break!" I'm already picturing myself twirling with a pistachio macaron in one hand and a raspberry one in the other.

Margot's eyes light up. "Do you think Daddy will let you?"

"Sure, it's culture. He'll have to let me." But it's true that I've never flown by myself before. And also I've never even left the country before. Would Margot meet me at the airport, or would I have to find my own way to the hostel?

Josh must see the sudden worry on my face because he says, "Don't worry. Your dad will definitely let you go if I'm with you."

I brighten. "Yeah! We can stay at hostels and just eat pastries and cheese for all our meals."

JENNY HAN

"We can go to Jim Morrison's grave!" Josh throws in.

"We can go to a *parfumerie* and get our personal scents done!" I cheer, and Josh snorts.

"Um, I'm pretty sure 'getting our scents done' at a *parfumerie* would cost the same as a week's stay at the hostel," he says. He nudges Margot. "Your sister suffers from delusions of grandeur."

"She is the fanciest of the three of us," Margot agrees.

"What about me?" Kitty whimpers.

"You?" I scoff. "You're the *least* fancy Song girl. I have to beg you to wash your feet at night, much less take a shower."

Kitty's face gets pinched and red. "I wasn't talking about that, you dodo bird. I was *talking* about Paris."

Airily, I wave her off. "You're too little to stay at a hostel."

She crawls over to Margot and climbs in her lap, even though she's nine and nine is too big to sit in people's laps. "Margot, you'll let me go, won't you?"

"Maybe it could be a family vacation," Margot says, kissing her cheek. "You and Lara Jean and Daddy could all come."

I frown. That's not at all the Paris trip I was imagining. Over Kitty's head Josh mouths to me, *We'll talk later*, and I give him a discreet thumbs-up.

It's later that night; Josh is long gone. Kitty and our dad are asleep. We are in the kitchen. Margot is at the table on her computer; I am sitting next to her, rolling cookie dough into balls and dropping them in cinnamon and sugar. Snicker-doodles to get back in Kitty's good graces. Earlier, when I went in to say good night, Kitty rolled over and wouldn't speak to me because she's still convinced I'm going to try to cut her out of the Paris trip. My plan is to put the snicker-doodles on a plate right next to her pillow so she wakes up to the smell of fresh-baked cookies.

Margot's being extra quiet, and then, out of nowhere, she looks up from her computer and says, "I broke up with Josh tonight. After dinner."

My cookie-dough ball falls out of my fingers and into the sugar bowl.

"I mean, it was time," she says. Her eyes aren't red-rimmed; she hasn't been crying, I don't think. Her voice is calm and even. Anyone looking at her would think she was fine. Because Margot is always fine, even when she's not.

"I don't see why you had to break up," I say. "Just 'cause you're going to college doesn't mean you have to break up."

"Lara Jean, I'm going to Scotland, not UVA. Saint Andrews is nearly four thousand miles away." She pushes up her glasses. "What would be the point?"

I can't even believe she would say that. "The point is, it's Josh. Josh who loves you more than any boy has ever loved a girl!"

Margot rolls her eyes at this. She thinks I'm being dra-matic, but I'm not. It's true—that's how much Josh loves Margot. He would never so much as look at another girl.

Suddenly she says, "Do you know what Mommy told me once?"

"What?" For a moment I forget all about Josh. Because

no matter what I am doing in life, if Margot and I are in the middle of an argument, if I am about to get hit by a car, I will always stop and listen to a story about Mommy. Any detail, any remembrance that Margot has, I want to have it too. I'm better off than Kitty, though. Kitty doesn't have one memory of Mommy that we haven't given her. We've told her so many stories so many times that they're hers now. "Remember that time . . . ," she'll say. And then she'll tell the story like she was there and not just a little baby.

"She told me to try not to go to college with a boyfriend. She said she didn't want me to be the girl crying on the phone with her boyfriend and saying no to things instead of yes."

Scotland is Margot's yes, I guess. Absently, I scoop up a mound of cookie dough and pop it in my mouth.

"You shouldn't eat raw cookie dough," Margot says.

I ignore her. "Josh would never hold you back from anything. He's not like that. Remember how when you decided to run for student-body president, he was your campaign manager? He's your biggest fan!"

At this, the corners of Margot's mouth turn down, and I get up and fling my arms around her neck. She leans her head back and smiles up at me. "I'm okay," she says, but she isn't, I know she isn't.

"It's not too late, you know. You can go over there right now and tell him you changed your mind."

Margot shakes her head. "It's done, Lara Jean." I release her and she closes her laptop. "When will the first batch be ready? I'm hungry."

I look at the magnetic egg timer on the fridge. "Four more minutes." I sit back down and say, "I don't care what you say, Margot. You guys aren't done. You love him too much."

She shakes her head. "Lara Jean," she begins, in her patient Margot voice, like I am a child and she is a wise old woman of forty-two.

I wave a spoonful of cookie dough under Margot's nose, and she hesitates and then opens her mouth. I feed it to her like a baby. "Wait and see, you and Josh will be back together in a day, maybe two." But even as I'm saying it, I know it's not true. Margot's not the kind of girl to break up and get back together on a whim; once she's decided something, that's it. There's no waffling, no regrets. It's like she said: when she's done, she's just done.

I wish (and this is a thought I've had many, many times, too many times to count) I was more like Margot. Because sometimes it feels like I'll never be done.

Later, after I've washed the dishes and plated the cookies and set them on Kitty's pillow, I go to my room. I don't turn the light on. I go to my window. Josh's light is still on.

2

THE NEXT MORNING, MARGOT IS MAKING
coffee and I am pouring cereal in bowls, and I say the thing
I've been thinking all morning. "Just so you know, Daddy
and Kitty are going to be really upset." When Kitty and I
were brushing our teeth just now, I was tempted to go ahead
and spill the beans, but Kitty was still mad at me from yesterday, so I kept quiet. She didn't even acknowledge my cookies, though I know she ate them because all that was left on
the plate were crumbs.

Margot lets out a heavy sigh. "So I'm supposed to stay
with Josh because of you and Daddy and Kitty?"

"No, I'm just telling you."

"It's not like he would come over here that much once I
was gone, anyway."

I frown. This didn't occur to me, that Josh would stop
coming over because Margot was gone. He was coming over
long before they were ever a couple, so I don't see why he
should stop. "He might," I say. "He really loves Kitty."

She pushes the start button on the coffee machine. I'm
watching her super carefully because Margot's always been the
one to make the coffee and I never have, and now that she's
leaving (only six more days), I'd better know how. With her
back to me she says, "Maybe I won't even mention it to them."

"Um, I think they'll figure it out when he's not at the airport, Gogo." Gogo is my nickname for Margot. As in go-go boots. "How many cups of water did you put in there? And how many spoons of coffee beans?"

"I'll write it all down for you," Margot assures me. "In the notebook."

We keep a house notebook by the fridge. Margot's idea, of course. It has all the important numbers and Daddy's schedule and Kitty's carpool. "Make sure you put in the number for the new dry cleaners," I say.

"Already done." Margot slices a banana for her cereal: each slice is perfectly thin. "And also, Josh wouldn't have come to the airport with us anyway. You know how I feel about sad good-byes." Margot makes a face, like *Ugh, emotions*.

I do know.

When Margot decided to go to college in Scotland, it felt like a betrayal. Even though I knew it was coming, because of course she was going to go to college somewhere far away. And of course she was going to go to college in Scotland and study anthropology, because she is Margot, the girl with the maps and the travel books and the plans. Of course she would leave us one day.

I'm still mad at her, just a little. Just a teeny-tiny bit. Obviously I know it's not her fault. But she's going so far away, and we always said we'd be the Song girls forever. Margot first, me in the middle, and my sister Kitty last. On her birth certificate she is Katherine; to us she is Kitty.

Occasionally we call her Kitten, because that's what I called her when she was born: she looked like a scrawny, hairless kitten.

We are the three Song girls. There used to be four. My mom, Eve Song. Evie to my dad, Mommy to us, Eve to everyone else. Song is, was, my mom's last name. Our last name is Covey—Covey like lovey, not like cove. But the reason we are the Song girls and not the Covey girls is my mom used to say that she was a Song girl for life, and Margot said then we should be too. We all have Song for our middle name, and we look more Song than Covey anyway, more Korean than white. At least Margot and I do; Kitty looks most like Daddy: her hair is light brown like his. People say I look the most like Mommy, but I think Margot does, with her high cheekbones and dark eyes. It's been almost six years now, and sometimes it feels like just yesterday she was here, and sometimes it feels like she never was, only in dreams.

She'd mopped the floors that morning; they were shiny and everything smelled like lemons and clean house. The phone was ringing in the kitchen, she came running in to answer it, and she slipped. She hit her head on the floor, and she was unconscious, but then she woke up and she was fine. That was her lucid interval. That's what they call it. A little while later she said she had a headache, she went to lie down on the couch, and then she didn't wake up.

Margot was the one who found her. She was twelve. She took care of everything: she called 911; she called Daddy; she told me to watch over Kitty, who was only three. I turned on the TV for Kitty in the playroom and I sat with her. That's all I did. I don't know what I would have done if Margot hadn't been there. Even though Margot is only two years older than me, I look up to her more than anybody.

When other adults find out that my dad is a single father of three girls, they shake their heads in admiration, like *How does he do it? How does he ever manage that all by himself?* The answer is Margot. She's been an organizer from the start, everything labeled and scheduled and arranged in neat, even rows.

Margot is a good girl, and I guess Kitty and I have followed her lead. I've never cheated or gotten drunk or smoked a cigarette or even had a boyfriend. We tease Daddy and say how lucky he is that we're all so good, but the truth is, we're the lucky ones. He's a really good dad. And he tries hard. He doesn't always understand us, but he tries, and that's the important thing. We three Song girls have an unspoken pact: to make life as easy as possible for Daddy. But then again, maybe it's not so unspoken, because how many times have I heard Margot say, "Shh, be quiet, Daddy's taking a nap before he has to go back to the hospital," or "Don't bother Daddy with that; do it yourself"?

I've asked Margot what she thinks it would have been like if Mommy hadn't died. Like would we spend more time with our Korean side of the family and not just on Thanksgiving and New Year's Day? Or—

Margot doesn't see the point in wondering. This is our life; there's no use in asking what if. No one could ever give you the answers. I try, I really do, but it's hard for me to accept this way of thinking. I'm always wondering about the what-ifs, about the road not taken.

Daddy and Kitty come downstairs at the same time. Margot pours Daddy a cup of coffee, black, and I pour milk in Kitty's cereal bowl. I push it in front of her, and she turns her head away from me and gets a yogurt out of the fridge. She takes it into the living room to eat in front of the TV. So she's still mad.

"I'm going to go to Costco later today, so you girls make a list for whatever you need," Daddy asks, taking a big sip of coffee. "I think I'll pick up some New York strips for dinner. We can grill out. Should I get one for Josh, too?"

My head whips in Margot's direction. She opens her mouth and closes it. Then she says, "No, just get enough for the four of us, Daddy."

I give her a reproving look, and she ignores me. I've never known Margot to chicken out before, but I suppose in matters of the heart, there's no predicting how a person will or won't behave.

3

SO NOW IT'S THE LAST DAYS OF SUMMER and our last days with Margot. Maybe it's not altogether such a bad thing that she broke up with Josh; this way we have more time with just us sisters. I'm sure she must have thought of that. I'm sure it was part of the plan.

We're driving out of our neighborhood when we see Josh run past. He joined track last year, so now he's always running. Kitty yells his name, but the windows are up, and it's no use anyway—he pretends not to hear. "Turn around," Kitty urges Margot. "Maybe he wants to come with us."

"This is a Song-girls-only day," I tell her.

We spend the rest of the morning at Target, picking up last minute things like Honey Nut Chex mix for the flight and deodorant and hair ties. We let Kitty push the cart so she can do that thing where she gets a running start and then rides the cart like she's pushing a chariot. Margot only lets her do it a couple of times before she makes her stop, though, so as not to annoy other customers.

Next we go back home and make chicken salad with green grapes for lunch and then it's nearly time for Kitty's swim meet. We pack a picnic dinner of ham-and-cheese sandwiches and fruit salad and bring Margot's laptop to watch movies on, because swim meets can go long into the night. We make a sign, too, that says *Go Kitty Go!* I draw a dog on it. Daddy ends up missing the swim meet because he is delivering a baby, and as far as excuses go, it's a pretty good one. (It was a girl, and they named her Patricia Rose after her two grandmothers. Daddy always finds out the first and middle name for me. It's the first thing I ask when he gets home from a delivery.)

Kitty's so excited about winning two first-place ribbons and one second place that she forgets to ask where Josh is until we're in the car driving back home. She's in the backseat and she's got her towel wrapped around her head like a turban and her ribbons dangling from her ears like earrings. She leans forward and says, "Hey! Why didn't Josh come to my meet?"

I can see Margot hesitate, so I answer before she can. Maybe the only thing I'm better at than Margot is lying. "He had to work at the bookstore tonight. He really wanted to make it, though." Margot reaches across the console and gives my hand a grateful squeeze.

Sticking out her lower lip, Kitty says, "That was the last regular meet! He promised he'd come watch me swim."

"It was a last-minute thing," I say. "He couldn't get out of working the shift because one of his coworkers had an emergency."

Kitty nods begrudgingly. Little as she is, she understands emergency shifts.

"Let's get frozen custards," Margot says suddenly.

Kitty lights up, and Josh and his imaginary emergency

shift is forgotten. "Yeah! I want a waffle cone! Can I get a waffle cone with two scoops? I want mint chip and peanut brittle. No, rainbow sherbet and double fudge. No, wait—"

I twist around in my seat. "You can't finish two scoops and a waffle cone," I tell her. "Maybe you could finish two scoops in a cup, but not in a cone."

"Yes, I can. Tonight I can. I'm *starving.*"

"Fine, but you better finish the whole thing." I shake my finger at her and say it like a threat, which makes her roll her eyes and giggle. As for me, I'll get what I always get—the cherry chocolate-chunk custard in a sugar cone.

Margot pulls into the drive-thru, and as we wait our turn, I say, "I bet they don't have frozen custard in Scotland."

"Probably not," she says.

"You won't have another one of these until Thanksgiving," I say.

Margot looks straight ahead. "Christmas," she says, correcting me. "Thanksgiving's too short to fly all that way, remember?"

"Thanksgiving's gonna suck." Kitty pouts.

I'm silent. We've never had a Thanksgiving without Margot. She always does the turkey and the broccoli casserole and the creamed onions. I do the pies (pumpkin and pecan) and the mashed potatoes. Kitty is the taste tester and the table setter. I don't know how to roast a turkey. And both of our grandmothers will be there, and Nana, Daddy's mother, likes Margot best of all of us. She says Kitty drains her and I'm too dreamy-eyed.

All of a sudden I feel panicky and it's hard to breathe and I couldn't care less about cherry chocolate-chunk custard. I can't picture Thanksgiving without Margot. I can't even picture next Monday without her. I know most sisters don't get along, but I'm closer to Margot than I am to anybody in the world. How can we be the Song girls without Margot?

4

MY OLDEST FRIEND CHRIS SMOKES, SHE hooks up with boys she doesn't know hardly at all, and she's been suspended twice. One time she had to go before the court for truancy. I never knew what truancy was before I met Chris. FYI, it's when you skip so much school you're in trouble with the law.

I'm pretty sure that if Chris and I met each other now, we wouldn't be friends. We're as different as different can be. But it wasn't always this way. In sixth grade Chris liked stationery and sleepovers and staying up all night watching John Hughes movies, just like me. But by eighth grade she was sneaking out after my dad fell asleep to meet boys she met at the mall. They'd drop her back off before it got light outside. I'd stay up until she came back, terrified she wouldn't make it home before my dad woke up. She always made it back in time though.

Chris isn't the kind of friend you call every night or have lunch with every day. She is like a street cat, she comes and goes as she pleases. She can't be tied down to a place or a person. Sometimes I won't see Chris for days and then in the middle of the night there will be a knock at my bedroom window and it'll be Chris, crouched in the magnolia tree. I keep my window unlocked for her in case. Chris and Margot can't stand each other. Chris thinks Margot is uptight, and Margot thinks Chris is bipolar. She thinks Chris uses me; Chris thinks Margot controls me. I think maybe they're both a little bit right. But the important thing, the real thing, is Chris and I understand each other, which I think counts for a lot more than people realize.

Chris calls me on the way over to our house; she says her mom's being a beotch and she's coming over for a couple hours and do we have any food?

Chris and I are sharing a bowl of leftover gnocchi in the living room when Margot comes home from dropping Kitty off at her swim team's end-of-season barbecue. "Oh, hey," she says. Then she spots Chris's glass of Diet Coke on the coffee table, sans coaster. "Can you please use a coaster?"

As soon as Margot's up the stairs, Chris says, "Gawd! Why is your sister such a beotch?"

I slide a coaster under her glass. "You think everyone's a beotch today."

"That's because everyone is." Chris rolls her eyes toward the ceiling. Loudly, she says, "She needs to pull that stick out of her ass."

From her room Margot yells, "I heard that!"

"I meant for you to!" Chris yells back, scraping up the last piece of gnocchi for herself.

I sigh. "She's leaving so soon."

Snickering, Chris says, "So is Joshy, like, going to light a candle for her every night until she comes back home?"

I hesitate. While I'm not sure if it's still supposed to be a secret, I *am* sure that Margot wouldn't want Chris knowing any of her personal business. All I say is, "I'm not sure."

"Wait a minute. Did she dump him?" Chris demands.

Reluctantly I nod. "Don't say anything to her, though," I warn. "She's still really sad about it."

"Margot? Sad?" Chris picks at her nails. "Margot doesn't have normal human emotions like the rest of us."

"You just don't know her," I say. "Besides, we can't all be like you."

She grins a toothy grin. She has sharp incisors, which make her look always a little bit hungry. "True."

Chris is pure emotion. She screams at the drop of a hat. She says sometimes you have to scream out emotions; if you don't, they'll fester. The other day she screamed at a lady at the grocery store for accidentally stepping on her toes. I don't think she's in any danger of her emotions festering.

"I just can't believe that in a few days she'll be gone," I say, feeling sniffly all of a sudden.

"She's not *dying*, Lara Jean. There's nothing to get all boo-hoo about." Chris pulls at a loose string on her red shorts. They're so short that when she's sitting, you can see her underwear. Which are red to match her shorts. "In fact, I think this is good for you. It's about time you did your own thing and stopped just listening to whatever Queen Margot says. This is your junior year, beotch. This is when it's supposed to get good. French some guys, live a little, you know?"

"I live plenty," I say.

"Yeah, at the nursing home." Chris snickers and I glare at her.

Margot started volunteering at the Belleview Retirement Community when she got her driver's license; it was her job to help host cocktail hour for the residents. I'd help sometimes. We'd set out peanuts and pour drinks and sometimes Margot would play the piano, but usually Stormy hogged that. Stormy is the Belleview diva. She rules the roost. I like listening to her stories. And Miss Mary, she might not be so good at conversation due to her dementia, but she taught me how to knit.

They have a new volunteer there now, but I know that at Belleview it really is the more the merrier, because most of the residents get so few visitors. I should go back soon; I miss going there. And I for sure don't appreciate Chris making fun of it.

"Those people at Belleview have lived more life than everyone we know combined," I tell her. "There's this one lady, Stormy, she was a USO girl! She used to get a hundred letters a day from soldiers who were in love with her. And there was this one veteran who lost his leg—he sent her a diamond ring!"

Chris looks interested all of a sudden. "Did she keep it?"

"She did," I admit. I think it was wrong of her to keep the ring since she had no intention of marrying him, but she showed it to me, and it was beautiful. It was a pink diamond, very rare. I bet it's worth so much money now.

"I guess Stormy sounds kind of like a badass," Chris says begrudgingly.

"Maybe you could come with me to Belleview sometime," I suggest. "We could go to their cocktail hour. Mr. Perelli loves to dance with new girls. He'll teach you how to fox-trot."

Chris makes a horrible face like I suggested we go hang out at the town dump. "No, thanks. How about I take *you* dancing?" She nudges her chin toward upstairs. "Now that your sister's leaving, we can have some real fun. You know I always have fun."

It's true, Chris does always have fun. Sometimes a little too much fun, but fun nonetheless.

5

THE NIGHT BEFORE MARGOT LEAVES, ALL three of us are in her room helping pack up the last little things. Kitty is organizing Margot's bath stuff, packing it nice and neat in the clear shower caddy. Margot is trying to decide which coat to bring.

"Should I bring my peacoat and my puffy coat or just my peacoat?" she asks me.

"Just the peacoat," I say. "You can dress that up or down." I'm lying on her bed directing the packing process. "Kitty, make sure the lotion cap is on tight."

"It's brand-new—course it's on tight!" Kitty growls, but she double-checks.

"It gets cold in Scotland sooner than it does here," Margot said, folding the coat and setting it on top of her suitcase. "I think I'll just bring both."

"I don't know why you asked if you already knew what you were going to do," I say. "Also, I thought you said you were coming home for Christmas. You're still coming home for Christmas, right?"

"Yes, if you'll stop being a brat," Margot says.

Honestly, Margot isn't even packing that much. She doesn't need a lot. If it was me, I'd have packed up my whole room, but not Margot. Her room looks the same, almost.

Margot sits down next to me, and Kitty climbs up and sits at the foot of the bed. "Everything's changing," I say, sighing.

Margot makes a face and puts her arm around me. "Nothing's changing, not really. We're the Song girls forever, remember?"

Our father stands in the doorway. He knocks, even though the door is open and we can clearly see it is him. "I'm going to start packing up the car now," he announces. We watch from the bed as he lugs one of the suitcases downstairs, and then he comes up for the other one. Drily he says, "Oh no, don't get up. Don't trouble yourselves."

"Don't worry, we won't," we sing out.

For the past week our father has been in spring-cleaning mode, even though it isn't spring. He's getting rid of everything—the bread machine we never used, CDs, old blankets, our mother's old typewriter. It's all going to Goodwill. A psychiatrist or someone could probably connect it to Margot's leaving for college, but I can't explain the exact significance of it. Whatever it is, it's annoying. I had to shoo him away from my glass-unicorn collection twice.

I lay down my head in Margot's lap. "So you really are coming home for Christmas, right?"

"Right."

"I wish I could come with you." Kitty pouts. "You're nicer than Lara Jean."

I give her a pinch.

"See?" she crows.

"Lara Jean will be nice," Margot says, "as long as you

behave. And you both have to take care of Daddy. Make sure he doesn't work too many Saturdays. Make sure he takes the car in for inspection next month. And make sure you buy coffee filters—you're always forgetting to buy coffee filters."

"Yes, drill sergeant," Kitty and I chorus. I search Margot's face for sadness or fear or worry, for some sign that she is scared to go so far away, that she will miss us as much as we will miss her. I don't see it, though.

The three of us sleep in Margot's room that night.

Kitty falls asleep first, as always. I lie in the dark beside her with my eyes open. I can't sleep. The thought that tomorrow night Margot won't be in this room—it makes me so sad I can hardly bear it. I hate change more than almost anything.

In the dark next to me Margot asks, "Lara Jean . . . do you think you've ever been in love before? Real love?"

She catches me off guard; I don't have an answer ready for her. I'm trying to think of one, but she's already talking again.

Wistfully, she says, "I wish I'd been in love more than once. I think you should fall in love at least twice in high school." Then she lets out a little sigh and falls asleep. Margot falls asleep like that—one dreamy sigh and she's off to never-never land, just like that.

I wake up in the middle of the night and Margot's not there. Kitty's curled up on her side next to me, but no Margot. It's pitch dark; only the moonlight filters through the curtains. I crawl out of bed and move to the window. My breath catches. There they are: Josh and Margot standing in the driveway. Margot's face is turned away from him, toward the moon. Josh is crying. They aren't touching. There's enough space between them for me to know that Margot hasn't changed her mind.

I drop the curtain and find my way back to the bed, where Kitty has rolled farther into the center. I push her back a few inches so there will be room for Margot. I wish I hadn't seen that. It was too personal. Too real. It was supposed to be just for them. If there was a way for me to unsee it, I would.

I turn on my side and close my eyes. What must it be like, to have a boy like you so much he cries for you? And not just any boy. Josh. Our Josh.

To answer her question: yes, I think I have been in real love. Just once, though. With Josh. Our Josh.

6

THIS IS HOW MARGOT AND JOSH GOT together. In a way I heard about it from Josh first.

It was two years ago. We were sitting in the library during our free. I was doing math homework; Josh was helping because he's good at math. We had our heads bent over my page, so close I could smell the soap he'd used that morning. Irish Spring.

And then he said, "I need your advice on something. I like someone."

For a split second I thought it was me. I thought he was going to say me. I hoped. It was the start of the school year. We'd hung out nearly every day that August, sometimes with Margot but mostly just by ourselves, because Margot had her internship at the Montpelier plantation three days a week. We swam a lot. I had a great tan from all the swimming. So for that split second I thought he was going to say my name.

But then I saw the way he blushed, the way he looked off into space, and I knew it wasn't for me.

Mentally, I ran through the list of girls it could be. It was a short list. Josh didn't hang out with a ton of girls; he had his best friend Jersey Mike, who had moved from New Jersey in middle school, and his other best friend, Ben, and that was it.

It could have been Ashley, a junior on the volleyball team. He'd once pointed her out as the cutest of all the junior girls. In Josh's defense, I'd made him do it: I asked him who was the prettiest girl in each grade. For prettiest freshman, my grade, he said Genevieve. Not that I was surprised, but it still gave me a little pinch in my heart.

It could have been Jodie, the college girl from the bookstore. Josh often talked about how smart Jodie was, how she was so cultured because she'd studied abroad in India and was now Buddhist. Ha! I was the one who was half-Korean; I was the one who'd taught Josh how to eat with chopsticks. He'd had kimchi for the first time at *my* house.

I was about to ask him who when the librarian came over to shush us, and then we went back to doing work and Josh didn't bring it up again and I didn't ask. Honestly, I didn't want to know. It wasn't me, and that was all I cared about.

I didn't think for one second that the girl he liked was Margot. Not that I didn't see her as a girl who could be liked. She'd been asked out before, by a certain type of guy. Smart guys who would partner up with her in chemistry and run against her for student government. In retrospect, it wasn't so surprising that Josh would like Margot, since he's that kind of guy too.

If someone were to ask me what Josh looks like, I would say he's just ordinary. He looks like the kind of guy you'd expect would be good at computers, the kind of guy who calls comic books graphic novels. Brown hair. Not a special brown, just regular brown. Green eyes that go muddy in the center. He's on the skinny side, but he's strong. I know because I sprained my ankle once by the old baseball field and he piggybacked me all the way home. He has freckles, which make him look younger than his age. And a dimple on his left check. I've always liked that dimple. He has such a serious face otherwise.

What was surprising, what was shocking, was that Margot would like him back. Not because of who Josh was, but because of who Margot was. I'd never heard her talk about liking a boy before, not even once. I was the flighty one, the flibbertigibbet, as my white grandma would say. Not Margot. Margot was above all that. She existed on some higher plane where those things—boys, makeup, clothes—didn't really matter.

The way it happened was sudden. Margot came home from school late that day in October; her cheeks were pink from the cold mountainy air and she had her hair in a braid and a scarf around her neck. She'd been working on a project at school, it was dinnertime, and I'd cooked chicken parmesan with thin spaghetti in watery tomato sauce.

She came into the kitchen and announced, "I have something to tell you." Her eyes were very bright; I remember she was unspooling the scarf from around her neck.

Kitty was doing her homework at the kitchen table, Daddy was on his way home, and I was stirring the watery sauce. "What?" Kitty and I asked.

"Josh likes me." Margot gave a pleased kind of shrug; her shoulders nearly went up to her ears.

I went very still. Then I dropped my wooden spoon into the sauce. "*Josh* Josh? Our Josh?" I couldn't even look at her. I was afraid that she would see.

"Yes. He waited for me after school today so he could tell me. He said—" Margot grinned ruefully. "He said I'm his dream girl. Can you believe that?"

"Wow," I said, and I tried to communicate happiness in that word, but I don't know if it came out that way. All I was feeling was despair. And envy. Envy so thick and so black I felt like I was choking on it. So I tried again, this time with a smile. "Wow, Margot."

"Wow," Kitty echoed. "So are you boyfriend and girl-friend now?"

I held my breath, waiting for her to answer.

Margot took a pinch of parmesan between her fingers and dropped it in her mouth. "Yeah, I think so." And then she smiled, and her eyes went all soft and liquid. I understood then that she liked him too. So much.

That night I wrote my letter to Josh.

Dear Josh . . .

I cried a lot. Just like that, it was over. It was over before I even had a chance. The important thing wasn't that Josh had chosen Margot. It was that Margot had chosen him.

So that was that. I cried my eyes out; I wrote my letter; I put the whole thing to rest. I haven't thought of him that way since. He and Margot are meant to be. They're MFEO. Made for each other.

I'm still awake when Margot comes back to bed, but I quickly shut my eyes and pretend to be asleep. Kitty's cuddled up next to me.

I hear a snuffly sound and I peek out of one eye to look at Margot. Her back is to us; her shoulders are shaking. She's crying.

Margot never cries.

Now that I've seen Margot cry over him, I believe it more than ever—they're not over.

7

THE NEXT DAY, WE DRIVE MARGOT TO THE airport. Outside, we load up her suitcases on a luggage carrier—Kitty tries to get on top and dance, but our father pulls her down right away. Margot insists on going in by herself, just like she said she would.

"Margot, at least let me get your bags checked," Daddy says, trying to maneuver the luggage carrier around her. "I want to see you go through security."

"I'll be fine," she repeats. "I've flown by myself before. I know how to check a bag." She stretches up on her toes and puts her arms around our dad's shoulders. "I'll call as soon as I get there, I promise."

"Call every day," I whisper. The lump in my throat is getting bigger, and a few tears leak out of my eyes. I'd hoped I wouldn't cry, because I knew Margot wouldn't, and it's lonely to cry alone, but I can't help it.

"Don't you dare forget us," Kitty warns.

That makes Margot smile. "I could never." She hugs us each one more time. She saves me for last, the way I knew she would. "Take good care of Daddy and Kitty. You're in charge now." I don't want to let go, so I hold on tighter; I'm still waiting and hoping for some sign, some indication that she will miss us as much as we'll miss her. And then she laughs and I release her.

"Bye, Gogo," I say, wiping my eyes with a corner of my shirt.

We all watch as she pushes the luggage carrier over to the check-in counter. I'm crying hard, wiping my tears with the back of my arm. Daddy puts one arm around me and one around Kitty. "We'll wait until she's in line for security," he says.

When she's done checking in, she turns back and looks at us through the glass doors. She lifts one hand and waves, and then she heads for the security line. We watch her go, thinking she might turn around one more time, but she doesn't. She already seems so far away from us. Straight-A Margot, ever capable. When it's my time to leave, I doubt I'll be as strong as Margot. But, honestly, who is?

I cry all the way home. Kitty tells me I'm a bigger baby than she is, but then from the backseat she grabs my hand and squeezes it, and I know she's sad too.

Even though Margot isn't a loud person, it feels quiet at home. Empty, somehow. What will it be like when I'm gone in two years? What will Daddy and Kitty do then? I hate the thought of the two of them coming home to an empty, dark house with no me and no Margot. Maybe I won't go away far; maybe I'll even live at home, at least for the first semester. I think that would be the right thing to do.

8

LATER THAT AFTERNOON CHRIS CALLS AND
tells me to meet her at the mall; she wants my opinion on
a leather jacket, and to get the full effect I have to see it in
person. I'm proud she's asking for my sartorial advice, and
it would be good to get out of the house and not be sad
anymore, but I'm nervous about driving to the mall alone.
I (or anyone, really) would consider myself a skittish driver.

I ask her if she'll just send me a picture instead, but Chris
knows me too well. She says, "Nuh-uh. You get your ass
down here, Lara Jean. You'll never get better at driving if
you don't just suck it up and do it."

So that's what I'm doing: I'm driving Margot's car to the
mall. I mean, I have my license and everything; I'm just not
very confident. My dad has taken me for lessons numerous
times, Margot too, and I'm basically fine with them in the car,
but I get nervous when I drive alone. It's the changing-lanes
part that scares me. I don't like taking my eyes away from
what's happening right in front of me, not for a second. Also
I don't like going too fast.

But the worst thing is I have a tendency of getting lost.
The only places I can get to with absolute certainty are
school and the grocery store. I've never had to know how
to get to the mall, because Margot always drove us there.

But now I have to do better, because I'm responsible for driving Kitty around. Though truthfully, Kitty is better with directions than I am; she knows how to get to loads of places. But I don't want to have to hear her tell me how to get somewhere. I want to feel like the big sister; I want her to relax in the passenger seat, safe in the knowledge that Lara Jean will get her where she needs to go, just like I did with Margot.

Sure, I could just use a GPS, but I would feel silly putting in directions to go to the mall when I've been there a million times. It should come to me intuitively, easy, where I don't even have to think about it. Instead I worry over every turn, second-guess every highway sign—is it north or is it south, do I turn right here or is it the next one? I've never had to pay attention.

But today, so far so good. I'm listening to the radio, bopping along, even driving with just one hand on the wheel. I do this to feign confidence, because the more I fake it, the more it's supposed to feel true.

Everything is going so well that I take the shortcut way instead of the highway way. I cut through the side neighborhood, and even as I'm doing it, I'm wondering if this was such a great idea. After a couple of minutes things aren't looking so familiar, and I realize I should have taken a left instead of a right. I push down the panic that's rising in my chest and I try to backtrack.

You can do it, you can do it.

There's a four-way stop sign. I don't see anyone, so I zip

ahead. I don't even see the car on my right; I feel it before I see it.

I scream my head off. I taste copper in my mouth. Am I bleeding? Did I bite my tongue off? I touch it and it's still there. My heart is racing; my whole body feels wet and clammy. I try to take deep breaths, but I can't seem to get air.

My legs shake as I get out of the car. The other guy is already out, inspecting his car with his arms crossed. He's old, older than my dad, and he has gray hair, and he's wearing shorts with red lobsters on them. His car is fine; mine has a huge dent in the side. "Didn't you see the stop sign?" he demands. "Were you texting on your phone?"

I shake my head; my throat is closing up. I just don't want to cry. As long as I don't cry . . .

He seems to sense this. The irritated furrow of his brow is loosening. "Well, my car looks fine," he says reluctantly. "Are you all right?"

I nod again. "I'm so sorry," I say.

"Kids need to be more careful," the man says, as if I haven't spoken.

The lump in my throat is getting bigger. "I'm very, very sorry, sir."

He makes a grunty sound. "You should call someone to come get you," the man says. "Do you want me to wait?"

"No, thank you." What if he's a serial killer or a child molester? I don't want to be alone with a strange man.

The man drives off.

As soon as he's gone, it occurs to me that maybe I should

have called the police while he was still here. Aren't you always supposed to call the police when you're in a car accident, no matter what? I'm pretty sure they told us that in driver's ed. So that's another mistake I made.

I sit down on the curb and stare at Margot's car. I've only had it for two hours and I've already wrecked it. I rest my head in my lap and sit in a tight bundle. My neck is starting to ache. This is when the tears start. My dad is not going to be happy. Margot is not going to be happy. They'll both probably agree that I have no business driving around town unsupervised, and maybe they're right. Driving a car is a lot of responsibility. Maybe I'm not ready for it yet. Maybe I'll never be ready. Maybe even when I'm old, my sisters or my dad will have to drive me around, because that's how useless I am.

I pull out my phone and call Josh. When he answers, I say, "Josh, can you do me a f-f-favor?" and my voice comes out so wobbly I'm embarrassed.

Which of course he hears, because he's Josh. He comes to attention immediately and says, "What's wrong?"

"I just got into a car accident. I don't even know where I am. Can you come get me?" *Wobble wobble.*

"Are you hurt?" he demands.

"No, I'm fine. I'm just—" If I say another word, I will cry.

"What street signs do you see? What stores?"

I crane my neck to look. "Falstone," I say. I look for the closet mailbox. "I'm at 8109 Falstone Road."

"I'm on my way. Do you want me to stay on the phone with you?"

"No, that's okay." I hang up and start to cry.

I don't know how long I've been sitting there crying when another car rolls up in front of me. I look up, and it's Peter Kavinsky's black Audi with the tinted windows. One of them rolls down. "Lara Jean? Are you okay?"

I nod my head yes and make a motion like he should just go. He rolls the window back up, and I think he's really going to drive off, but then he pulls over to the side and parks. He climbs out and starts inspecting my car. "You really messed it up," he says. "Did you get the other guy's insurance info?"

"No, his car was fine." Furtively, I wipe my cheeks with my arm. "It was my fault."

"Do you have Triple A?"

I nod.

"So you called them already?"

"No. But someone's coming."

Peter sits down next to me. "How long have you been sitting here crying by yourself?"

I turn my head and wipe my face again. "I'm not crying."

Peter Kavinsky and I used to be friends, back before he was Kavinsky, when he was Peter K. There was a whole gang of us in middle school. The boys were Peter Kavinsky and John Ambrose McClaren and Trevor Pike. The girls were Genevieve and me and Allie Feldman who lived down the block and sometimes Chris. Growing up, Genevieve lived two streets away from me. It's funny how much of childhood is about proximity. Like who your best friend is is directly correlated to how close your houses are; who you sit next to in music is all about how close your names are in the alphabet. Such a game of chance. In eighth grade Genevieve moved to a different neighborhood, and we stayed friends a little while longer. She'd come back to the neighborhood to hang out, but something was different. By high school Genevieve had eclipsed us. She was still friends with the boys, but the girls' crew was over. Allie and I stayed friends until she moved last year, but there was always something just a little bit humiliating about it, like we were two leftover heels of bread and together we made a dry sandwich.

We're not friends anymore. Me and Genevieve or me and Peter. Which is why it's so weird to be sitting next to him on somebody's curb like no time has passed.

His phone buzzes and he takes it out of his pocket. "I've gotta go."

I sniffle. "Where are you headed?"

"To Gen's."

"You'd better get going then," I say. "Genevieve will be mad if you're late."

Peter makes a *pfft* sound, but he sure does get up fast. I wonder what it's like to have that much power over a boy. I don't think I'd want it; it's a lot of responsibility to hold a person's heart in your hands. He's getting into his car when, as an afterthought, he turns around and asks, "Want me to call Triple A for you?"

"No, that's okay," I say. "Thanks for stopping, though. That was really nice of you."

Peter grins. I remember that about Peter—how much he likes positive reinforcement. "Do you feel better now?"

I nod. I do, actually.

"Good," he says.

He has the look of a Handsome Boy from a different time. He could be a dashing World War I soldier, handsome enough for a girl to wait years for him to come back from war, so handsome she could wait forever. He could be wearing a red letterman's jacket, driving around in a Corvette with the top down, one arm on the steering wheel, on his way to pick up his girl for the sock hop. Peter's kind of wholesome good looks feel more like yesterday than today. There's just something about him girls like.

He was my first kiss. It's so strange to think of it now. It feels like forever ago, but really it was just four years.

Josh shows up about a minute later, as I'm texting Chris that I'm not going to make it to the mall after all. I stand up. "It took you long enough!"

"You told me 8109. This is 8901!"

Confidently I say, "No, I definitely said 8901."

"No, you definitely said 8109. And why weren't you answering your phone?" Josh gets out of his car, and when he sees the side of my car, his jaw drops. "Holy crap. Did you call Triple A yet?"

"No. Can you?"

Josh does, and then we sit in his car in the air-conditioning while we wait. I almost get into the backseat, when I remember.

Margot isn't here anymore. I've ridden in his car so many times, and I don't think I've ever once sat up front in the passenger seat.

"Um . . . you know Margot's going to kill you, right?"

I whip my head around so fast my hair slaps me in the face. "Margot's not going to find out, so don't you say a word!"

"When would I even talk to her? We're broken up, remember?"

I frown at him. "I hate when people do that—when you ask them to keep something a secret and instead of saying yes or no, they say, 'Who would I tell?'"

"I didn't say, 'Who would I tell?'!"

"Just say yes or no and mean it. Don't make it conditional."

"I won't tell Margot anything," he says. "It'll just be between you and me. I promise. All right?"

"All right," I say. And then it gets quiet with neither of us saying anything; there's just the sound of cool air coming out of the A/C vents.

My stomach feels queasy thinking about how I'm going to tell my dad. Maybe I should break the news to him with tears in my eyes so he feels sorry for me. Or I could say something like, I have good news and bad news. The good news is, I'm fine, not a scratch on me. The bad news is, the car is wrecked. Maybe "wrecked" isn't the right word.

I'm mulling over the right word choice in my head when Josh says, "So just because Margot and I broke up, you're not going to talk to me anymore either?" Josh sounds jokingly bitter or bitterly joking, if there is such a combination.

I look over at him in surprise. "Don't be dumb. Of course I'm still going to talk to you. Just not in public." This is the role I play with him. The part of the pesky little sister. As if I am the same as Kitty. As if we aren't only a year apart. Josh doesn't crack a smile, he just looks glum, so I bump my forehead against his. "That was a joke, dummy!"

"Did she tell you she was going to do it? I mean, was it always her plan?" When I hesitate, he says, "Come on. I know she tells you everything."

"Not really. Not this time anyway. Honestly, Josh. I didn't know a thing about it. Promise." I cross my heart.

Josh absorbs this. Chewing on his bottom lip he says, "Maybe she'll change her mind. That's possible, right?"

I don't know if it's more heartless for me to say yes or no, because he'll be hurt either way. Because while I'm 99.99999 percent sure that she will get back together with him, there's that tiny chance she won't, and I don't want to get his hopes up. So I don't say anything.

He swallows, his Adam's apple bobbing up and down. "No, you're right. When Margot makes up her mind, she doesn't go back on it."

Please please please don't cry.

I rest my head on his shoulder and say, "You never know, Joshy."

Josh stares straight ahead. A squirrel is darting up the big oak tree in the yard. Up and down and back up again. We both watch. "What time does she land?"

"Not for hours."

"Is . . . is she coming home for Thanksgiving?"

"No. They don't get off for Thanksgiving. It's Scotland, Josh. They don't celebrate American holidays, hello!" I'm teasing again, but my heart's not in it.

"That's right," he says.

I say, "She'll be home for Christmas, though," and we both sigh.

"Can I still hang out with you guys?" Josh asks me.

"Me and Kitty?"

"Your dad, too."

"We're not going anywhere," I assure him.

Josh looks relieved. "Good. I'd hate to lose you, too."

As soon as he says it, my heart does this pause, and I forget to breathe, and just for that one second I'm dizzy. And then, just as quickly as it came, the feeling, the strange flutter in my chest, is gone, and the tow truck arrives.

When we pull into my driveway, he says, "Do you want me to be there when you tell your dad?"

I brighten up and then I remember how Margot said I'm in charge now. I'm pretty sure taking responsibility for one's mistakes is part of being in charge.

9

DADDY ISN'T SO MAD AFTER ALL. I GO
through my whole good news–bad news spiel and he just
sighs and says, "As long as you're all right."

The car needs a special part that has to be flown in
from Indiana or Idaho, I can't remember which. In the
meantime I'll have to share the car with Daddy and take
the bus to school or ask Josh for rides, which was already
my plan.

Margot calls later that night. Kitty and I are watching TV
and I scream for Daddy to come quick. We sit on the couch
and pass the phone around and take turns talking to her.

"Margot, guess what happened today!" Kitty shouts.

Frantically, I shake my head at her. *Don't tell her about the
car,* I mouth. I give her warning eyes.

"Lara Jean got into . . ." Kitty pauses tantalizingly. "A fight
with Daddy. Yeah, she was mean to me and Daddy told her
to be nice, so they had a fight."

I grab the phone out of her hand. "We didn't have a fight,
Gogo. Kitty's just being annoying."

"What did you guys have for dinner? Did you cook the
chicken I defrosted last night?" Margot asks. Her voice
sounds so far away.

I push the volume up on the phone. "Yes, but never mind

about that. Are you settled into your room? Is it big? What's your roommate like?"

"She's nice. She's from London and she has a really fancy accent. Her name is Penelope St. George-Dixon."

"Gosh, even her name sounds fancy," I say. "What about your room?"

"The room is about the same as that dorm we saw at UVA; it's just older."

"What time is it over there?"

"It's almost midnight. We're five hours ahead, remember?"

We're five hours ahead, like she's already considering Scotland her home, and she's only been gone a day, not even! "We miss you already," I tell her.

"Miss you too."

After dinner I text Chris to see if she wants to come over, but she doesn't text back. She's probably out with one of the guys she hooks up with. Which is fine. I should catch up on my scrapbooking.

I was hoping to be done with Margot's scrapbook before she left for college, but as anyone who's ever scrapbooked knows, Rome wasn't built in a day. You could spend a year or more working on one scrapbook.

I've got Motown girl-group music playing, and my supplies are laid out all around me in a semicircle. My heart hole punch, pages and pages of scrapbook paper, pictures I've cut out of magazines, glue gun, my tape dispenser with all my different colored washi tapes. Souvenirs like the playbill from when we saw *Wicked* in New York, receipts, pictures. Ribbon, buttons, stickers, charms. A good scrap-book has texture. It's thick and chunky and doesn't close all the way.

I'm working on a Josh-and-Margot page. I don't care what Margot says. They're getting back together, I know it. And even if they aren't, not right away, it's not like Margot can just erase him from her history. He was such a big part of her senior year. And, like, her life. The only compromise I'm willing to make is I was saving my heart washi tape for this page, but I can just do a regular plaid tape instead. But then I put the plaid tape up against the pictures and the colors don't look as good.

So I go ahead and use the heart tape. And then, swaying to the music, I use my heart template to cut out a picture of the two of them at prom. Margot's going to love this.

I'm carefully gluing a dried rose petal from Margot's cor-sage when my dad raps on the door. "What are you up to tonight?" he asks me.

"This," I say, gluing another petal. "If I keep at it, it'll probably be done by Christmas."

"Ah." My dad doesn't move. He just hovers there in the doorway, watching me work. "Well, I'm going to watch that new Ken Burns documentary in a bit, if you want to join me."

"Maybe," I say, just to be nice. It'll be too much of a pain to bring all my supplies downstairs and get set up again. I'm in a good rhythm right now. "Why don't you get it started without me?"

"All righty. I'll leave you to it, then." Daddy shuffles down the stairs.

It takes me most of the night, but I finish the Josh-and-Margot page, and it comes out really nice. Next is a sister page. For this one I use flowered paper for the background, and I glue in a picture of the three of us from a long time ago. Mommy took it. We're standing in front of the oak tree in front of our house in our church clothes. We're all wearing white dresses, and we have matching pink ribbons in our hair. The best thing about the picture is Margot and I are smiling sweetly and Kitty is picking her nose.

I smile to myself. Kitty's going to pitch a fit when she sees this page. I can't wait.

10

MARGOT SAYS THAT JUNIOR YEAR IS THE
most important year, the busiest year, a year so crucial that
everything else in life hinges upon it. So I figure I should
get in all the pleasure reading I can before school starts
next week and junior year officially begins. I'm sitting
on my front steps, reading a 1980s romantic British spy
novel I got for seventy-five cents at the Friends of the
Library sale.

I'm just getting to the good stuff (Cressida must seduce
Nigel to gain access to the spy codes!) when Josh walks
out of his house to get the mail. He sees me too; he lifts
his hand like he's just going to wave and not come over,
but then he does.

"Hey, nice onesie," he says as he makes his way across
the driveway.

It's faded light blue with sunflowers and it ties around
the neck. I got it from the vintage store, 75 percent off.
And it's not a onesie. "This is a *sunsuit*," I tell him, going
back to my book. I try to subtly hide the cover with my
hand. The last thing I need is Josh giving me a hard time
for reading a trashy book when I'm just trying to enjoy a
relaxing afternoon.

I can feel him looking at me, his arms crossed, waiting. I look up. "What?"

"Wanna see a movie tonight at the Bess? There's a Pixar movie playing. We can take Kitty."

"Sure, text me when you want to head over," I say, turning the page of my book. Nigel is unbuttoning Cressida's blouse and she's wondering when the sleeping pill she slipped in his Merlot will kick in, while simultaneously hoping it won't kick in too soon, because Nigel is actually quite a good kisser.

Josh reaches down and tries to get a closer look at my book. I slap his hand away, but not before he reads out loud, "Cressida's heart raced as Nigel moved his hand along her stockinged thigh." Josh cracks up. "What the heck are you reading?"

My cheeks are burning. "Oh, be quiet."

Chuckling, Josh backs away. "I'll leave you to Cressida and Noel then."

To his back, I call out, "For your information, it's *Nigel*!"

Kitty's over the moon about hanging out with Josh. When Josh asks the girl at the concession stand to layer the butter on the popcorn (bottom, middle, top), we both give an approving nod. Kitty sits in the middle of us, and at the funny parts she laughs so hard she kicks her legs up in the air. She weighs so little that the seat keeps tipping up. Josh and I share smiles over her head.

Whenever Josh, Margot, and I went to the movies, Margot always sat in the middle too. It was so she could whisper to both of us. She never wanted me to feel left out because she had a boyfriend and I didn't. She was so careful about this that it made me worry at first, that she sensed something from before. But she's not someone to hold back or pretty up the truth. She's just a really good big sister. The best.

There were times I felt left out anyway. Not in a romantic way, but a friend way. Josh and I had always been friends. But those times when he'd put his arm around Margot when we were in line for popcorn, or in the car when they'd talk softly to each other and I felt like the kid in the backseat who can't hear what the adults are talking about, it made me feel a little bit invisible. They made me wish I had someone to whisper to in the backseat.

It's strange to be the one in the front seat now. The view isn't so different from the backseat. In fact, everything feels good and normal and the same, which is a comfort.

Chris calls me later that night while I'm painting my toenails different-colored pinks. It's so loud in the background she has to yell. "Guess what!"

"What? I can barely hear you!" I'm doing my pinky toe a fruit-punch color called Hit Me with Your Best Shot.

"Hold up." I can hear Chris moving rooms, because it gets quieter. "Can you hear me now?"

"Yes, much better."

"Guess who broke up."

I've moved on to a mod pink color that looks like Wite-Out with a drop of red in it. "Who?"

"Gen and Kavinsky! She dumped his ass."

My eyes go huge. "Whoa! Why?"

"Apparently, she met some UVA guy at that hostessing job she had. I guarantee you she was cheating on Kavinsky the whole summer." A guy calls Chris's name, and Chris says, "I gotta go. It's my turn at bocce." Chris hangs up without saying good-bye, which is her way.

I actually met Chris through Genevieve. They're cousins: their moms are sisters. Chris used to come over sometimes when we were little, but she and Gen didn't get along even back then. They'd argue over whose Barbie had dibs on Ken, because there was only one Ken. I didn't even try to fight for Ken, even though he was technically mine. Well, Margot's. At school some people don't even know Gen and Chris are cousins. They don't look alike, like at all: Gen is petite with fit arms and sunny blond hair the color of margarine. Chris is blond too, but peroxide blond, and she's taller and has broad swimmer's shoulders. Still, there is a sameness to them.

Chris was pretty wild our freshman year. She went to every party, got drunk, hooked up with older boys. That year a junior guy from the lacrosse team told everyone that Chris had sex with him in the boys' locker room, and it wasn't even true. Genevieve made Peter threaten to kick his ass if he didn't tell everybody the truth. I thought it was a really nice thing Genevieve did for Chris, but Chris insisted that Gen had only done it so people wouldn't think she was related to a slut. After that Chris stopped hanging out and pretty much did her own thing, with people from another school.

She still has that freshman-year reputation though. She acts like she doesn't care, but I know she does, at least a little.

11

ON SUNDAY, DADDY MAKES LASAGNA. HE does that thing where he puts black-bean salsa in it to jazz it up, and it sounds gross but it's actually good and you don't notice the beans. Josh comes over too, and he has three helpings, which Daddy loves. When Margot's name comes up over dinner, I look over at Josh and see how stiff he gets, and I feel sorry for him. Kitty must notice too, because she changes the subject over to dessert, which is a batch of peanut-butter brownies I baked earlier in the afternoon.

Since Daddy cooked, us kids have kitchen duty. He uses every pot in the kitchen when he makes lasagna, so it's the worst cleanup, but worth it.

After, the three of us are relaxing in the TV room. It's Sunday night, but there's not that Sunday night feeling in the air, because tomorrow is Labor Day and we have one last day before school starts. Kitty's working on her dog collage, *quelle surprise.*

"What kind do you want most of all?" Josh asks her.

Kitty answers back lightning fast. "An Akita."

"Boy or girl?"

Again her answer is prompt. "Boy."

"What'll you name him?"

Kitty hesitates, and I know why. I roll over and tickle

Kitty's bare foot. "I know what you'll name him," I say in a singsong voice.

"Be quiet, Lara Jean!" she screeches.

I have Josh's full attention now. "Come on, tell us," Josh begs.

I look at Kitty and she is giving me evil glowy red eyes. "Never mind," I say, feeling nervous all of a sudden. Kitty might be the baby of the family, but she is not someone to trifle with.

Then Josh tugs on my ponytail and says, "Aw, come on, Lara Jean! Don't leave us in suspense."

I prop myself up on my elbows, and Kitty tries to put her hand over my mouth. Giggling, I say, "It's after a boy she likes."

"Shut up, Lara Jean, shut up!"

Kitty kicks me, and in doing so she accidentally rips one of her dog pictures. She lets out a cry and drops to her knees and examines it. Her face is red with the effort of not crying. I feel like such a jerk. I sit up and try to give her an *I'm sorry* hug, but she twists away from me and kicks at my legs, so hard I yelp. I pick the picture up and try to tape it back, but before I can, Kitty snatches it out of my hands and gives it to Josh. "Josh, fix it," she says. "Lara Jean ruined it."

"Kitty, I was only teasing," I say lamely. I wasn't going to say the name of the boy. I would never ever have said it.

She ignores me, and Josh smooths the paper back out with a coaster, and with the concentration of a surgeon he tapes the two pieces together. He wipes his brow. "Phew. I think this one will make it."

I clap, and I try to catch Kitty's eye, but she won't look at me. I know I deserve it. The boy Kitty has a crush on—it's Josh.

Kitty whisks her collage away from Josh. Stiffly she says, "I'm going upstairs to work on this. Good night, Josh."

"Night, Kitty," Josh says.

Meekly, I say, "Good night, Kitty," but she's already running up the stairs, and she doesn't reply.

When we hear the sound of her bedroom door closing, Josh turns to me and says, "You're in so much trouble."

"I know," I say. I've got a sick feeling in the pit of my stomach. Why did I do that? Even as I was doing it, I knew it was wrong. Margot would never have done that to me. That's not how big sisters are supposed to treat their little sisters, especially not when I'm so much older than Kitty.

"Who's this kid she likes?"

"Just a boy from school."

Josh sighs. "Is she really old enough to have crushes on boys? I feel like she's too young for all that."

"I had crushes on boys when I was nine," I tell him. I'm still thinking about Kitty. I wonder how I can make it so she isn't mad at me anymore. Somehow I don't think snickerdoodles will cut it this time.

"Who?" Josh asks me.

"Who what?" Maybe if I can somehow convince Daddy to buy her a puppy . . .

"Who was your first crush?"

"Hmm. My first *real* crush?" I had kindergarten and

first- and second-grade crushes aplenty, but they don't really count. "Like the first one that really mattered?"

"Sure."

"Well . . . I guess Peter Kavinsky."

Josh practically gags. "Kavinsky? Are you kidding me? He's so obvious. I thought you'd be into someone more . . . I don't know, subtle. Peter Kavinsky's such a cliché. He's like a cardboard cutout of a 'cool guy' in a movie about high school."

I shrug. "You asked."

"Wow," he says, shaking his head. "Just . . . wow."

"He used to be different. I mean, he was still very Peter, but less so." When Josh looks unconvinced, I say, "You're a boy, so you can't understand what I'm talking about."

"You're right. I don't understand!"

"Hey, you're the one who had a crush on Ms. Rothschild!"

Josh turns red. "She was really pretty back then!"

"Uh-huh." I give him a knowing look. "She was really 'pretty.'" Our across-the-street neighbor Ms. Rothschild used to mow her lawn in terry-cloth short shorts and a string bikini top. The neighborhood boys would conveniently come and play in Josh's yard on those days.

"Anyway, Ms. Rothschild wasn't my first crush."

"She wasn't?"

"No. You were."

It takes me a few seconds to process this. Even then, all I can manage is, "Huh?"

"When I first moved here, before I knew your true personality." I kick him in the shin for that, and he yelps. "I was twelve and you were eleven. I let you ride my scooter, remember? That scooter was my pride and joy. I saved up for it for two birthdays. And I let *you* take it for a ride."

"I thought you were just being generous."

"You crashed it and you got a big scratch on the side," he continues. "Remember that?"

"Yeah, I remember you cried."

"I didn't *cry*. I was justifiably upset. And that was the end of my little crush." Josh gets up to go and we walk to the foyer.

Before he opens the front door, Josh turns around and says to me, "I don't know what I would've done if you hadn't been around after . . . Margot dumped me." A blush blooms pink across his face, underneath each sweetly freckled cheek. "You're keeping me going, Lara Jean." Josh looks at me and I feel it all, every memory, every moment we've ever shared. Then he gives me a quick, fierce hug and disappears into the night.

I'm standing there in the open door and the thought flies in my head, so quick, so unexpected, I can't stop myself from thinking it: *If you were mine, I would never have broken up with you, not in a million years.*

12

THIS IS HOW WE MET JOSH. WE WERE HAV-
ing a teddy-bear, tea-party picnic on the back lawn with
real tea and muffins. It had to be in the backyard so no one
would see. I was eleven, way too old for it, and Margot was
thirteen, way, way too old. I got the idea in my head because
I read about it in a book. Because of Kitty I could pretend
it was for her and persuade Margot into playing with us.
Mommy had died the year before and ever since, Margot
rarely said no to anything if it was for Kitty.

We had everything spread out on Margot's old baby
blanket, which was blue and nubby with a squirrel print. I
laid out a chipped tea set of Margot's, mini muffins studded
with blueberries and granules of sugar that I made Daddy
buy at the grocery store, and a teddy bear for each of us.
We were all wearing hats, because I insisted. "You have to
wear a hat to a tea party," I kept saying until Margot finally
put hers on just so I'd stop. She had on Mommy's straw
gardening hat, and Kitty was wearing a tennis visor, and I'd
fancied up an old fur hat of Grandma's by pinning a few
plastic flowers on top.

I was pouring lukewarm tea out of the thermos and into
cups when Josh climbed up on the fence and watched us.
The month before, from the upstairs playroom, we'd watched

Josh's family move in. We'd hoped for girls, but then we saw the movers unload a boy bike and we went back to playing.

Josh sat up on the fence, not saying anything, and Margot was really stiff and embarrassed; her cheeks were red, but she kept her hat on. Kitty was the one to call out to him. "Hello, boy," she said.

"Hi," he said. His hair was shaggy, and he kept shaking it out of his eyes. He was wearing a red T-shirt with a hole in the shoulder.

Kitty asked him, "What's your name?"

"Josh."

"You should play with us, Josh," Kitty commanded.

So he did.

I didn't know it then, how important this boy would become to me and to the people I love the most. But even if I had known, what could I have done differently? It was never going to be me and him. Even though.

13

I THOUGHT I WAS OVER HIM.

When I wrote my letter, when I said my good-byes, I meant it, I swear I did. It wasn't even that hard, not really. Not when I thought about how much Margot liked him, how much she cared. How could I begrudge Margot a first love? Margot, who'd sacrificed so much for all of us. She always, always put Kitty and me before herself. Letting go of Josh was my way of putting Margot first.

But now, sitting here alone in my living room, with my sister four thousand miles away and Josh next door, all I can think is, *Josh Sanderson, I liked you first. By all rights, you were mine. And if it had been me, I'd have packed you in my suitcase and taken you with me, or, you know what, I would have stayed. I would have never left you. Not in a million years, not for anything.*

Thinking these kinds of thoughts, feeling these kinds of feelings, it's more than disloyal. I know that. It's downright traitorous. It makes my soul feel dirty. Margot's been gone less than a week and look at me, how fast I cave. How fast I covet. I'm a betrayer of the worst kind, because I'm betraying my own sister, and there's no greater betrayal than that. But what now? What am I supposed to do with all these feelings?

I suppose there's only one thing I *can* do. I'll write him

another letter. A postscript with as many pages as it takes to X away whatever feelings I have left for him. I'll put this whole thing to rest, once and for all.

I go to my room and I find my special writing pen, the one with the really smooth inky-black ink. I take out my heavy writing paper, and I begin to write.

P.S. I still love you.

I still love you and that's a really huge problem for me and it's also a really huge surprise. I swear I didn't know. All this time, I thought I was over it. How could I not be, when it's Margot you love? It's always been Margot . . .

When I'm done, I put the letter in my diary instead of in my hat box. I have a feeling I'm not done-done yet, that there's still more I need to say, I just haven't thought of it yet.

14

KITTY'S STILL MAD AT ME. IN THE WAKE OF the Josh revelation, I'd forgotten all about Kitty. She ignores me all morning, and when I ask if she wants me to take her to the store for school supplies, she snaps, "With what car? You wrecked Margot's."

Ouch. "I was going to take Daddy's when he comes back from Home Depot." I back away from her, far enough away that she can't lash out at me with a kick or a hit. "There's no need to be nasty, Katherine."

Kitty practically growls, which is exactly the reaction I was hoping for. I hate when Kitty goes mad and silent. But then she flounces away, and with her back to me she says, "I'm not speaking to you. You know what you did, so don't bother trying to get back on my good side." I follow her around, trying to provoke her into talking to me, but there's really no use. I've been dismissed. So I give up and go back to my room and put on the *Mermaids* soundtrack. I'm organizing my first-week back-to-school outfits on my bed when I get a text from Josh. A little thrill runs up my spine to see his name on my phone, but I sternly remind myself of my vow. *He is still Margot's, not yours.* It doesn't matter that they're broken up. He was hers first, which means he's hers always.

Wanna go for a bike ride on that trail by
the park?

Biking is a Margot-type activity. She loves going on trails
and hikes and bikes. Not me. Josh knows it too. I don't even
own my own bike anymore, and Margot's is too big for me.
Kitty's is more my size.

I write back that I can't; I have to help my dad around
the house. It's not a total lie. My dad did ask me to help him
repot some of his plants. And I said only if he was making
me and if I had no say in the matter, then sure.

What does he need help with?

What to say? I have to be careful about my excuses; Josh
can easily look out the window and see if I'm home or not.
I text back a vague *Just some random chores.* Knowing Josh,
he would show up with a shovel or a rake or whatever tool
the chore entailed. And then he'd stay for dinner, because he
always stays for dinner.

He said I was keeping him going. Me, Lara Jean. I want
to be that person for him, I want to be the one who keeps
him going during this difficult time. I want to be his light-
house keeper while we wait for Margot's return. But it's
hard. Harder than I thought.

15

I WAKE UP HAPPY BECAUSE IT'S THE FIRST
day of school. I've always loved the first day of school better
than the last day of school. Firsts are best because they are
beginnings.

While Daddy and Kitty are upstairs washing up, I make
whole-wheat pancakes with sliced bananas, Kitty's favorite.
First-day-of-school breakfast was always a big thing with my
mom, and then Margot took over, and now I guess it's my
turn. The pancakes are a little dense, not quite as light and
fluffy as Margot's. And the coffee . . . well, is coffee supposed
to be light brown like cocoa? When Daddy comes down, he
says in a merry voice, "I smell coffee!" And then he drinks it
and gives me a thumbs-up, but I notice he only has the one
sip. I guess I'm a better baker than I am a cook.

"You look like a farm girl," Kitty says with a touch of
meanness, and I know she's still at least a little bit mad at me.

"Thank you," I say. I'm wearing faded shortalls and a
scoop-neck floral shirt. It does look farm-girlish, but I think
in a nice way. Margot left her brown lace-up combat boots,
and they're only a half size too big. With thick socks, they're
a perfect fit. "Will you braid my hair to the side?" I ask her.

"You don't deserve a braid from me," Kitty says,
licking her fork. "Besides, a braid would take it too far."

Kitty is only nine, but she has good fashion sense.

"Agreed," my dad says, not looking up from his paper.

I put my plate in the sink and then put Kitty's bag lunch down next to her plate. It's got all her favorite things: a Brie sandwich, barbecue chips, rainbow cookies, the good kind of apple juice.

"Have a great first day," my dad chirps. He pops out his cheek for a kiss, and I bend down and give him one. I try to give Kitty one too, but she turns her cheek.

"I got your favorite kind of apple juice and your favorite kind of Brie," I tell her pleadingly. I really don't want us to start the school year off on a bad note.

"Thank you," she sniffs.

Before she can stop me, I throw my arms around her and squeeze her so tight she yelps. Then I get my new floral back-to-school book bag and head out the front door. It's a new day, a new year. I have a feeling it's going to be a good one.

Josh is already in the car, and I run over and open the door and slide inside.

"You're on time," Josh says. He lifts his hand up for a high five, and when I slap it, our hands make a satisfying smack. "That was a good one," he says.

"An eight at least," I agree. We whizz past the pool, the sign for our neighborhood, then past the Wendy's.

"Has Kitty forgiven you yet for the other night?"

"Not quite, but hopefully soon."

"Nobody can hold a grudge like Kitty," Josh says, and I

nod wholeheartedly. I can never stay mad for long, but Kitty will nurse a grudge like her life depended on it.

"I made her a good first-day-of-school lunch, so I think that'll help," I say.

"You're a good big sister."

I pipe up with "As good as Margot?" and together we chorus, "Nobody's as good as Margot."

16

SCHOOL HAS OFFICIALLY BEGUN AND FOUND
its own rhythm. The first couple of days of school are always
throwaway days of handing out books and syllabuses and fig-
uring out where you're sitting and who you're sitting with.
Now is when school really begins.

For gym, Coach White set us loose outside to enjoy the
warm sun while we still have it. Chris and I are walking the
track field. Chris is telling me about a party she went to over
Labor Day weekend. "I almost got into a fight with this girl
who kept saying I was wearing extensions. It's not my fault
my hair is fabulous."

As we round the corner for our third lap, I catch Peter
Kavinsky looking at me. I thought I was imagining it at first,
him staring in my direction, but this is the third time. He's
playing ultimate Frisbee with some of the guys. When we
pass them, Peter jogs over to us and says, "Can I talk to you
for a minute?"

Chris and I look at each other. "Her or me?" she asks.

"Lara Jean."

Chris puts her arm around my shoulder protectively. "Go
ahead. We're listening."

Peter rolls his eyes. "I want to talk to her in private."

"Fine," she snaps, and she flounces away. Over her shoulder

she looks back at me with wide eyes, like *What?* I shrug back, like *I have no idea!*

In a low, quiet voice, Peter says, "Just so you know, I don't have any STDs."

What in the world? I stare at him, my mouth open. "I never said you had an STD!"

His voice is still low but actually furious. "I also don't always take the last piece of pizza."

"What are you talking about?"

"That's what you said. In your letter. How I'm an egotistical guy who goes around giving girls STDs. Remember?"

"What letter? I never wrote you any letter!"

Wait. Yes I did. I did write him a letter, about a million years ago. But that's not the letter he's talking about. It couldn't be.

"Yes. You. Did. It was addressed to me, from you."

Oh, God. No. No. This isn't happening. This isn't reality. I'm dreaming. I'm in my room and I'm dreaming and Peter Kavinsky is in my dream, glaring at me. I close my eyes. Am I dreaming? Is this real?

"Lara Jean?"

I open my eyes. I'm not dreaming, and this is real. This is a nightmare. Peter Kavinsky is holding my letter in his hand. It's my handwriting, my envelope, my everything. "How—how did you get that?"

"It came in the mail yesterday." Peter sighs. Gruffly he says,

"Listen, it's no big deal; I just hope you're not going around telling people—"

"It came in the mail? To your house?"

"Yeah."

I feel faint. I actually feel faint. Please let me faint right now, because if I faint I will no longer be here, in this moment. It will be like in movies when a girl passes out from the horror of it all and the fighting happens while she is asleep and she wakes up in a hospital bed with a bruise or two, but she's missed all the bad stuff. I wish that was my life instead of this.

I can feel myself start to sweat. Rapidly I say, "You should know that I wrote that letter a really long time ago."

"Okay."

"Like, years ago. Years and years ago. I don't even remember what I said." *Up close, your face wasn't so much handsome as beautiful.* "Seriously, that letter's from middle school. I don't even know who would have sent it. Can I see it?" I reach for the letter, trying to stay calm and not sound desperate. Just casual cool.

He hesitates and then grins his perfect Peter grin. "Nah, I want to keep it. I never got a letter like this before."

I leap forward, and quick like a cat I snatch it out of his hand.

Peter laughs and throws up his hands in surrender. "All right, fine, have it. Geez."

"Thanks." I start to back away from him. The paper is shaking in my hand.

"Wait." He hesitates. "Listen, I didn't mean to steal your first kiss or whatever. I mean, that wasn't my intention—"

I laugh, a forced and fake laugh that sounds crazy even to my own ears. People turn around and look at us. "Apology accepted! Ancient history!" And then I bolt. I run faster than I've ever run. All the way to the girls' locker room.

How did this even happen?

I sink to the floor. I've had the going-to-school-naked dream before. I've had the going-to-school-naked-forgot-to-study-for-an-exam-in-a-class-I-never-signed-up-for combo, the naked-exam-somebody-trying-to-kill-me combo. This is all that times infinity.

And then, because there's nothing left for me to do, I take the letter out of the envelope and I read it.

Dear Peter K,

First of all I refuse to call you Kavinsky. You think you're so cool, going by your last name all of a sudden. Just so you know, Kavinsky sounds like the name of an old man with a long white beard.

Did you know that when you kissed me, I would come to love you? Sometimes I think yes. Definitely yes. You know why? Because you think EVERYONE loves you, Peter. That's what I hate about you. Because

everyone <u>does</u> love you. Including me. I did.
Not anymore.

Here are all your worst qualities:

You burp and you don't say excuse me. You just
assume everyone else will find it charming.
And if they don't, who cares, right? Wrong!
You do care. You care a lot about what people
think of you.

You always take the last piece of pizza. You
never ask if anyone else wants it. That's rude.

You're so good at everything. Too good. You
could've given other guys a chance to be good,
but you never did.

You kissed me for no reason. Even though
I knew you liked Gen, and you knew you
liked Gen, and Gen knew you liked Gen.
But you still did it. Just because you could.
I really want to know: Why would you do
that to me? My first kiss was supposed
to be something special. I've read about it,
what it's supposed to feel like—fireworks
and lightning bolts and the sound of waves
crashing in your ears. I didn't have any of

that. Thanks to you it was as unspecial as a kiss could be.

The worst part of it is, that stupid nothing kiss is what made me start liking you. I never did before. I never even thought about you before. Gen has always said that you are the best-looking boy in our grade, and I agreed, because sure, you are. But I still didn't see the allure of you. Plenty of people are good-looking. That doesn't make them interesting or intriguing or cool.

Maybe that's why you kissed me. To do mind control on me, to _make_ me see you that way. It worked. Your little trick worked. From then on, I saw you. Up close, your face wasn't so much handsome as beautiful. How many beautiful boys have you ever seen? For me it was just one. You. I think it's a lot to do with your lashes. You have really long lashes. Unfairly long.

Even though you don't deserve it, fine, I'll go into all the things I like(d) about you:

One time in science, nobody wanted to be partners with Jeffrey Suttleman because he has BO, and you volunteered like it was no big deal. Suddenly everybody thought Jeffrey wasn't so bad.

You're still in chorus, even though all the other boys take band and orchestra now. You even sing solos. And you dance, and you're not embarrassed.

You were the last boy to get tall. And now you're the tallest, but it's like you earned it. Also, when you were short, no one even cared that you were short—the girls still liked you and the boys still picked you first for basketball in gym.

After you kissed me, I liked you for the rest of seventh grade and most of eighth. It hasn't been easy, watching you with Gen, holding hands and making out at the bus loop. You probably make her feel very special. Because that's your talent, right? You're good at making people feel special.

Do you know what it's like to like someone so much you can't stand it and know that they'll never feel the same way? Probably not. People like you don't have to suffer through those kinds of things. It was easier after Gen moved and we stopped being friends. At least then I didn't have to hear about it.

And now that the year is almost over, I know for sure that I am also over you. I'm immune to you now, Peter. I'm really proud to say that I'm the only girl in this school who has been immunized to the charms of Peter Kavinsky. All because I had a really bad dose of you in seventh grade and most of eighth. Now I never ever have to worry about catching you again. What a relief! I bet if I did ever kiss you again, I would definitely catch something, and it wouldn't be love. It would be an STD!

Lara Jean Song

17

IF I COULD CRAWL INTO A HOLE AND BURROW
in it comfortably and live out the rest of my days in it, well,
then that is what I would do.

Why did I have to bring up that kiss? Why?

I still remember everything about that day at John
Ambrose McClaren's house. We were in the basement, and
it smelled like mildew and laundry detergent. I was wearing
white shorts and an embroidered blue-and-white halter top
I stole out of Margot's closet. I had on a strapless bra for the
first time ever. It was one of Chris's, and I kept adjusting it
because it felt unnatural.

It was one of our first boy-girl hangouts on a weekend
and at night. That was a weird thing too, because it felt pur-
poseful. Not the same as going over to Allie's house after
school and neighborhood boys are there hanging out with
her twin brother. Also not the same as going to the arcade
at the mall knowing we would probably run into boys. This
was making a plan, getting dropped off, wearing a special
bra, all on a Saturday night. No parents around, just us in
John's ultraprivate basement. John's older brother was supposed to be watching us, but John paid him ten dollars to
stay in his room.

Not that anything exciting happened, for instance an

impromptu game of spin the bottle or seven minutes in heaven—two possibilities for which us girls had prepared for with gum and lip gloss. All that happened was the boys played video games and us girls watched and played on our phones and whispered to each other. And then people's moms and dads were picking them up, and it was so anti-climactic after all that planning and anticipation. It was disappointing for me, not because I liked anyone, but because I liked romance and drama and I was hoping something exciting would happen to someone.

Something did.

To me!

Peter and I were downstairs alone, the last two people to be picked up. We were sitting on the couch. I kept texting my dad, Where are uuuuuu? Peter was playing a game on his phone.

And then, out of nowhere, he said, "Your hair smells like coconuts."

We weren't even sitting that close. I said, "Really? You can smell it from there?"

He scooted closer and took a sniff, nodding. "Yeah, it reminds me of Hawaii or something."

"Thanks!" I said. I wasn't positive it was a compliment, but it seemed like enough of one to say thanks. "I've been switching between this coconut one and my sister's baby shampoo, to do an experiment on which makes my hair softer—"

Then Peter Kavinsky leaned right in and kissed me, and I was stunned.

I'd never thought of him any kind of way before that kiss. He was too pretty, too smooth. Not my type of boy at all. But after he kissed me, he was all I could think about for months after.

What if Peter is just the beginning? What if . . . what if my other letters somehow got sent too? To John Ambrose McClaren. Kenny from camp. Lucas Krapf.

Josh.

Oh my God, Josh.

I leap up off the floor. I've got to find that hatbox. I've got to find those letters.

I go back outside to the track. I don't see Chris anywhere, so I guess she is smoking behind the field house. I go straight over to Coach, who is sitting on the bleachers with his phone.

"I can't stop throwing up," I whimper. I double over and cradle my arms to my stomach. "Can I please go to the nurse's office?"

Coach barely looks up from his phone. "Sure."

As soon as I'm out of his eye line, I make a run for it. Gym's my last period of the day, and my house is only a couple of miles from school. I run like the wind. I don't think I've ever run so hard or so fast in my life, and I likely never will again. I run so hard, a couple of times I have to stop because I feel like I really am going to throw up. And then I remember the letters, and Josh, and *Up close, your face wasn't so much handsome as beautiful*, and I'm off and running again.

As soon as I get home, I dash upstairs and go into my closet for my hatbox. It's not sitting on the top shelf where it usually sits. It's not on the floor, or behind my stack of board games. It's not anywhere. I get on my hands and knees and start rifling through piles of sweaters, shoe boxes, craft supplies. I look in places it could not possibly be, because it's a hatbox and it's big, but I look anyway. My hatbox is nowhere.

I collapse onto the floor. This is a horror movie. My life has become a horror movie. Next to me my phone buzzes. It's Josh. Where are you? Did you get a ride home with Chris?

I turn my phone off and go down to the kitchen and call Margot on the house phone. It's still my first impulse, to go to her when things get bad. I'll just leave out the Josh part of it and focus on the Peter part. She'll know what to do; she always knows what to do. I'm all set to burst out, *Gogo, I miss you so much and everything's a mess without you*, but when she picks up the phone, she sounds sleepy, and I can tell that I've woken her up. "Were you sleeping?" I ask.

"No, I was just lying down," she lies.

"Yes you *were* sleeping! Gogo, it's not even ten o'clock over there! Wait, is it? Did I calculate wrong again?"

"No, you're right. I'm just so tired. I've been up since five, because . . ." Her voice trails off. "What's wrong?"

I hesitate. Maybe it's better not to burden Margot with all of this. I mean, she just got to college: this is what she's worked for; this is her dream come true. She should be having fun and not worrying over how things are going back home without her. Besides, what would I even say? I wrote a bunch of love letters and they got sent out, including one I wrote to your boyfriend? "Nothing's wrong," I say. I'm doing what Margot would do, which is figure it out on my own.

"It definitely sounds like something's wrong." Margot yawns. "Tell me."

"Go back to sleep, Gogo."

"Okay," she says, yawning again.

We hang up and I make myself an ice cream sundae right in the carton: chocolate sauce, whipped cream, chopped nuts. The works. I take it back up to my room and eat it lying down. I feed it to myself like medicine, until I've eaten the whole thing, every last bite.

18

A LITTLE WHILE LATER I WAKE UP TO KITTY standing at the foot of my bed. "You've got ice cream on your sheets," she informs me.

I groan and turn over to my side. "Kitty, that's the least of my problems today."

"Daddy wants to know if you want chicken for dinner or hamburgers. My vote is chicken."

I sit straight up. Daddy's home! Maybe he knows something. He was on that cleaning binge, throwing things away. Maybe he's spirited my hatbox away somewhere safe, and the Peter letter was just an unfortunate fluke!

I jump out of bed and run downstairs, my heart thumping hard in my chest. My dad's in his study, wearing his glasses and reading a thick book on Audubon paintings.

All in one breath I ask, "Daddy-have-you-seen-my-hatbox?"

He looks up; his face is hazy and I can tell he is still with Audubon's birds and not at all focused on my frenzied state. "What box?"

"My teal hatbox Mommy gave me!"

"Oh, that . . . ," he says, still looking confused. He takes off his glasses. "I don't know. It might have gone the way of your roller skates."

"What does that mean? What are you even saying?"

"Goodwill. There's a slight possibility I took them to Goodwill."

When I gasp, my dad says defensively, "Those roller skates don't even fit you anymore. They were just taking up space!"

I sink to the floor. "They were pink and they were vintage and I was saving them for Kitty . . . and that's not even the point. I don't care about the roller skates. I care about my hatbox! Daddy, you don't even know what you've done." My dad gets up and tries to pull me off the floor. I resist him and flop onto my back like a goldfish.

"Lara Jean, I don't even know that I got rid of it. Come on, let's have a look around the house, all right? Don't let's panic yet."

"There's only one place it could be, and it's not there. It's gone."

"Then I'll check Goodwill tomorrow on my way to work," he says, squatting down next to me. He's giving me that look—sympathetic but also exasperated and mystified, like *How is it possible that my sane and reasonable DNA created such a crazy daughter?*

"It's too late. It's too late. There's no point."

"What was in that box that's so important?"

I can feel my ice cream sundae curdling in my stomach. For the second time today I feel like I'm going to be sick. "Only everything."

He grimaces. "I really didn't realize your mother had given it to you or that it was so important." As he retreats off to the kitchen, he says, "Hey, how about an ice cream sundae before dinner? Will that cheer you up?"

As if dessert before dinner would be the thing that cheers me up, as if I am Kitty's age and not sixteen going on seventeen. I don't even bother dignifying it with an answer. I just lie there on the floor, my cheek against the cool hardwood. Besides, there isn't any ice cream left anyway, but he'll find that out soon enough.

I don't even want to think about Josh reading that letter. I don't even want to think it. It's too terrible.

After dinner (chicken, per Kitty's request), I'm in the kitchen doing dishes when I hear the doorbell ring. Daddy opens the door, and I hear Josh's voice. "Hey, Dr. Covey. Is Lara Jean around?"

Oh, no. No no no no. I can't see Josh. I know I have to at some point, but not today. Not right this second. I can't. I just can't.

I drop the plate back into the sink and make a run for it, out the back door, down the porch steps, across the backyard to the Pearces' yard. I scramble up the wooden ladder and into Carolyn Pearce's old tree house. I haven't been in this tree house since middle school. We used to hang out up here sometimes, at night—Chris and Genevieve and Allie and me, the boys a couple of times.

I peek through the wooden slats, crouched in a ball, waiting until I see Josh walk back to his house. When I'm sure he's inside, I climb down the ladder and run back to mine. I sure have been doing a lot of running today. I'm exhausted, now that I think of it.

19

I WAKE UP THE NEXT MORNING RENEWED. I am a girl with a plan. I'm just going to have to avoid Josh forever. It's as simple as that. And if not forever, then at least until this dies down and he forgets about my letter. There's still the tiny chance he never even got it. Perhaps whoever mailed Peter's only sent the one! You never know.

My mom always said optimism was my best trait. Both Chris and Margot have said it's annoying, but to that I say looking on the bright side of life never killed anybody.

When I get downstairs, Daddy and Kitty are already at the table eating toast. I make myself a bowl of cereal and sit down with them.

"I'm going to stop by Goodwill on my way to work," my dad says, crunching on his toast from behind his newspaper. "I'm sure the hatbox will turn up there."

"Your hatbox is missing?" Kitty asks me. "The one Mommy gave you?"

I nod and shovel cereal into my mouth. I have to leave soon or else I'll risk running into Josh on my way out.

"What was in the box, anyway?" Kitty asks.

"That's private," I say. "All you need to know is the contents are precious to me."

"Will you be mad at Daddy if you never get the hatbox

back?" Kitty answers her own question before I can. "I doubt it. You never stay mad for long."

This is true. I never can stay mad for long.

Peering over his newspaper, he asks Kitty, "What in the world was in that hatbox?"

Kitty shrugs. Her mouth full of toast, she says, "Probably more French berets?"

"No, not more berets." I give them both a mean look. "Now if you'll excuse me, I don't want to be late for school."

"Aren't you leaving a little early?"

"I'm taking the bus today," I say. And probably every day until Margot's car is fixed, but they don't need to know that.

20

THE WAY IT HAPPENS IS A STRANGE SORT of serendipity. A slow-motion train wreck. For something to go this colossally wrong, everything must intersect and collide at the exact right, or in this case, wrong, moment.

If the bus driver hadn't had trouble backing out of the cul-de-sac, taking four extra minutes to get to school, I never would have run into Josh.

If Josh's car had started up and he hadn't had to get a jump from *his* dad, he wouldn't have been walking by my locker.

And if Peter hadn't had to meet Ms. Wooten in the guidance office, he would not have been walking down the hallway ten seconds later. And maybe this whole thing would not have happened. But it did.

I'm at my locker; the door is jammed, and I'm trying to yank it open. I finally get the door loose and there's Josh, standing right there.

"Lara Jean . . ." He has this shell-shocked, confused expression on his face. "I've been trying to talk to you since last night. I came by, and nobody could find you. . . ." He holds out my letter. "I don't understand. What is this?"

"I don't know . . . ," I hear myself say. My voice feels

far away. It's like I'm floating above myself, watching it all unfold.

"I mean, it's from you, right?"

"Oh, wow." I take a breath and accept the letter. I fight the urge to tear it up. "Where did you even get this?"

"It got sent to me in the mail." Josh jams his hands into his pockets. "When did you write this?"

"Like, a long time ago," I say. I let out a fake little laugh. "I don't even remember when. It might have been middle school." Good job, Lara Jean. Keep it up.

Slowly he says, "Right . . . but you mention going to the movies with Margot and Mike and Ben that time. That was a couple of years ago."

I bite my bottom lip. "Right. I mean, it was *kind* of a long time ago. In the grand scheme of things." I can feel tears coming on so close that if I break concentration even for a second, if I waver, I will cry and that will make everything worse, if such a thing is possible. I must be cool and breezy and nonchalant now. Tears would ruin that.

Josh is staring at me so hard I have to look away. "So then . . . Do you . . . or did you have feelings for me or . . . ?"

"I mean, yes, sure, I did have a crush on you at one point, before you and Margot ever started dating. A million years ago."

"Why didn't you ever say anything? Because, Lara Jean . . . God. I don't know." His eyes are on me, and they're confused, but there's something else, too. "This is crazy. I feel kind of blindsided."

The way he's looking at me now, I'm suddenly in a time warp back to a summer day when I was fourteen and he was fifteen, and we were walking home from somewhere. He was looking at me so intently I was sure he was going to try to kiss me. I got nervous, so I picked a fight with him and he never looked at me like that again.

Until this moment.

Don't. Just please, don't.

Whatever he's thinking, whatever he wants to say, I don't want to hear it. I will do anything, literally anything, not to hear it.

Before he can, I say, "I'm dating someone."

Josh's jaw goes slack. "What?"

What?

"Yup. I'm dating someone, someone I really really like, so please don't worry about this." I wave the letter like it's just paper, trash, like once upon a time I didn't literally pour my heart onto this page. I stuff it into my bag. "I was really confused when I wrote this; I don't even know how it got sent out. Honestly, it's not worth talking about. So please, please don't say anything to Margot about it."

He nods, but that's not good enough. I need a verbal commitment. I need to hear the words come out of his mouth. So I add, "Do you swear? On your life?" If Margot was to ever find out . . . I would want to die.

"All right, I swear. I mean, we haven't even spoken since she left."

I let out a huge breath. "Great. Thanks." I'm about to walk away, but then Josh stops me.

"Who's the guy?"

"What guy?"

"The guy you're dating."

That's when I see him. Peter Kavinsky, walking down the hallway. Like magic. Beautiful, dark-haired Peter. He deserves background music, he looks so good. "Peter. Kavinsky. Peter Kavinsky!" The bell rings, and I sail past Josh. "I've gotta go! Talk later, Josh!"

"Wait!" he calls out.

I run up to Peter and launch myself into his arms like a shot out of a cannon. I've got my arms around his neck and my legs hooked around his waist, and I don't even know how my body knows how, because I've for sure never touched a boy like this in my life. It's like we're in a movie and the music is swelling and waves are crashing around us. Except for the fact that Peter's expression is registering pure shock and disbelief and maybe a drop of amusement, because Peter likes to be amused. Raising his eyebrows, he says, "Lara Jean? What the—?"

I don't answer. I just kiss him.

My first thought is: I have muscle memory of his lips.

My second thought is: I hope Josh is watching. He has to be watching or it's all for nothing.

My heart is beating so fast I forget to be afraid of doing it wrong. Because for about three seconds, he's kissing me back. Peter Kavinsky, the boy of every girl's dreams, is kissing me back.

I haven't kissed that many boys before. Peter Kavinsky, John Ambrose McClaren, Allie Feldman's cousin with the weird eye, and now Peter again.

I open my eyes and Peter's staring at me with that same expression on his face. Very sincerely I say, "Thank you." He replies, "You're welcome," and I hop out of his arms and sprint off in the opposite direction.

It takes all of history class and most of English for my heart rate to slow down. I kissed Peter Kavinsky. In the hallway, in front of everybody. In front of Josh.

I didn't think this thing through, obviously. That's what Margot would say, including and especially the "obviously." If I *had* thought it through, I would have made up a boyfriend and not picked an actual person. More specifically, I would not have picked Peter K. He is literally the worst person I could have picked, because everybody knows him. He's Peter Kavinsky, for Pete's sake. Kavinsky of Gen and Kavinsky. It doesn't matter that they're broken up. They're an institution at this institution.

I spend the rest of the day hiding out. I even eat my lunch in the girls' bathroom.

My last class of the day is gym. With Peter. Coach White gives us a reintroduction to the weight room, and we have to practice using the machines. Peter and his friends already know how to use them, so they separate off from

JENNY HAN

the group and have a free-throw contest, and I don't get a chance to talk to him. At one point he catches me looking at him and he winks, which makes me want to shrivel up and die.

After class is over, I wait for Peter outside the boys' locker room, planning out what I'm going to say, how I'm going to explain it. I'll start out with, "So about this morning . . . ," and then I'll give a little laugh, like how hilarious was that!

Peter's the last one to come out. His hair is wet from a shower. It's weird that boys take showers at school, since girls never do. I wonder if they have stalls in there, or just a bunch of shower heads and no privacy.

"Hey," he says when he sees me, but he doesn't stop.

To his back I hurriedly say, "So about this morning . . ." I laugh, and Peter turns around and just looks at me.

"Oh yeah. What was that all about?"

"It was a dumb joke," I begin.

Peter crosses his arms and leans against the lockers. "Did it have anything to do with that letter you sent me?"

"No. I mean, yes. Tangentially."

"Look," he says kindly. "I think you're cute. In a quirky way. But Gen and I just broke up, and I'm not in a place right now where I want be somebody's boyfriend. So . . ."

My mouth drops. Peter Kavinsky is giving me the brush-off! I don't even like him, and he's giving me the brush-off. Also, "quirky"? How am I "quirky"? "Cute in a quirky way" is an insult. A total insult!

He's still talking, still giving me the kind eyes. "I mean, I'm definitely flattered. That you would like me all this time—it's flattering, you know?"

That's enough. That's plenty enough. "I don't like you," I say, loudly. "So there's no reason you should feel flattered."

Now it's Peter's turn to look taken aback. He quickly looks around to see if anyone heard. He leans forward and whispers, "Then why did you kiss me?"

"I kissed you *because* I don't like you," I explain, like this should be obvious. "See, my letters got sent out by someone. Not me."

"Wait a minute. 'Letters'? How many of us are there?"

"Five. And the guy I *do* like got one too—"

Peter frowns. "Who?"

Why should I tell him anything? "That's . . . personal."

"Hey, I think I have a right to know, since you pulled me into this little drama," Peter says with a pointed look. I suck in my top lip and shake my head and he adds, "If there even really is a guy."

"There is so a guy! It's Josh Sanderson."

"Doesn't he go out with your sister?"

I nod. I'm surprised he even knows this. I didn't think Josh and Margot would be on his radar. "They're broken up now. But I don't want him to know I have feelings for him . . . for obvious reasons. So . . . I told him you were my boyfriend."

"So you used me to save face?"

"I mean, basically." Basically exactly.

"You're a funny girl."

First I'm cute in a quirky way; now I'm a funny girl. I know what that means. "Anyway, thanks for going along with it, Peter." I flash him what I hope is a winning smile and turn on my heel to go. "See ya!"

Peter reaches out and grabs me by the backpack. "Wait— so Sanderson thinks I'm your boyfriend now, right? So what are you going to tell him?"

I try to shrug him loose, but he won't let go. "I haven't figured that part out yet. But I will." I lift my chin. "I'm quirky like that."

Peter laughs out loud, his mouth open wide. "You really are funny, Lara Jean."

21

MY PHONE VIBRATES NEXT TO ME. IT'S CHRIS.

"Is it true?" I can hear her puffing on her cigarette.

"Is what true?"

I'm lying on my bed, on my stomach. My mom told me that if my stomach hurt, I should lie on my stomach and it would warm up and feel better. I don't think it's helping, though. My stomach's been in knots all day.

"Did you run up to Kavinsky and kiss him like a maniac?"

I close my eyes and whimper. I wish I could say no, because I'm not the kind of person to do that. But I did do it, so I guess I am. But my reasons were really good! I want to tell Chris the truth, but the whole thing is just so embarrassing. "Yeah. I went up to Peter Kavinsky and kissed him. Like a maniac."

Chris exhales. "Damn!"

"I know."

"What the hell were you thinking?"

"Honestly? I don't even know. I just . . . did it."

"Shit. I didn't know you had it in you. I'm kind of impressed."

"Thanks."

"But you know Gen's gonna come after you, right? They may be broken up, but she still thinks she owns his ass."

My stomach lurches. "Yeah. I know. I'm scared, Chris."

"I'll do my best to protect you from her, but you know how she is. You better watch your back." Chris hangs up.

I feel even worse than before. If Margot was here, she'd probably say that writing those letters was pointless in the first place, and she'd get on me about telling such a big lie. Then she'd help me figure out a solution. But Margot's not here, she's in Scotland—and even bigger than that, she's the one person I can't talk to. She can never-never-never know how I felt about Josh.

After a while I get out of bed and wander into Kitty's room. She's on the floor rifling through her bottom drawer. Without looking up, she says, "Have you seen my pajamas with the hearts?"

"I washed them yesterday, so they're probably in the dryer. Tonight do you wanna watch a movie and play Uno?" I could use a cheer-up night.

Kitty scrambles up. "Can't. I'm going to Alicia Bernard's birthday. It's in the schedule notebook."

"Who's Alicia Bernard?" I plop down on Kitty's unmade bed.

"She's the new girl. She invited all the girls in our class. Her mom's making us crepes for breakfast. Do you know what a crepe is?"

"Yes."

"Have you ever had one? I heard they can be salty or sweet."

"Yes, I had one with Nutella and strawberries once." Josh and Margot and I drove down to Richmond because Margot wanted to go to the Edgar Allan Poe museum. We ate lunch at a café downtown and that's what I had.

Kitty's eyes go big and greedy. "I hope that's the kind her mom makes." Then she dashes off, I guess to find her pajamas in the laundry room downstairs.

I pick up Kitty's stuffed pig and cuddle it in my arms. So even my nine-year-old sister has plans on a Friday night. If Margot was here, we'd be going to the movies with Josh, or stopping by the cocktail hour at the Belleview retirement home. If my dad was home, I could maybe get up the courage to take his car or have him drop me off, but I can't even do that.

After Kitty gets picked up, I go back to my room and organize my shoe collection. It's a little early in the season to switch out my sandals for my winter shoes, but I go ahead and do it because I'm in the mood. I think about doing my clothes too, but that's no small undertaking. Instead I sit down and write Margot a letter on stationery my grandma bought me in Korea. It's pale blue with a border of fluffy white lambs. I talk about school, and Kitty's new teacher, and a lavender skirt I ordered from a Japanese website that I'm sure she'll want to borrow, but I don't tell her any of the real things.

I miss her so much. Nothing's the same without her. I'm realizing now that the year is going to be a lonely one, because I don't have Margot, and I don't have Josh, and it's just me alone. I have Chris, but not really. I wish I'd made more friends. If I had more friends, maybe I wouldn't have done something as stupid as kiss Peter K. in the hallway and tell Josh he's my boyfriend.

22

I WAKE UP TO THE SOUND OF THE LAWN mower.

It's Saturday morning and I can't fall back to sleep, so now I'm lying in my bed staring at my walls, at all the pictures and things I've saved. I'm thinking I want to shake things up. I'm thinking maybe I should paint my room. The only question is, what color? Lavender? Cotton-candy pink? Something bold, like turquoise? Maybe just an accent wall? Maybe one marigold wall, one salmon pink. It's a lot to consider. I should probably wait for Margot to come home before I make such a momentous decision. Plus I've never painted a room before, and Margot has, with Habitat for Humanity. She'll know what to do.

On Saturdays we usually have something good for breakfast, like pancakes or frittata with frozen shredded potato and broccoli. But since there's no Kitty and no Margot, I just eat cereal instead. Who ever heard of making pancakes or frittata for just one person? My dad's been awake for hours; he's outside mowing the lawn. I don't want to get roped into helping him do yard work, so I make myself busy in the house and clean the downstairs. I Swiffer and DustBust and wipe the tables down, and all the while my wheels are turning about how I'm going to get myself out of this Peter K. situation with even a sliver of dignity. The wheels turn and turn, but no good solutions come to mind.

When Kitty gets dropped off, I'm folding laundry. She plops down on the couch on her belly and asks me, "What'd you do last night?"

"Nothing. I just stayed home."

"And?"

"I organized my closet." It's humiliating to say that out loud. Hastily I change the subject. "So did Alicia's mom make sweet crepes or salty ones?"

"She made both. First we had ham and cheese and then we had Nutella. How come we never have any Nutella?"

"I think maybe because hazelnuts make Margot's throat itch."

"Can we get some next time?"

"Sure," I say. "We'll just have to eat the whole jar before Margot comes home."

"No problem," Kitty says.

"On a scale of one to ten, how badly do you miss Gogo?" I ask her.

Kitty thinks this over. "A six point five," she says at last.

"Only a six point five?"

"Yeah, I've been really busy," she says, rolling over and kicking her legs up in the air. "I've hardly had time to miss Margot. You know, if you got out more, maybe you wouldn't miss her so much."

I boomerang a sock at her head and Kitty explodes into a giggle fit. I'm tickling her armpits when Daddy comes in from outside with a stack of mail. "Something came back return to sender for you, Lara Jean," he says, handing me an envelope.

It's got my handwriting! I scramble up and snatch it out of his hands. It's my letter to Kenny from camp. It came back to me!

"Who's Kenny?" Daddy wants to know.

"Just a boy I met at church camp a long time ago," I say, tearing the envelope open.

Dear Kenny,

It's the last day of camp and possibly the last time I will ever see you because we live so far apart. Remember on the second day, I was scared to do archery and you made a joke about minnows and it was so funny I nearly peed my pants?

I stop reading. A joke about *minnows*? How funny could it have been?

I was really homesick but you made me feel better. I think I might've left camp early if it hadn't been for you, Kenny. So, thank you. Also you're a really amazing swimmer and I like your laugh. I wish it had been me you kissed at the bonfire last night and not Blaire H.

Take care, Kenny. Have a really good rest of the summer and a really good life.

Love, Lara Jean

I clutch the letter to my chest.

This is the first love letter I ever wrote. I'm glad it came back to me. Though, I suppose it wouldn't have been so bad if Kenny Donati got to know that he helped two people at camp that summer—the kid who almost drowned in the lake and twelve-year-old Lara Jean Song Covey.

23

WHEN MY DAD HAS A DAY OFF, HE COOKS Korean food. It's not exactly authentic, and sometimes he just goes to the Korean market and buys ready-made side dishes and marinated meat, but sometimes he'll call our grandma for a recipe and he'll try. That's the thing: Daddy tries. He doesn't say so, but I know it's because he doesn't want us to lose our connection to our Korean side, and food is the only way he knows how to contribute. After Mommy died, he used to try to make us have play dates with other Korean kids, but it always felt awkward and forced. Except I did have a crush on Edward Kim for a minute there. Thank God the crush never escalated into full-on love—or else I'd have written him a letter too, and that'd be just one more person I'd have to avoid.

My dad's made bo ssam, which is pork shoulder you slice up and then wrap in lettuce. He brined it last night in sugar and salt and it's been roasting in the oven all day. Kitty and I keep checking on it; it smells so good.

When it's finally time to eat, my dad has everything laid out on the dining room table so pretty. A silver bowl of butter-lettuce leaves, just washed, with the water beads still clinging to the surface; a cut-glass bowl of kimchi he bought from Whole Foods; a little bowl of pepper paste; soy sauce with scallions and ginger.

My dad's taking arty pictures of the table. "I'm sending a pic to Margot so she can see," he says.

"What time is it over there?" I ask him. It's a cozy day: it's nearly six o'clock, and I'm still in my pj's. I'm hugging my knees to me, sitting in the big dining-room chair with the armrests.

"It's eleven. I'm sure she's still up," my dad says, snapping away. "Why don't you invite Josh over? We're going to need help finishing all this food."

"He's probably busy," I say quickly. I still haven't figured out what I'm going to say to him about me and Peter, much less me and him.

"Just try him. He loves Korean food." Daddy moves the pork shoulder so it's more centered. "Hurry, before my bo ssam gets cold!"

I pretend to text him on my phone. I feel a tiny bit guilty for lying, but Daddy would understand if he knew all the facts.

"I don't understand why you kids text when you could just call. You'd get an answer right away instead of waiting for one."

"You're so old, Daddy," I say. I look down at my phone. "Josh can't come over. Let's just eat. Kitty! Dinner bell!"

"Co-ming!" Kitty screams from upstairs.

"Well, maybe he'll come over later and take some leftovers," Daddy says.

"Daddy, Josh has his own life now. Why would he come over when Margot's not here? Besides, they're not even together anymore, remember?"

My dad makes a confused face. "What? They're not?"

I guess Margot didn't tell him after all. Though you'd have thought he could have sussed it out for himself when Josh didn't come with us to the airport to drop Margot off. Why don't dads know anything? Does he not have eyes and ears? "No, they're not. And by the way, Margot is at college in Scotland. And my name is Lara Jean."

"All right, all right, your dad is clueless," Daddy says. "I get it. No need to rub it in." He scratches his chin. "Geez, I could have sworn Margot never mentioned anything. . . ."

Kitty comes crashing into the dining room. "Yum yum yum." She slams into her chair and starts spearing pork onto her plate.

"Kitty, we have to pray first," my dad says, settling into his chair.

We only ever pray before we eat when we eat in the dining room, and we only ever eat in the dining room when Daddy cooks Korean or on Thanksgiving or Christmas. Mommy used to take us to church when we were little, and after she died, Daddy tried to keep it going, but he has Sunday shifts sometimes and it became less and less.

"Thank you, God, for this food you have blessed us with. Thank you for my beautiful daughters, and please watch over our Margot. In Jesus's name we pray, amen."

"Amen," we echo.

"Looks pretty great, right, girls?" My dad is grinning as he assembles a lettuce leaf with pork and rice and kimchi. "Kitty, you know how to do it, right? It's like a little taco."

Kitty nods and copies him.

I make my own lettuce-leaf taco and nearly spit it out. The pork is really really salty. So salty I could cry. But I keep chewing, and across the table Kitty's making a horrible face at me, but I give her a *shush* look. Daddy hasn't tried his yet; he's taking a picture of his plate.

"So good, Daddy," I say. "It tastes like at the restaurant."

"Thanks, Lara Jean. It came out just like the picture. I can't believe how beautiful and crispy the top looks." My dad finally takes a bite, and then he frowns. "Is this salty to you?"

"Not really," I say.

He takes another bite. "This tastes really salty to me. Kitty, what do you think?"

Kitty's chugging water. "No, it tastes good, Daddy."

I give her a secret thumbs-up.

"Hmm, no, it definitely tastes salty." He swallows. "I followed the recipe exactly . . . maybe I used the wrong kind of salt for the brine? Lara Jean, taste it again."

I take a teeny-tiny bite, which I try to hide by putting the lettuce in front of my face. "Mmm."

"Maybe if I cut more from the center . . ."

My phone buzzes on the table. It's a text from Josh. Was coming back from a run and saw the light on in the dining room. A totally normal text, as if yesterday never happened.

Korean food??

Josh has some sixth sense of when my dad's cooking Korean food, because he'll come sniffing around right when we're sitting down to eat. He loves Korean food. When my grandma comes to visit, he won't leave her side. He'll even watch Korean dramas with her. She cuts him pieces of apple and peels clementines for him like he's a baby. My grandma likes boys better than girls.

Now that I think of it, all the women in my family really do love Josh. Except for Mommy, who never got to meet him. But I'm sure she'd love him too. She'd love anyone who's as good to Margot as Josh is, was, to her.

Kitty cranes her neck to look over my shoulder. "Is that Josh? Is he coming over?"

"No!" I set down my phone and it buzzes again. Can I come over?

"It says he wants to come over!"

My dad perks up. "Tell him to come over! I want to get his opinion on this bo ssam."

"Listen, everyone in this family needs to accept that Josh is no longer a part of it. He and Margot are donzo—" I hesitate. Does Kitty still not know? I can't remember if it's still supposed to be a secret. "I mean now that Margot's at college and they're long distance . . ."

"I know they're broken up," Kitty says, making a lettuce wrap with just rice. "Margot told me over video chat."

Across the table my dad makes a sad face and stuffs a piece of lettuce in his mouth.

Her mouth full, Kitty continues, "I just don't see why we can't still be friends with him. He's all of our friend. Right, Daddy?"

"Right," my dad agrees. "And look, relationships are incredibly amorphous. They could get back together. They could stay friends. Who's to say what will happen in the future? I say we don't count Josh out just yet."

We're finishing up dinner when I get another text from Josh. Never mind, it says.

We are stuck eating that salty pork shoulder for the rest of the weekend. The next morning, my dad makes fried rice and cuts the pork into tiny pieces and says to "think of it like bacon." For dinner I test that theory by mixing it with Kraft macaroni and cheese, and I end up throwing out the whole batch because it tastes like slop. "If we had a dog . . . ," Kitty keeps saying. I make a batch of regular macaroni instead.

After dinner I take Sadie the Sweetheart for a walk. That's what my sisters and I call Sadie; she's a golden retriever that lives down the street. The Shahs are out of town for the night, so they asked me to feed her and walk her. Normally, Kitty would beg to be the one to do it, but there's some movie on TV that she's been waiting to see.

Sadie and I are doing the usual route around our cul-de-sac when Josh jogs up to us in his running clothes. Crouching down to pet Sadie, he says, "So how are things going with Kavinsky?"

Funny you should bring that up, Josh. 'Cause I've got my story locked and loaded. Peter and I had a fight via video chat this morning (in case Josh has noticed I haven't left the house all weekend), and we broke up, and I'm devastated about the whole thing, because I've been in constant love with Peter Kavinsky since the seventh grade, but *c'est la vie.*

"Actually, Peter and I broke up this morning." I bite my lip and try to look sad. "It's just, really hard, you know? After I liked him for so long and then finally he likes me back. But it's just not meant to be. I don't think he's over his breakup yet. I think maybe Genevieve still has too strong a hold on him, so there's no room in his heart for me."

Josh gives me a funny look. "That's not what he was saying today at McCalls."

What in the world was Peter K. doing at a bookstore? He's not the bookstore type. "What did he say?" I try to sound casual, but my heart is pounding so loudly I'm pretty sure Sadie can hear it.

Josh keeps petting Sadie.

"What did he say?" Now I'm just trying not to sound shrill. "Like, what was said exactly?"

"When I was ringing him up, I asked him when you

guys started going out, and he said recently. He said he really liked you."

What . . .

I must look as shocked as I feel, because Josh straightens up and says, "Yeah, I was kind of surprised too."

"You were surprised that he would like me?"

"Well, kind of. Kavinsky just isn't the kind of guy who would date a girl like you." When I stare back at him, sour and unsmiling, he quickly tries to backtrack. "I mean, because you're not, you know . . ."

"I'm not what? As pretty as Genevieve?"

"No! That's not what I'm saying. What I'm trying to say is, you're like this sweet, innocent girl who likes to be at home with her family, and I don't know, I guess Kavinsky doesn't strike me as someone who would be into that."

Before he can say another word, I grab my phone out of my jacket pocket and say, "That's Peter calling me right now, so I guess he does like homely girls."

"I didn't say homely! I said you like to be at home!"

"Later, Josh." I speed walk away, dragging Sadie with me. Into my phone I say, "Oh hey, Peter."

24

IN CHEM, PETER SITS A ROW IN FRONT OF ME.

I write him a note. *Why would you tell Josh that we're—* I hesitate and then finish with *a thing?*

I kick the back of his chair, and he turns around and I hand him the note. He slouches in his seat to read it; then I watch as he scribbles something. He tips back in his chair and drops the note on my desk without looking at me.

A thing? Haha.

I press down so hard my pencil tip chips off. *Please answer the question.*

We'll talk later.

I let out a frustrated sigh and Matt, my lab partner, gives me a funny look.

After class Peter is swept away with all his friends; they leave in a big group. I'm packing up my backpack when he returns, alone. He hops up on the table. "So let's talk," he says, super casual.

I clear my throat and try to gather my bearings. "Why did you tell Josh we were—" I almost say "a thing" again, but then change it to "together?"

"I don't get what you're so upset about. I did you a favor. I could have just as easily blown up your spot."

I pause. He's right. He could have. "So why didn't you?"

"You've sure got a funny way of saying thank you. You're welcome, by the way."

Automatically I say, "Thank you." Wait. Why am I thanking him? "I appreciate you letting me kiss you, but—"

"You're welcome," he says again.

Ugh! He's so insufferable. Just for that I'm going to toss a little dig his way. "That was . . . really generous of you. To let me do that. But I've already explained to Josh that it's not going to work out with us because Genevieve has you whipped, so it's all good. You can stop pretending now."

Peter glares at me. "I'm not whipped."

"But aren't you, though? I mean, you guys have been together since the seventh grade. You're basically her property."

"You don't know what you're talking about," Peter scoffs.

"There was a rumor last year that she made you get a tattoo of her initials on your butt for her birthday." I pause. "So did you?" I reach around him and fake try to lift up the back of his shirt. He yelps and jumps away from me, and I collapse in a fit of giggles. "So you *do* have a tattoo!"

"I don't have a tattoo!" he yells. "And we're not even together anymore, so can you stop with this shit? We broke up. We're over. I'm done with her."

"Wait, didn't *she* break up with *you*?" I ask.

Peter shoots me a dirty look. "It was mutual."

Hastily I say, "Well, I'm sure you'll get back together soon. You've broken up before, right? Only to get back together again, like immediately. It's probably because you were each other's firsts. That's why you can't let each other go. I've heard that's how it is with firsts, especially with guys."

Peter's mouth drops. "How do you know—"

"Oh, everybody knows. You guys did it freshman year in her parents' basement, right?"

He gives a grudging nod.

"See? Even I know, and I'm a nobody. Even if you do stay broken up for real this time, which I doubt, it's not like any other girl can date you." Meaningfully I say, "Let's not forget what happened to Jamila Singh."

Peter and Genevieve broke up for a month last year, so Peter started dating Jamila Singh. Jamila might even be prettier than Genevieve—a different kind of pretty, anyway. More like hot. She has long wavy black hair and a little waist and a big butt. Let's just say it didn't end well for her. Not only did Genevieve cut her out of the group, but she told everyone that Jamila's family had an Indonesian slave living with them, when really it was just her cousin. And I'm pretty sure it was Genevieve who started a rumor online that Jamila washed her hair only once a month. The final straw was when Jamila's parents got an anonymous e-mail saying that she was having sex with Peter. Her parents transferred her right out and put her in private school. Genevieve and Peter were back together by spring formal.

"Gen says she didn't have anything to do with that."

I give him a *get real* look. "Please, Peter. I know her well and so do you. Well, I did know her well. But I don't think people change at the core. They are who they are."

Slowly Peter says, "That's right. You two were BFFs back in the day."

"We were friends," I agree. "I wouldn't call us BFFs, but . . ." Wait a minute, why are we talking about me again? "Everybody knows it was Genevieve who told Jamila's parents. You don't have to be a detective to figure out that Genevieve was jealous of her. Jamila was the prettiest girl in our grade, next to Genevieve. Gen was always a very jealous person. I remember this one time my dad bought me a . . ."

Peter's staring at me in a thoughtful way, and it's all of a sudden making me nervous.

"What?"

"Let's just do this for a little while."

"Do what?"

"Let's let people think we're a couple."

Wait . . . what?

"It's driving Gen crazy not knowing what's up with you and me. Why don't we let her sit with it a little longer? It's actually kind of perfect. You date me first, and then Gen will get it that we're over. You'll be breaking the seal." He raises an eyebrow at me. "Do you even know what breaking the seal means?"

"Yes, of course I know what that means." I have no idea what that means. I make a mental note to ask Chris the next time I see her.

Peter comes up close to me, and I scoot backward. He laughs and cocks his head to the side and puts his hands on my shoulders. "So then break my seal."

I let out a nervous laugh. "Ha-ha, sorry, Peter, but I'm not interested. In you."

"Well, yeah. That's the whole point. I'm not interested in

you, either. Like, at all." Peter shudders. "So what do you say?"

I shrug my shoulders so his hands fall away. "Hello, I just got through explaining to you how Gen will kill any girl that goes near you!"

Peter dismisses this. "Gen's all talk. She'd never do anything to anybody. You just don't know her like I do." When I don't say anything, he takes my silence as encouragement, and he says, "It would help you out too, you know. With that kid Josh. Weren't you so worried about losing face in front of him? This could save you from more humiliation. Because why would you be with him when you could be with me? Well, pretend be with me. Strictly business, though. I can't have you falling in love with me, too."

It gives me great pleasure to look up into his Handsome Boy face and sweetly say, "Peter, I don't even want to be your pretend girlfriend, much less your real one."

He blinks. "Why not?"

"You read my letter. You're not my type. Nobody would ever believe I would like you."

"It's up to you. I'm just trying to do us both a favor." Then he shrugs and looks over my shoulder, like he's bored with this conversation. "But Josh definitely believed it."

In a flash, without even thinking, I say, "Okay. Let's do it."

Hours later, I'm lying in bed that night still marveling about it all. What people will say when they see me walking down the hall with Peter Kavinsky.

25

THE NEXT MORNING, PETER IS WAITING IN the parking lot for me when I get off the bus. "Hey," he says. "Are you seriously taking the bus every day?"

"My car is being fixed, remember? My accident?"

He sighs like this is somehow offensive to him, me taking the bus to school. Then he grabs my hand and holds it as we walk into school together.

This is the first time I've walked down the school hall-way holding hands with a boy. It should feel momentous, special, but it doesn't, because it's not real. Honestly, it feels like nothing.

Emily Nussbaum does a double take when she sees us. Emily is Gen's best friend. She's staring so hard I'm surprised she doesn't take a quick pic on her phone to send to Gen.

Peter keeps stopping to say hi to people, and I stand there smiling like it's the most natural thing in the world. Me and Peter Kavinsky.

At one point I try to let go of his hand, because mine is starting to feel sweaty, but he tightens his grip. "Your hand is too hot," I hiss.

Through clenched teeth he says, "No, your hand is."

I'm sure Genevieve's hands are never sweaty. She could probably hold hands for days without getting overheated.

When we get to my locker, we finally drop hands so I can dump my books inside. I'm shutting my locker door when Peter leans in and tries to kiss me on the mouth. I'm so startled I turn my head, and we hit foreheads.

"Ow!" Peter rubs his forehead and glares at me.

"Well, don't just sneak up on me like that!" My forehead hurts too. We really banged them hard, like cymbals. If I looked up right now, I would see blue cartoon birdies.

"Lower your voice, dummy," he says through clenched teeth.

"Don't you call me a dummy, you dummy," I whisper back.

Peter heaves a big sigh like he's really annoyed with me. I'm about to snap at him that it's his fault, not mine, when I catch a glimpse of Genevieve gliding down the hallway. "Gotta go," I say, and I dart off in the opposite direction.

"Wait!" Peter calls out.

But I keep darting.

I'm lying on my bed with my pillow over my face reliving the horrible kiss-that-wasn't. I keep trying to block it out, but it just keeps coming back.

I put my hand to my forehead. I don't think I can do this. It's all so . . . I mean, the kissing, the sweaty hands, everybody looking. It's too much.

I'm just going to have to tell him I changed my mind, and I don't want to do this anymore, and that'll be that. I don't have his number, and I don't want to say any of this in an e-mail, either. I'll have to go to his house. It's not far; I still remember the way.

I run downstairs, passing Kitty, who is balancing a plate of Oreos and a glass of milk on a tray. "I'm borrowing your bike!" I yell as I fly past her. "I'll be back soon!"

"You better not let anything happen to it!" Kitty yells back.

I grab her helmet and the bike and tear out of the yard, pedaling as fast as I can. My knees hit my chest a little, but I'm not that much taller than Kitty, so it isn't so bad. Peter lives two neighborhoods away. It takes me less than twenty minutes to get there.

When I do, there aren't any cars in the driveway. Peter's not home. My heart sinks to the pavement. What do I do now? Sit and wait for him on the front porch like some kind of stalker? What if his mom comes home first?

I take off my helmet and sit for a minute so I can rest. My hair is damp and sweaty from the ride over, and I'm exhausted. I try to run my fingers through my hair, smooth it out. It's a lost cause.

As I'm contemplating texting Chris and seeing if she can come get me, Peter's car comes roaring down the street and up the driveway. I drop my phone and then scramble to pick it up.

Peter climbs out of his car and raises his eyebrows at me. "Look who's here. My adoring girlfriend."

I stand up and wave at him. "Can I talk to you for a minute?"

He slings his backpack over his shoulder and takes his time sauntering over. He sits down on the front step like a prince on his throne, and I stand in front of him, my helmet in one hand and my phone in the other. "So what's up?" he drawls. "Let me guess. You're here to back out on me, am I right?"

He's so smug, so sure of himself. I don't want to give him the satisfaction of being right.

"I just wanted to go over our game plan with you," I say, sitting down. "Get our story straight before people start asking questions."

He raises his eyebrows. "Oh. Okay. Makes sense. So how *did* we get together?"

I clasp my hands in my lap and recite, "When I got in that car accident last week, you happened to be driving by, and you waited for Triple A with me and then you drove me home. You were really nervous the whole time, because you've actually had kind of a thing for me since middle school. I was your first kiss. So this was your big chance—"

"*You* were *my* first kiss?" he interrupts. "How about *I* was *your* first kiss. That's a lot more believable."

I ignore him and continue on. "This was your big chance. So you took it. You asked me out that very day and we've been hanging out ever since and now we're basically a couple."

"I don't think Gen's going to buy this," he says, shaking his head.

"Peter," I say in my most patient voice, "the most believable lies are the ones that are at least a little bit true. I did get into a car accident; you did stop and sit with me; we did kiss in middle school."

"It's not that."

"Then what?"

"Gen and I hooked up that day after I saw you."

I sigh. "Okay. Spare me the details. My story still works, though. After the car accident, you couldn't get me out of your mind, so you asked me out as soon as Genevieve dumped—I mean, as soon as you guys broke up." I clear my throat. "Since we're on the topic, I'd also like to set some ground rules."

"What kind of ground rules?" he asks, leaning back.

I press my lips together and take a breath. "Well . . . I don't want you trying to kiss me again."

Peter curls his lip at me. "Trust me, I don't want to do it either. My forehead still hurts from this morning. I think I have a bruise." He pushes his hair off his forehead. "Do you see a bruise?"

"No, but I see a receding hairline."

"*What?*"

Ha. I knew that would get him. Peter's so vain. "Calm down, I'm only kidding. Do you have a piece of paper and a pen?"

"You're gonna write this down?"

Primly I say, "It'll help us remember."

Rolling his eyes, Peter reaches into his backpack, pulls out a notebook, and hands it to me. I turn to a clean page and write at the top, *Contract*. Then I write *No kissing*.

"Are people really gonna buy it if we never touch each other in public?" Peter asks, looking skeptical.

"I don't think relationships are just about physicality. There are ways to show you care about someone, not just using your lips." Peter's smiling, and he looks like he's about to crack a joke, so I swiftly add, "Or any other body part."

He groans. "You've gotta give me something here, Lara Jean. I have a reputation to uphold. None of my friends will believe I suddenly turned into a monk to date you. How about at least a hand in your back jean pocket? Trust me, it'll be strictly professional."

I don't say what I'm thinking, which is that he cares way too much what people think about him. I just nod and write down, *Peter is allowed to put a hand in Lara Jean's back jean pocket.* "But no more kissing," I say, keeping my head down so he can't see me blush.

"You're the one who started it," he reminds me. "And also, I don't have any STDs, so you can get that out of your head."

"I don't think you have any STDs." I look back up at him. "The thing is . . . I've never had a boyfriend before. I've never been on a real date before, or held hands walking down the hallway. This is all new for me, so I'm sorry about the forehead thing this morning. I just . . . wish all of these firsts were happening for real and not with you."

Peter seems to be thinking this over. He says, "Huh. Okay. Let's just save some stuff, then."

"Yeah?"

"Sure. We'll save some stuff for you to do when it's the real thing and not for show."

I'm touched. Who knew Peter could be so thoughtful and generous?

"Like, I won't pay for stuff. I'll save that for a guy who really likes you."

My smile fades. "I wasn't expecting you to pay for anything!"

Peter's on a roll. "And I won't walk you to class or buy you flowers."

"I get the picture." It seems to me like Peter's less concerned about me and more concerned about his wallet. He sure is cheap. "So when you were with Genevieve, what kinds of things did she like you to do?"

I'm afraid he's going to take this opportunity to make a joke, but instead he stares off into space and says, "She was always bitching at me to write her notes."

"Notes?"

"Yeah, at school. I didn't get why I couldn't just text her. It's immediate, it's efficient. Why not use the technology that's available to us?"

This I understand perfectly. Genevieve didn't want notes. She wanted letters. Real letters written in his handwriting on actual paper that she could hold and keep and read whenever the mood struck her. They were proof, solid and tangible, that someone was thinking about her.

"I'll write you a note a day," Peter says suddenly, with gusto. "That'll drive her ass crazy."

I write down, *Peter will write Lara Jean one note every day.*

Peter leans in. "Write down that you have to go to some parties with me. And write down no rom coms."

"Who said anything about rom coms? Not every girl wants to watch rom coms."

"I can just tell that you're the kind of girl who does."

I'm annoyed that he has this perception of me, and even more annoyed that he's right. I write, *NO DUMB ACTION MOVIES.*

"Then what does that leave us with?" Peter demands.

"Superhero movies, horror movies, period films, documentaries, foreign films—"

Peter makes a face, grabs the pen and paper from me, and writes down, *NO FOREIGN FILMS.* He also writes, *Lara Jean will make Peter's picture her phone wallpaper.* "And vice versa!" I say. I point my phone at him. "Smile."

Peter smiles, and ugh, it's annoying how handsome he is. Then he reaches for his phone and I stop him. "Not right now. My hair looks sweaty and gross."

"Good point," he says, and I want to punch him.

"Can you also write down that under no circumstances can either of us tell anyone the truth?" I ask him.

"The first rule of Fight Club," Peter says knowingly.

"I've never seen that movie."

"Of course you haven't," he says, and I make a face at him. Also: mental note, watch *Fight Club.*

Peter writes it down, and then I sit next to him and take the pen and underline "under no circumstances" twice. "What about an end date?" I ask suddenly.

"What do you mean?"

"I mean, how long are we going to do this for? Like, two weeks? A month?"

Peter shrugs. "For as long as we feel it."

"But—don't you think we should have something set—"

He cuts me off. "You need to relax, Lara Jean. Life doesn't have to be so *planned*. Just roll with it and let it happen."

I sigh and say, "Words of wisdom from the great Kavinsky," and Peter wiggles his eyebrows at me. "Just as long as it's over by the time my sister comes back for Christmas break. She can always tell when I'm lying."

"Oh, we'll definitely be done by then," he says.

"Good," I say, and then I sign the paper, and so does he, and we have our contract.

I'm too proud to ask for a ride, and Peter doesn't offer, so I put my helmet back on and ride Kitty's bike back home. I'm halfway there when I realize we never exchanged phone numbers. I don't even know my own supposed boyfriend's phone number.

26

I'M AT MCCALLS BOOKSTORE, PICKING UP a copy of *The Glass Menagerie* for English and scanning the store for Josh. Now that Peter and I have everything worked out, I can triumphantly crow all about it. That'll show him for thinking I'm just a homebody no boy would want to date.

I spot him setting up a display of new books in the nonfiction section. He doesn't see me, so I sneak up behind and yell, "Boo!"

He jumps and drops a book on the floor. "You scared the crap out of me!"

"That was the point, Joshy!" I'm having a giggle fit. The look on his face! I wonder, why is it so deliciously funny to sneak up on people?

"All right, all right. Quit laughing. What are you here for?"

I hold up my book and wave it in his face. "I have Mr. Radnor for English. You had him, right?"

"Yeah, he's good. He's strict but fair. I still have my notes if you want them."

"Thanks," I say. Brightly I add, "So guess what. Peter and I aren't broken up after all. It was just a misunderstanding."

"Oh yeah?" Josh starts stacking books into a column.

"Mm-hmm. I saw him yesterday and we talked and talked,

for hours. I feel like I could talk to him about anything, you know? He just really gets me."

Josh's forehead wrinkles. "What do you guys talk about?"

"Oh, everything. Movies, books, the usual stuff."

"Huh. I never saw him as the reading type." He squints and looks over my shoulder. "Hey, I've gotta go help Janice out at the counter. When you're ready to check out, come to my register so I can give you my discount."

Hmm, this isn't exactly the reaction I was hoping for. I barely even got a chance to crow. "Sounds good," I say, but he's already walking away.

I hug my book to my chest. Now that Josh knows I'm not in love with him anymore and I'm with Peter, I guess everything will slide right back into place and be normal again. Like my letter never happened.

27

"MARGOT CALLED WHEN YOU WERE OUT today," my dad says over dinner.

Dinner is just salad. Salad for me and Daddy and cereal for Kitty. There were supposed to be chicken breasts, but I forgot to take them out of the freezer this morning, so there's just lettuce and carrot with balsamic dressing. Daddy's supplementing his with two boiled eggs, and I have a piece of buttered toast. Some dinner. Cereal and lettuce. I need to get to the grocery store stat.

Since Margot left, I've only spoken to her twice, and once was over video chat with all of us crowded around my laptop. I didn't get to ask her about the good stuff—the real deal, all the adventures she's been going on and the people she's been meeting. I think I heard that British people drink absinthe at pubs. I wonder if she's tried it by now. I've e-mailed Margot so many times and have only gotten back one e-mail in return so far. I understand that she is busy, but the least she can do is e-mail back once a day. For all she knows, I could be dead in a ditch. "What did she say?" I ask as I cut my carrot into tiny pieces.

"She's thinking about trying out for the shinty club team," my dad says, wiping salad dressing off his chin.

"What's shinty?" Kitty asks me, and I shrug.

"It's a Scottish sport that's similar to field hockey," Daddy explains. "It started out as safe swordfight practice in medieval Scotland."

Boring. Before Daddy can get started on telling us more about medieval Scotland, I say, "Let's send Gogo a care package! Stuff she can't get over there."

"Yeah!" Kitty cheers.

"What should we send?" I ask. "I say we all contribute something."

Daddy chews and taps his finger to his chin. "I'll send gummy vitamins," he says. "And Advil. I think she only took a small bottle of Advil, and you know how she gets migraines sometimes."

"I approve." I point my fork at Kitty. "And what about you?"

"I've got something I could send," Kitty says. "Should I go get it?"

Daddy and I look at each other and shrug. "Sure."

Kitty comes running back with a picture she's drawn of Margot. Petting a dog. The exact breed of dog Kitty wants. Akita. I have to laugh.

Kitty frowns. "What's so funny?"

"Nothing," I say.

"Do you think it's good enough?" Kitty asks me. "Good enough to hang up on her wall?"

"Definitely," I say.

"No, I want you to really look at it," she says. "Critique it. I can always do better. Margot won't want it if it's not my best work."

"Kitty, it definitely is," I say. "Why would I lie?"

She sighs. "I just don't know if it's finished yet."

"Only the artist knows," Daddy says with a sage nod.

"What do you think about the dog?" she asks him. "Isn't it cute?"

Daddy takes the picture from me and looks at it closely. "Yes, the dog is undeniably a good-looking dog."

"I'm Asian too," she says. Kitty sits back down and takes a bite of cereal and tries not to smile. She is doing her inception thing. Planting positive associations about dogs in Daddy's head. The kid never rests. She always has an angle.

"What else is going in the care package?" Kitty wants to know.

I start ticking off with my fingers. "Tampons because I don't know if they have our brand in Scotland, flannel pj's, thick socks, Girl Scout cookies—"

"Where are we going to get Girl Scout cookies this time of year?" Daddy asks.

"I have a box of Thin Mints hidden in the freezer," I say.

He gives me a hurt look. "Hidden from who?" Thin Mints are his favorite. If there are Thin Mints in the house, forget about it. Daddy is a Thin Mint Monster.

I give an enigmatic shrug. "Also I'm sending Margot's favorite kind of roller-ball pen, and . . . I think that's it."

"Don't forget her brown boots," my dad reminds me. "She specifically requested we send her brown boots with the laces."

"Did she?" I was hoping Margot hadn't noticed she'd left them behind. "When did she say that?"

"She e-mailed me yesterday."

"I'll see if I can find them."

My dad says, "Weren't you wearing them this weekend?" and at the same time Kitty says, "They're in your closet."

I throw up my hands. "All right, all right!"

"If you get the box together tonight, I can drop it off at the post office tomorrow morning on my way to work," Daddy offers.

I shake my head. "I want to send the scarf I've been knitting, and it won't be ready in time. Maybe in another week or two?"

Slurping her milk, Kitty waves a hand at me and advises, "Just give up on the scarf already. Knitting isn't your thing."

I open my mouth to argue and then close it. Maybe she's right. If we wait for my scarf to be done to send the care package, Margot will probably be out of college already. "All right," I say. "We'll send the care package sans scarf. I'm not saying I'm giving up on knitting, though. I'll keep chugging along on it and have it ready for you for your Christmas gift, Kitty." I smile at her sweetly. "It's pink. Your favorite."

Kitty's eyes go wide with horror. "Or Margot. You could also give it to Margot."

Kitty slides a piece of paper under my door that night. It's her Christmas list. It's only September—Christmas is still months away! "Puppy" is written at the top in capital block letters. She also wants an ant farm and a skateboard and a TV in her room. Yeah, that TV's not going to happen. I could buy her the ant farm, though. Or maybe I could talk to Daddy about the puppy. She hasn't said so, but I think she misses Margot a lot. In a way, Margot is the only mother she's known. It must be hard for Kitty having her so far away. I'll just have to remind myself to be more patient with her, more attentive. She needs me now.

I go to her room and climb into her bed. She's just turned the lights off but is already halfway to sleep. "What if we got a kitten?" I whisper.

Her eyes fly open. "No way in heck."

"Don't you think we're more of a kitten family?" Dreamily I say, "A fluffy gray-and-white kitten with a bushy tail. We could name him Prince if it's a boy. Ooh, or Gandalf the Gray! Wouldn't that be cute? Or if it's a girl, maybe Agatha. Or Tilly. Or Boss. It really depends on her personality."

"Quit it," Kitty warns. "We're not getting a cat. Cats are blah. They're also very manipulative."

Impressed, I say, "Where'd you learn that word?"

"TV."

"A puppy is a lot of work. Who's going to feed him and walk him and house-train him?"

"I'll do it. I'll do it all. I'm responsible enough to take care of it on my own."

I snuggle closer to her. I love the way Kitty's head smells after she's had a bath. "Ha! You don't even do the dishes ever. And you never clean your room. And when have you ever helped fold laundry even once in your life? I mean, really, if you don't do any of those things, how you can be responsible for another living creature?"

Kitty shoves me off. "Then I'll help more!"

"I'll believe it when I see it."

"If I help out more, will you help me convince Daddy about the puppy?"

"If you help out more," I agree. "If you can prove to me you're not a baby anymore." Kitty will be ten in January. That's plenty old enough to help out around the house. Margot babies her too much, I think. "I'm putting you in charge of emptying the upstairs trash cans once a week. And helping with the laundry."

"So . . . would I get a raise in my allowance?"

"No. The incentive is me helping you convince Daddy to get a dog, and also you not being so babyish anymore." I fluff up my pillow. "By the way, I'm sleeping in here tonight."

Kitty gives me a swift kick and I almost fall out of the bed. "You're the babyish one, not me, Lara Jean."

"Just let me sleep in here one night!"

"You take up all the covers."

Kitty tries to kick me again, but I make my body heavy and pretend I'm already asleep. Soon we both fall asleep for real.

Sunday night I'm doing my homework in bed when I get a call from a number I don't recognize. "Hello?"

"Hey. What are you doing?"

"Um . . . sorry, but who's this?"

"It's Peter!"

"Oh. How did you get my number?"

"Don't worry about it."

There's a longish silence. It's agonizing, every millisecond that ticks by with neither of us talking, but I don't know what to say. "So, what did you want?"

Peter laughs. "You're so awk, Covey. Your car's in the shop, right? So how about I pick you up for school?"

"Okay."

"Seven thirty."

"Okay."

"O-kay . . ."

"Bye," I say, and I hang up.

28

THE NEXT MORNING, I WAKE KITTY UP EARLY so she can braid my hair. "Leave me alone," she says, rolling on to her other side. "I'm sleeping."

"Please please please can I get a braid crown?" I ask her, squatting in front of her bed.

"No. You can have a side braid and that's it."

Swiftly Kitty braids my braid, and then she falls right back to sleep and I'm on my way to figure out clothes. Now that Peter and I are official, people will be noticing me more, so I should wear something good. I try on a polka-dot puffy-sleeved dress with tights, but it doesn't look right. Neither does my favorite heart sweater with the little pom-poms. Everything looks so kiddish all of a sudden. I finally settle on a floral babydoll dress I ordered off a Japanese street fashion site, with ankle boots. Sort of a seventies London look.

When I run downstairs at seven twenty-five, Kitty is sitting at the kitchen table with her jean jacket on waiting for me. "Why are you downstairs already?" I ask her. Her bus doesn't come until eight.

"I have my field trip today, so I have to go to school early. Remember?"

I run and look at the calendar on the refrigerator. There it is, in my handwriting: *Kitty's Field Trip*. Shoot.

I was supposed to drive her, but that was before my car accident. Daddy had an overnight shift at the hospital and he's not home yet, so I don't have a car. "Can one of the carpool moms come get you?"

"It's too late. The bus leaves at seven forty." Kitty's face is getting splotchy and her chin is starting to quiver. "I can't miss the bus, Lara Jean!"

"Okay, okay. Don't get upset. I've got a ride coming for us right now. Don't worry, okay?" I pluck a greenish banana from the banana hammock. "Let's go outside and wait for him."

"Who?"

"Just hurry."

Kitty and I are waiting on the front steps sharing the greenish banana. We both prefer an unripe, greenish banana to a brown speckled one. It's Margot who likes the speckled ones. I'll try to save them for banana bread, but Margot gobbles them up, mushy bruised parts and all. I shudder to even think of it.

There's a chill in the air, even though it's still September and therefore practically still summer. Kitty rubs her legs to keep warm. She says she'll wear shorts all the way to October; that's her plan.

It's past seven thirty now and no Peter yet. I'm starting to get nervous, but I don't want Kitty to worry. I decide that if he's not here in exactly two minutes, I'll go next door to Josh's and ask him to run Kitty over to school.

Across the street, our neighbor Ms. Rothschild waves at us

as she locks her front door, a big coffee thermos in her hand. She dashes toward her car.

"Good morning, Ms. Rothschild," we chorus. I elbow Kitty and say, "Five, four, three—"

"Damn it!" Ms. Rothschild shrieks. Ms. Rothschild has spilled coffee on her hand. She does this at least twice a week. I don't know why she doesn't just slow down or maybe just put the top on the thermos or not fill it up so high.

Just then Peter drives up, and his black Audi is even shinier in the daylight. I get up and say, "Come on, Kitty," and she trails behind me.

"Who's that?" I hear her whisper.

His windows are down. I come up close to the passenger side and stick my head in. "Is it okay if we drop my little sister off at the elementary school?" I ask. "She has to be there early today for a field trip."

Peter looks annoyed. "Why didn't you mention it yesterday?"

"I didn't know about it yesterday!" Behind me I can feel rather than hear Kitty fidgeting.

"This is a two-seater," Peter says, as if I can't see with my own two eyes.

"I know that. I'll just put Kitty in my lap and the seat belt over us." Which my dad would kill me for if he knew, but I'm not telling, and neither will Kitty.

"Yeah, 'cause that sounds really safe." He's being sarcastic. I hate when people are sarcastic. It's so cheap.

"It's two miles!"

He sighs. "Fine. Get in."

I open the door and slide in, laying my bag at my feet. "Come on, Kitty." I make space for her between my legs, and she climbs in. I strap us in tight, my arms around her. "Don't tell Daddy," I say.

"Duh," she says.

"Hey. What's your name?" Peter asks her.

Kitty hesitates. More and more this happens. With new people she has to decide if she'll be Kitty or Katherine.

"Katherine."

"But everyone calls you Kitty?"

"Everyone who knows me," Kitty says. "You can call me Katherine."

Peter's eyes light up. "You're tough," he says admiringly, which Kitty ignores, but she keeps sneaking peeks at him. He has that effect on people. On girls. Women, even.

We drive through the neighborhood in silence. At last Kitty says, "So who are you?"

I look over at him and he's looking straight ahead. "I'm Peter. Your sister's, um, boyfriend."

My mouth drops. We never said anything about lying to our families! I thought this was going to be an at-school-only thing.

Kitty goes completely still in my arms. Then she twists around to look at me and shrieks, "*He's* your *boyfriend*? Since *when*?"

"Since last week." At least that much is the truth. Sort of.

"But you never said anything! Not one frigging word, Lara Jean!"

Automatically I say, "Don't say 'frig.'"

"Not one frigging word," Kitty repeats with a shake of her head.

Peter cracks up, and I give him a dirty look. "It all happened really fast," he offers. "There was barely time to tell anybody—"

"Was I talking to you?" Kitty snaps. "No, I don't think so. I was talking to my sister."

Peter's eyes widen, and I can see him trying to keep a straight face.

"Does Margot know?" she asks me.

"Not yet, and don't you go mentioning it to her before I have a chance to."

"Hmph." This seems to appease Kitty a tiny bit. Knowing something first, before Margot, is a big deal.

Then we're at the elementary school, and thank God the bus is still there in the parking lot. All the kids are lined up in front of it. I let out the breath I've been holding the whole way over, and Kitty is already untangling herself from me and bounding out of the car. "Have a good time on the field trip!" I call out.

She spins back around and points an accusing finger at me. "I want to hear the *whole* story when I get home!" With that decree she's off running for the bus loop.

I rebuckle my seat belt. "Um, I don't remember us deciding to tell our families that we're boyfriend-girlfriend."

"She was going to have to find out at some point, with me chauffeuring you and her around town."

"You didn't have to say 'boyfriend.' You could've just said 'friend.'" We're getting close to school now, just two more lights. I give my side braid a nervous tug. "Um, so have you talked to Genevieve at all?"

Peter frowns. "No."

"She hasn't said a word to you about it?"

"Nope. But I'm sure she will soon."

Peter speeds into the parking lot and zooms into a space. When we get out of the car and head for the entrance, Peter's fingers lace through mine. I think he's going to drop me off at my locker like he did before, but he leads us in the opposite direction.

"Where are we going?" I ask him.

"Cafeteria."

I'm about to protest, but before I can, he says firmly, "We need to start hanging out in public more. The caf is where we'll get the most bang for our buck."

Josh won't be in the cafeteria—that's for popular people—but I know who will most certainly be there: Genevieve.

When we walk in, she's holding court at their lunch table—her and Emily Nussbaum and Gabe and Darrell from the lacrosse team. They're all eating breakfast and drinking coffee. She must have a sixth sense where Peter is concerned, because she beams lasers at us immediately. I start slowing down, which Peter doesn't seem to notice. Peter makes a beeline for the table, but at the last second I chicken out. I tug on his hand and say, "Let's sit over here," and point to an empty table in their line of vision.

"Why?"

"Just—please." I think fast. "Because, you see, it would be too blatantly jerky of you to bring a girl to the table after you've only been broken up for, like, a minute. And this way Genevieve can watch from afar and wonder for just a little bit longer." And also, I'm terrified.

As I drag Peter over to the table, he waves to his friends, shrugging his shoulders like *Whaddareyougonnado?* I sit down and Peter sits down next to me. He pulls my chair closer to his. Raising his eyebrows, he asks, "Are you that afraid of her?"

"No." Yes.

"You're going to have to face her sometime." Peter leans forward and grabs my hand again and starts tracing the lines on my palm.

"Quit," I say. "You're creeping me out."

He flashes me a hurt look. "Girls love it when I do that."

"No, *Genevieve* loves it. Or she pretends to love it. You know, now that I think of it, you actually don't have *that* much experience when it comes to girls. Just one girl." I take my hand away from his and perch it on the table. "I mean, everybody thinks you're this big ladies' man, when in reality you've only ever been with Genevieve and then Jamila for like a month—"

"Okay, okay. I get it. Enough already. They're watching us."

"Who is? Your table?"

Peter shrugs. "Everyone."

I do a quick look around. He's right. Everyone is watching us. Peter's so used to people watching him, but I'm not. It feels funny, like a new sweater that makes my skin feel itchy. Because no one ever watches me. It's like being onstage. And the funny thing, the really strange thing is, it's not an altogether unpleasant feeling.

I'm pondering this when my eyes meet Genevieve's. There's this very brief moment of recognition between us, like *I know you*. Then she looks away and whispers something to Emily. Genevieve is looking at me like I am a tasty morsel and she is going to eat me alive and then spit out my bones. And then, just as quickly, the look is gone and she's smiling.

I shiver. The truth is, Genevieve scared me even when we were kids. One time I was playing at her house, and Margot called looking for me to come home for lunch, and Genevieve told her I wasn't there. She wouldn't let me leave because she wanted to keep playing dollhouse. She kept blocking the door. I had to call for her mom.

The clock reads five minutes past eight. The bell's going to ring soon. "We should get going," I say, and when I stand up, my knees feel shaky. "Ready?"

He's distracted because he was looking over at his table of friends. "Yeah, sure." Peter gets up and propels me toward the door; he keeps one hand on the small of my back. With his other hand he waves at his friends. "Smile," he whispers to me, so I do.

I have to admit, it's not a bad feeling, having a boy sweep

you along, usher you through crowds. It's the feeling of being cared for. It's kind of like walking in a dream. I'm still me and Peter's still Peter, but everything around me feels fuzzy and unreal, like the time Margot and I snuck champagne on New Year's Eve.

I never knew it before, but I think maybe all this time I've been invisible. Just someone who was there. Now that people think I'm Peter Kavinsky's girlfriend, they're wondering about me. Like, why? What about me made Peter like me? What do I have? What makes me so special? I would be wondering too.

I am now a Mysterious Girl. Before I was just a Quiet Girl. But becoming Peter's girlfriend has elevated me to Mysterious Girl.

I take the bus home from school because Peter has to go to lacrosse practice. I sit in the front the way I've been doing, but today people have questions for me. Underclassmen, mostly, because hardly any upperclassmen take the bus.

"What's with you and Kavinsky?" a sophomore girl named Manda asks me. I pretend like I don't hear her.

Instead I sink lower into my seat and open up the note Peter left for me in my locker.

Dear Lara Jean,

Good job today.

Peter

I start to smile and then I hear Manda whisper to her friend, "It's so weird that Kavinsky would like her. I mean . . . look at her and then look at Genevieve." I can feel myself shrink. Is that what everyone thinks? Maybe it's not that I'm a Mysterious Girl. Maybe it's that I'm a Not Good Enough Girl.

When I get home, I go straight to my room, put on a soft nightgown, and release my braid. It's sweet relief to let it out. My scalp is tingling with gratitude. Then I lie in my bed and stare out the window until it gets dark. My phone keeps buzzing, and I'm sure it's Chris, but I don't lift my head to look.

Kitty barges in at one point and says, "Are you sick? Why are you still lying in bed like you have cancer like Brielle's mom did?"

"I need peace," I say, closing my eyes. "I need to replenish myself with peace."

"Well . . . then what are we eating for dinner?"

I open my eyes. That's right. It's a Monday. I'm in charge of dinner on Mondays now. Ugh, Margot, where *are* you? It's dark already, there's not enough time to defrost anything. Maybe Mondays should be pizza nights. I eye her. "Do you have any money?"

We both get an allowance—Kitty gets five dollars a week and I get twenty, but Kitty always has more money than me. She saves everything like a wily squirrel. I don't know where she keeps it, because she locks the door whenever she goes to take any out of her stash. And she'll lend it, but she charges interest. Margot has a credit card that she's allowed to use for groceries and gas, but she took that with her. I should probably ask Daddy about getting me one too, now that I'm the oldest sister.

"Why do you need money?"

"Because I want to order a pizza for dinner." Kitty opens her mouth to negotiate, but before she can get a word in, I say, "Daddy will pay you back when he gets home, so don't even think about charging me interest. The pizza's for you, too, you know. A twenty ought to do it."

Kitty crosses her arms. "I'll give you the money, but first you have to tell me about that boy from this morning. Your *boyfriend*."

I groan. "What do you want to know?"

"I want to know how you got together."

"We used to be friends back in middle school, remember? We'd all hang out in the Pearces' tree house sometimes." Kitty gives me a blank shrug. "Well, remember that day I got in a car accident?" Kitty nods. "Well, Peter was driving by, and he stopped and helped me. And we just . . . reconnected. It was fate." Actually, this is good practice, telling Kitty this story. I'll tell Chris the same story tonight.

"That's it? That's the whole story?"

"Hey, that's a pretty good story," I say. "I mean, a car accident is very dramatic, plus our history together."

Kitty just says, "Hmm," and she leaves it at that.

We have sausage and mushroom pizza for dinner, and when I broach the idea of Pizza Mondays, Daddy is quick to agree. I think he's remembering my bo ssam mac and cheese.

It's a relief that Kitty spends most of dinner talking about her field trip and all I have to do is chew on my pizza. I'm still thinking about what Manda said and wondering if maybe this wasn't such a good idea after all.

When Kitty pauses to inhale her slice, Daddy turns to me and says, "Did anything interesting happen to you today?"

I swallow my mouthful of pizza. "Um . . . not really."

Later that night I fix myself a bubble bath and soak in the tub for so long Kitty bangs on the door twice to check if I've fallen asleep. Once I almost do.

I've just drifted off when my phone buzzes. It's Chris. I hit ignore, but then it keeps buzzing, and buzzing, and buzzing. I finally just pick up.

"Is it true?" she screams.

I hold the phone away from my ear. "Yes."

"Oh my gawd. Tell me everything."

"Tomorrow, Chris. I'll tell you everything tomorrow. Good night."

"Wait—"

"Night!"

29

THAT FRIDAY I GO TO MY FIRST EVER
football game. I've never had even the tiniest bit of interest
in it before, and I still don't. I'm sitting high in the stands
with Peter and his friends, and as far as I can tell, there's not
a lot to see. It just seems like a lot of waiting and huddling
and not a lot of action. Nothing at all like football games in
the movies and on TV shows.

By nine thirty the game's almost over, I hope, and I'm
yawning into my coat when Peter suddenly throws his arm
around me. I nearly choke on my yawn.

Down below, Genevieve is cheering with the rest of the
squad. She is shimmying and shaking her pom-poms. She
looks up in the stands, and when she sees us, she stops for just
a half second before launching into a new cheer, eyes blazing.

I glance at Peter, who has a satisfied smirk on. When
Genevieve's back on the sidelines, he drops his arm and suddenly seems to remember I'm there. He says, "Eli's having
people over tonight. Wanna go?"

I don't even know who Eli is. I yawn again, a big one for
show. "Um . . . I'm really tired. So . . . no. No, thank you. Can
you just drop me off on the way there?"

Peter gives me a look, but he doesn't argue.

On the way home, we pass by the diner and Peter suddenly

says, "I'm hungry. Do you want to stop and get something?" Pointedly he adds, "Or are you too tired?"

I ignore the dig and say, "Sure, I can eat."

So Peter turns the car around and we go to the diner. We get a booth up front. Whenever I used to come here with Margot and Josh, we would always sit in the back near the jukebox so we could put coins in. Half the time the jukebox was broken, but we still liked sitting near it. It's weird to be here without them. We have so many traditions here. The three of us would get two grilled-cheese sandwiches and cut them up into squares, and we'd order a bowl of tomato soup to dip the squares in, and then Josh and I would share a waffle with extra whipped cream for dessert and Margot would have a bowl of tapioca pudding. Gross, I know. I'm pretty sure only grandmas like tapioca pudding.

Our waitress is Kelly, who's a student at the college. She was gone all summer, and I guess now she's back. She eyes Peter as she sets down our waters. "Where are your friends tonight?" she asks me.

I say, "Margot's left for Scotland, and Josh . . . isn't here." Which Peter rolls his eyes at.

Then Peter orders blueberry pancakes and bacon and scrambled eggs. I get a grilled cheese with fries on the side and a black-cherry soda.

When Kelly leaves to put in our orders, I ask him, "Why do you hate Josh so much?"

"I don't hate him," Peter scoffs. "I barely know the guy."

"Well, you certainly don't like him."

Peter scowls at me. "What's to like? That kid turned me in once for cheating in seventh grade."

Peter cheated? My stomach twists a little. "What kind of cheating was it? Like, homework?"

"No, a Spanish test. I wrote down the answers in my calculator, and Josh freaking told on me. Who does that?"

I search his face for some sign of embarrassment or shame at having cheated, but I don't see even an iota. "What are you so high and mighty for? You're the one who cheated!"

"It was seventh grade!"

"Well, do you still cheat?"

"No. Hardly ever. I mean, I have." He frowns at me. "Would you quit looking at me like that?"

"Like what?"

"With judgey eyes. Look, I'm going to school on a lacrosse scholarship anyway, so what does it matter?"

I have a sudden revelation. I lower my voice and say, "Wait . . . can you read?"

He bursts out laughing. "Yes, I can read! Geez, Lara Jean. Not everything has a story behind it, okay? I'm just lazy." He snorts. "*Can I read?* I've written you multiple notes! You're hilarious."

I can feel my face get flushed. "It wasn't that funny." I squint at him. "Is everything a joke to you?"

"Not everything, but most things, sure."

I drop my chin. "Then maybe that's a character flaw that you should work on," I say. "Because some things are serious and they should be taken seriously. Sorry if you think that's me being judgey."

"Yup, I think that's judgey. I think you're judgey in general. That's a character flaw that *you* should work on. I also think you need to learn how to kick back and have fun."

I'm listing off all the ways I have fun—biking (which I hate), baking, reading; I consider saying knitting but I'm pretty sure he'll only make fun of me—when Kelly drops off our food and I stop so I can bite into my grilled cheese while it's still oozy.

Peter steals one of my french fries. "So who else?"

"Who else what?"

With his mouth full, he says, "Who else got letters?"

"Um, that's really private." I shake my head at him, like *Wow, how rude.*

"What? I'm just curious." Peter dips another fry into my little ramekin of ketchup. Smirking, he says, "Come on, don't be shy. You can tell me. I know I'm number one, obviously. But I want to hear who else made the cut."

He's practically flexing, he's so sure of himself. Fine, if he wants to know so bad, I'll tell him. "Josh, you—"

"Obviously."

"Kenny."

Peter snorts. "Kenny? Who's he?"

I prop my elbows up on the table and rest my chin on my hands. "A boy I met at church camp. He was the best swimmer of the whole boys' side. He saved a drowning kid once. He swam out to the middle of the lake before the lifeguards even noticed anything was wrong."

"So what'd he say when he got the letter?"

"Nothing. It was sent back return to sender."

"Okay, who's next?"

I take a bite of sandwich. "Lucas Krapf."

"He's gay," Peter says.

"He's not gay!"

"Dude, quit dreaming. The kid is gay. He wore an ascot to school yesterday."

"I'm sure he was wearing it ironically. Besides, wearing an ascot doesn't make someone gay." I give him a look like *Wow, so homophobic.*

"Hey, don't give me that look," he objects. "My favorite uncle's gay as hell. I bet you fifty bucks that if I showed my uncle Eddie a picture of Lucas, he'd confirm it in half a second."

"Just because Lucas appreciates fashion, that doesn't make him gay." Peter opens his mouth to argue but I lift up a hand to quiet him. "All it means is he's more of a city guy in the midst of all this . . . this boring suburbia. I bet you he ends up going to NYU or some other place in New York. He could be a TV actor. He's got that look, you know. Svelte with fine-boned features. Very sensitive features. He looks like . . . like an angel."

"So what did Angel Boy say about the letter, then?"

"Nothing . . . I'm sure because he's a gentleman and didn't want to embarrass me by bringing it up." I give him a meaningful look. *Unlike some people* is what I'm saying with my eyes.

Peter rolls his eyes. "All right, all right. Whatever, I don't care." He leans back in his seat and stretches his arm out on the back of the empty seat next to him. "That's only four. Who's the fifth?"

I'm surprised he's been keeping count. "John Ambrose McClaren."

Peter's eyes widen. "McClaren? When did you like him?"

"Eighth grade."

"I thought you liked me in eighth grade!"

"There may have been a little bit of overlap," I admit. Stirring my straw, I say, "There was this one time, in gym . . . he and I had to pick up all the soccer balls, and it started to rain . . ." I sigh. "It was probably the most romantic thing that ever happened to me."

"What is it with girls and rain?" Peter wonders.

"I don't know . . . I guess maybe because everything feels more dramatic in the rain," I say with a shrug.

"Did anything actually happen with you two, or were you just standing out in the rain picking up soccer balls?"

"You wouldn't understand." Someone like Peter could never understand.

Peter rolls his eyes. "So did McClaren's letter get sent to his old house?" he prompts.

"I think so. I never heard anything back from him." I take a long sip of my soda.

"Why do you sound so sad about it?"

"I'm not!"

Maybe I am, a little. Besides Josh, I think John Ambrose McClaren matters the most to me of all the boys I've loved. There was just something so sweet about him. It was the promise of maybe, maybe one day. I think John Ambrose McClaren must be the One That Got Away. Out loud I say, "I mean, either he never got my letter or he did, and . . ." I shrug. "I just always wondered how he turned out. If he's still the same. I bet he is."

"You know what, I think maybe he mentioned you once." Slowly he says, "Yeah, he definitely did. He said he thought you were the prettiest girl in our grade. He said his one regret from middle school was not asking you to the eighth-grade formal."

My whole body goes still and I think I even stop breathing. "For real?" I whisper.

Peter busts up laughing. "Dude! You're so gullible!"

My stomach squeezes. Blinking, I say, "That was really mean. Why would you say that?"

Peter stops laughing and says, "Hey, I'm sorry. I was just kidding—"

I reach across the table and punch him in the shoulder, hard. "You're a jerk."

He rubs his shoulder and cries out, "Ow! That hurt!"

"Well, you deserved it."

"Sorry," he says again. But there's still a trace of laughter in his eyes, so I turn my head away from him. "Hey, come on. Don't be mad. Who knows? Maybe he did like you. Let's call him and find out."

My head snaps up. "You have his phone number? You have John Ambrose McClaren's number?"

Peter pulls out his cell phone. "Sure. Let's call him right now."

"No!" I try to grab his phone away from him, but he's too quick. He holds his phone above my head and I can't reach. "Don't you dare call him!"

"Why not? I thought you were so curious about what ever happened to him."

I shake my head fervently.

"What are you so afraid of? That he doesn't remember you?" Something changes in his face, some dawning realization about me. "Or that he does?"

I shake my head.

"That's it." Peter nods to himself; he tips back in his chair, his hands linked around his head.

I don't like the way he's looking at me. Like he thinks he's figured me out. I hold my palm out to him. "Give me your phone."

Peter's jaw drops. "You're going to call him? Right now?"

I like that I've surprised him. It makes me feel like I've won something back. I think throwing Peter off guard could be a fun hobby for me. In a commanding voice I've only ever used with Kitty, I say, "Just give me your phone." Peter hands me his phone, and I copy John's number into mine. "I'll call him when *I* feel like it, not because *you* feel like it."

Peter gives me a look of grudging respect. Of course I'm never going to call John, but Peter K. doesn't need to know that.

That night, I'm lying in bed still thinking about John. It's fun to think of the what-if. Scary, but fun. It's like, I thought this door was closed before, but here it is open just the tiniest crack. What if? What would that be like, me and John Ambrose McClaren? If I close my eyes, I can almost picture it.

30

MARGOT AND I ARE ON THE PHONE; IT'S Saturday afternoon here and Saturday night there. "Have you lined up an internship for the spring?"

"Not yet . . ."

Margot lets out a sigh. "I thought you were going to try and do something at Montpelier. I know they need help in the archives. Do you want me to call Donna for you?"

Margot did an internship at Montpelier for two summers and she loved it. She was there for some important dig where they found a shard of Dolley Madison's china plate, and you'd have thought they found diamonds or a dinosaur bone. Everybody loves Margot over there. When she left, they gave her a plaque for all her hard work. Daddy hung it up in the living room.

"Montpelier's too far of a drive," I say.

"What about volunteering at the hospital?" she suggests. "You could get a ride with Daddy on the days you have to go in."

"You know I don't like the hospital."

"Then the library! You like the library."

"I've already filled out an application," I lie.

"Have you really?"

"Or I was just about to."

"I shouldn't have to push you to want things. You should want them for yourself. You need to take the initiative. I'm not always going to be beside you to push you."

"I know that."

"I mean, do you realize how important this year is, Lara Jean? It's kind of everything. You don't get a do-over: this is junior year."

I can feel tears and panic building up inside me. If she asks me another question, it will be too much, and I'll cry.

"Hello?"

"I'm still here." My voice comes out tiny, and I know Margot knows how close I am to crying.

She pauses. "Look, you still have time, okay? I just don't want you to wait too long and have all the good placements go to other people. I'm just worried about you is all. But everything's fine; you're still okay."

"Okay." Even just that one little word is an effort.

"How's everything else?"

I started out this conversation wishing I could tell her about Peter and everything that's been going on with me, but now I'm just feeling relieved that there are all these miles between us and she can't see what I'm up to. "Everything's good," I say.

"How's Josh? Have you talked to him lately?"

"Not really," I say. Which I haven't. I've been so busy with Peter I haven't really had a chance.

31

KITTY AND I ARE ON THE FRONT STEPS.
She's drinking her Korean yogurt drink and I'm working on that scarf for Margot while I wait for Peter. Kitty's waiting for Daddy to come out. He's dropping her off at school today.

Ms. Rothschild hasn't come outside yet. Maybe she's sick today or maybe she's running even later than usual.

We've got our eyes locked on her front door when a minivan drives down our street and slows in front of our house. I squint my eyes. It's Peter Kavinsky. Driving a tan minivan. He ducks his head out the window. "Are you coming or not?"

"Why are you driving *that*?" Kitty calls out.

"Never mind that, Katherine," Peter calls back. "Just get in."

Kitty and I look at each other. "Me too?" Kitty asks me.

I shrug. Then I lean back and open the front door and yell out, "Kitty's getting a ride with me, Daddy!"

"Okay!" he yells back.

We stand up, but just then Ms. Rothschild comes dashing out of the house in her navy blue suit, briefcase in one hand, coffee in the other. Kitty and I look at each other gleefully. "Five, four, three—"

"Damn it!"

Giggling, we hurl ourselves toward Peter's minivan. I hop into the passenger seat and Kitty climbs into the back. "What were you guys laughing about?" he asks.

I'm about to tell him when Josh walks out of his house. He stops and stares at us for a second before he waves. I wave back and Kitty hangs her head out the window and yells, "Hi, Josh!"

"What up," Peter calls out, leaning over me.

"Hey," Josh says back. Then he gets in his car.

Peter pokes me in the side and grins and puts the car in reverse. "Tell me why you guys were laughing."

Clicking into my seat belt, I say, "At least once a week, Ms. Rothschild runs out to her car and spills hot coffee all over herself."

Kitty pipes up, "It's the funniest thing in the world."

Peter snorts. "You guys are sadistic."

"What's sadistic?" Kitty wants to know. She puts her head between us.

I push her back and say, "Put your seat belt on."

Peter puts the car in reverse. "It means seeing other people in pain makes you happy."

"Oh." She repeats it to herself softly. "Sadistic."

"Don't teach her weird stuff," I say.

"I like weird stuff," Kitty protests.

Peter says, "See? The kid likes weird stuff." Without turning around, he lifts his hand up for a high five and Kitty leans forward and slaps it heartily. "Hey, gimme a sip of whatever it is you're drinking back there."

"It's almost gone, so you can have the rest," she says.

Kitty hands it over, and Peter tips back the plastic container in his mouth. "This is good," he says.

"It's from the Korean grocery store," Kitty tells him. "They come in a pack and you can put them in the freezer and if you pack it for lunch, it'll be icy and cold when you drink it."

"Sounds good to me. Lara Jean, bring me one of these tomorrow morning, will you? For services rendered."

I shoot him a dirty look and Peter says, "I mean the rides! Geez."

"I'll bring you one, Peter," Kitty says.

"That's my girl."

"As long as you give me a ride to school tomorrow, too," Kitty finishes, and Peter hoots.

32

BEFORE FOURTH PERIOD, I'M AT MY LOCKER, trying to repin my milkmaid braid in the little mirror hanging from the door.

"Lara Jean?"

"Yes?"

I peek around the door and it's Lucas Krapf, wearing a thin V-neck sweater in brilliant blue and stone-colored khakis. "I've had this for a while now . . . I wasn't going to say anything, but then I thought maybe you'd want it back." He puts a pink envelope in my hand. It's my letter. So Lucas got his, too.

I drop it into my locker, make a *yikes* face at myself in the mirror, and then close the door. "So you're probably wondering what this is all about," I begin. And then I immediately falter. "It's um, well, I wrote it a long time ago, and—"

"You don't have to explain."

"Really? You're not curious?"

"No. It was just really nice to get a letter like that. I was actually pretty honored."

I let out a relieved sigh and sag against my locker. Why is Lucas Krapf just so exactly right? He knows how to say the perfect thing.

And then Lucas gives me a half grimace, half smile. "But the thing is . . ." He lowers his voice. "You know I'm gay, right?"

"Oh, right, totally," I say, trying not to sound disappointed. "No, I totally knew." So Peter was right after all.

Lucas smiles. "You're so cute," he says, and I perk up again. Then he says, "Listen, can you not tell anybody, though? I mean, I'm out, but I'm not *out* out yet. You know what I mean?"

"Totally," I say, super confident.

"For instance, my mom knows but my dad only kind of knows. I haven't outright told him."

"Got it."

"I just let people believe what they please. I don't feel like it's my responsibility to quantify myself for them. I mean, you get what I'm talking about. As a biracial person, I'm sure people are always asking you what race you are, right?"

I haven't thought of it that way before, but yes yes yes! Lucas just gets it. "Exactly. It's like, why do you need to know?"

"Exactly."

We smile at each other and I feel that wonderful sensation of being known by someone. We walk together in the same direction; he has Mandarin class and I have French. At one point he asks me about Peter, and I'm tempted to tell him the truth, because I'm feeling so close to him. But Peter and I made that pact: we explicitly said we would never tell anyone. I don't want to be the one to break it. So when Lucas says, "Hey, so what's the deal with you and Kavinsky?" I just shrug and give him an enigmatic smile.

JENNY HAN

"It's crazy, right? Because he's so . . ." I search for the exact right word, but I can't think of it. "I mean, he could play the part of a handsome guy in a movie." Hastily I add, "So could you, though. You'd play the guy the girl *should* pick."

Lucas laughs, but I can tell he likes it.

Dear Lucas,

I never met a boy with manners as good as yours. You ought to have a British accent. At homecoming, you wore a cravat and it suited you so well I think you could wear one all the time and get away with it.

Oh, Lucas! I wish I knew what kind of girls you liked. As far as I can tell, you haven't dated anyone . . . unless you have a girlfriend at another school. You're just so mysterious. I hardly know a thing about you. The things I know are so unsubstantial, so unsatisfying, like that you eat a chicken sandwich every day at lunch, and you're on the golf team. I guess the one remotely real thing I know about you is you're a good writer, which must mean you have deep reserves of emotion. Like that short story you wrote in creative writing about the poisoned well, and it was from a six-year-old boy's perspective. It was so sensitive, so keen!

That story made me feel like I knew you at least a little bit. But I don't <u>know</u> you, and I wish I did.

I think you're very special. I think you are probably one of the most special people at our school, and I wish more people knew that about you. Or maybe I don't, because sometimes it's nice to be the only one who knows something.

Love, Lara Jean

33

AFTER SCHOOL, CHRIS AND I ARE HANGING out in my room. She's in trouble with her mom for staying out all night, so she's hiding out over here until her mom leaves for book club. We're sharing a big bag of Kitty's Pirate Booty, which I'm going to have to replace because she'll complain if it's missing from her lunch on Monday.

Chris stuffs a handful of Pirate Booty puffs in her mouth. "Just tell me, Lara Jean. How far have you guys gone?"

I almost choke. "We've gone nowhere! And we have no plans to go anywhere in the near future." Or ever.

"Seriously? Not even over-the-bra action? A quick swipe across your chest?"

"No! I told you, me and my sister aren't like that."

Chris snorts. "Are you joking me? Of course Margot and Josh have had sex. Quit being so naive, Lara Jean."

"This isn't me being naive," I tell her. "I know for a fact that he and Margot haven't done it."

"How? How do you know 'for a fact'? I'd love to hear this."

"I'm not telling you."

If I tell Chris, she'll only laugh more. She doesn't understand; she only has a little brother. She doesn't know how it is with sisters. Margot and I, we made a pact, back in middle school. We swore we wouldn't have sex until we were married or we were really, really in love and at least twenty-one. Margot might be really, really in love, but she's not married and she's not twenty-one. She'd never go back on her word. With sisters a pact is everything.

"No, I'd really love to know." Chris has that hungry glint in her eyes, and I know she's just getting warmed up.

"You just want to make fun of it, and I'm not going to let you," I say.

Chris rolls her eyes. "Fine. But there's no way they haven't boned."

I think Chris talks like that on purpose to get a reaction from me. She loves a reaction, so I'm careful to not give her one. I calmly say, "Can you please stop talking about my sister and Josh having sex. You know I don't like it."

Chris takes a permanent marker out of her bag and starts to color in her thumbnail. "You need to stop being such a scaredy-cat. Seriously, you've built it up in your head to be this huge, life-changing moment, but it's actually done in under five, and it's not even the best part."

I know she's waiting for me to ask what the best part is, and I am curious, but I ignore her and say, "I think permanent marker is toxic for your nails," to which she shakes her head at me like I'm a lost cause.

I wonder, though . . . what *would* it be like? To be that close to a boy and have him see all of you, no holding back. Would it be scary only for a second or two, or would it be scary the whole time? What if I didn't like it at all? Or what if I liked it too much? It's a lot to think about.

34

"*DO YOU THINK IF A GUY AND A GIRL HAVE* been dating for a long time, they've automatically had sex?" I ask Peter. We're sitting on the floor of the library, our backs against the wall of the reference section nobody ever goes to. It's after school, the library's empty, and we're doing homework. Peter gets Cs and Ds in chemistry, so I've been helping him study.

Peter looks up from his chem book, suddenly interested. He tosses the book aside and says, "I need more information. How long have they been dating?"

"A long time. Like two years, something like that."

"How old are they? Our age?"

"About."

"Then most likely but not necessarily. It depends on the girl and the guy. But if I had to put money on it, yeah."

"But the girl's not like that. The guy isn't either."

"Who are we talking about here?"

"That's a secret." I hesitate, and then say, "Chris thinks there's no way they haven't. She says it's impossible."

Peter snorts. "Why are you going to her for advice? That girl is a train wreck."

"She is not a train wreck!"

He gives me a look. "Freshman year she got wasted on

Four Loko and she climbed up on Tyler Boylan's roof and did a striptease."

"Were you there?" I demand. "Did you see it with your own two eyes?"

"Damn straight. Fished her clothes out of the pool like the gentleman I am."

I blow out my cheeks. "Well, Chris never mentioned that story to me, so I can't really speak to that. Besides, didn't they ban Four Loko or whatever it's called?"

"They still make it, but a shitty watered-down version. You can dump Five-Hour Energy in it to get the same effect." I shudder, which makes Peter smile. "What do you and Chris even talk about?" he asks. "You have nothing in common."

"What do *we* talk about?" I counter.

Peter laughs. "Point taken." He pushes away from the wall and puts his head in my lap, and I go completely still.

I try to make my voice sound normal as I say, "You're in a really strange mood today."

He raises an eyebrow at me. "What kind of mood am I in?" Peter sure loves to hear about himself. Normally, I don't mind, but today I'm not in the mood to oblige him. He already has too many people in his life telling him how great he is.

"The obnoxious kind," I say, and he laughs.

"I'm sleepy." He closes his eyes and snuggles against me. "Tell me a bedtime story, Covey."

"Don't flirt," I tell him.

His eyes fly open. "I wasn't!"

"Yes, you were. You flirt with everyone. It's like you can't help yourself."

"Well, I don't ever flirt with you." Peter sits back up and checks his phone, and suddenly I'm wishing I didn't say anything at all.

35

I'M IN FRENCH CLASS, LOOKING OUT THE window as I am wont to do, and that's when I see Josh walking toward the bleachers by the track. He's carrying his lunch, and he's alone. Why is he eating alone? He has his comic-book group; he has Jersey Mike.

But I guess he and Jersey Mike didn't hang out so much last year. Josh was always with Margot and me. The trio. And now we're not even a duo, and he's all alone. Part of it's Margot's fault for leaving, but I can see my part in it too—if I'd never started liking him, I wouldn't have had to make up this whole Peter K. story. I could just be his good friend Lara Jean like always.

Maybe this is why Mommy told Margot not to go to college with a boyfriend. When you have a boyfriend or a girlfriend, you only want to be with that person, and you forget about everybody else, and then when the two of you break up, you've lost all your friends. They were off doing fun stuff without you.

All I can say is, Josh sure is a lonely figure eating his sandwich on the very top bleacher.

I take the bus home from school because Peter had to leave early for a lacrosse game with his club team. I'm in front of the house, taking the mail out of our mailbox, when Josh pulls into his driveway. "Hey!" he calls out. He climbs out of his car and jogs over to me, his backpack slung over his shoulder.

"I saw you on the bus," he says. "I waved, but you were doing your daydreaming thing. So how long's your car going to be in the shop?"

"I don't know. It keeps changing. They had to order a part from, like, Indiana."

Josh gives me a knowing look. "So you're secretly relieved, right?"

"No! Why would I be relieved?"

"Come on. I know you. You hate driving. You're probably glad to have the excuse not to drive."

I start to protest, but then I stop. There's no use. Josh knows me too well. "Well, maybe I'm a teeny-tiny bit relieved."

"If you ever need a ride, you know you can call me."

I nod. I do know that. I wouldn't call him for myself, but I would for Kitty, in an emergency.

"I mean, I know you have Kavinsky now, but I'm right next door. It's way more convenient for me to give you a ride to school than him. I mean, it's more environmentally responsible." I don't say anything, and Josh scratches the back of his neck. "I want to say something to you, but I feel weird bringing it up. Which is also weird, because we've always been able to talk to each other."

"We can still talk to each other," I say. "Nothing's changed." That's the biggest lie I've ever told him, even bigger than the lie about my so-called dead twin Marcella. Until a couple of years ago Josh thought I had a twin sister named Marcella who died of leukemia.

"Okay. I feel like . . . I feel like you've been avoiding me ever since . . ."

He's going to say it. He's actually going to say it. I look down at the ground.

"Ever since Margot broke up with me."

My head snaps up. That's what he thinks? That I'm avoiding him because of Margot? Did my letter really make that little of an impact? I try to keep my face still and expressionless when I say, "I haven't been avoiding you. I've just been busy."

"With Kavinsky. I know. You and I have known each other a long time. You're one of my best friends, Lara Jean. I don't want to lose you, too."

It's the "too" that's the sticking point. The "too" is what stops me in my tracks. It sticks in my craw. Because if he hadn't said "too," it would be about me and him. Not about me and him and Margot.

"That letter you wrote—"

Too late. I don't want to talk about the letter anymore. Before he can say another word, I say, "I'll always be your friend, Joshy." And then I smile at him, and it takes a lot of effort. It takes so much effort. But if I don't smile, I'll cry.

Josh nods. "Okay. Good. So . . . so can we hang out again?"

"Sure."

Josh reaches out and chucks my chin. "So can I give you a ride to school tomorrow?"

"Okay," I say. Because wasn't that kind of the whole point of this? To be able to hang out with Josh again without that letter hanging over our heads? To just be his good friend Lara Jean again?

After dinner I teach Kitty how to do laundry. She resists me at first, but I tell her that this is a job we are all sharing from now on, so she'd better just accept it.

"When the buzzer goes off, that means it's done and you have to fold it right away or it'll get wrinkled."

To both of our surprise, Kitty likes doing laundry. Mostly because she can sit in front of the TV and fold and watch her shows in peace.

"Next time I'll teach you how to iron."

"Ironing, too? Who am I, Cinderella?"

I ignore her. "You'll be good at ironing. You like precision and clean lines. You'll probably be better at it than me."

This piques her interest. "Yeah, maybe. Your stuff always looks wrinkled no matter what."

After we finish the laundry, Kitty and I are washing up in the bathroom we share. There are two sinks; Margot had the one on the left and Kitty and I used to fight over who the sink on the right belonged to. It's hers now.

Kitty's brushing her teeth and I'm putting on a cucumber-aloe face mask, when Kitty says to me, "Do you think if I asked, Peter would take us to McDonald's tomorrow on the way to school?"

I rub another dollop of green face mask onto my cheeks.

"I don't want you getting used to Peter giving us rides. You're taking the bus from now on, okay?"

Kitty pouts. "Why!"

"Because. Besides, Peter's not giving me a ride tomorrow, Josh is."

"But won't Peter be mad?"

My face is getting tight from the mask drying. Through clenched teeth I say, "Nah. He's not the jealous type."

"Then who's the jealous type?"

I don't have a good answer for that. Who *is* the jealous type? I'm mulling this over when Kitty giggles at me in the mirror and says, "You look like a zombie."

I hold my hands out to her face and she ducks away. In my best zombie voice I say, "I want to eat your brains."

Kitty runs away, screaming.

When I'm back in my room, I text Peter that I don't need a ride to school tomorrow. I don't tell him Josh is giving me a ride. Just in case.

36

TODAY'S NOTE FROM PETER SAYS, Tart and Tangy *after school?*

He's drawn two boxes, a yes or a no. I check yes and drop the note in his locker.

After school ends, I meet Peter at his car, and we caravan with his lacrosse friends to Tart and Tangy. I order an original frozen yogurt with Cap'n Crunch and strawberries and kiwi and pineapple, and Peter gets key lime with crushed-up Oreos. I pull out my wallet to pay for my yogurt, but Peter stops me. He winks at me and says, "I got this."

I whisper, "I thought you weren't ever paying for anything."

"My boys are here. I can't look like a cheap-ass in front of my boys." Then he puts his arm around me and says loudly, "For as long as you're my girl, you don't pay for frozen yogurt."

I roll my eyes, but I'm not going to say no to a free frozen yogurt. No boy has ever paid for me before. I could get used to this kind of nice treatment.

I was bracing myself to see Genevieve here, but she doesn't show. I think Peter's wondering too, because he keeps his eyes on the door. With Genevieve, I keep waiting for the other shoe to drop. So far she's been eerily, disturbingly quiet. She's hardly ever in the cafeteria during lunch because she and Emily Nussbaum have been eating off campus, and when I see her in the hallways, she fake smiles at me without showing her teeth, which is somehow more menacing.

When is she going to strike back against me? When will I have my Jamila Singh moment? Chris says Genevieve's too obsessed with her college boyfriend to care about me and Peter, but I don't believe it. I've seen the way she looks at him. Like he's hers.

The boys put a few tables together and we basically take over the place. It's just like at the lunch table, with them being loud, talking about the football game coming up on Friday. I don't think I say two words. I don't really have anything to add. I just eat my free frozen yogurt and enjoy the fact that I'm not at home organizing my shoe closet or watching the Golf Channel with my dad.

We're walking to our cars when Gabe says, "Hey, Lara Jean, did you know that if you say your name really fast, it sounds like Large? Try it! Larajean."

Dutifully I repeat, "Larajean. Larjean. Largy. Actually I think it sounds more like Largy, not Large."

Gabe nods to himself and announces, "I'm going to start calling you Large. You're so little it's funny. Right? Like those big guys who go by the name Tiny?"

I shrug. "Sure."

Gabe turns to Darrell. "She's so little she could be our mascot."

"Hey, I'm not *that* small," I protest.

"How tall are you?" Darrell asks me.

"Five two," I fib. It's more like five one and a quarter.

Tossing his spoon in the trash, Gabe says, "You're so little you could fit in my pocket!" All the guys laugh. Peter's smiling in a bemused way. Then Gabe suddenly grabs me and throws me over his shoulder like I'm a kid and he's my dad.

"Gabe! Put me down!" I shriek, kicking my legs and pounding on his chest.

He starts spinning around in a circle, and all the guys are cracking up. "I'm going to adopt you, Large! You're going to be my pet. I'll put you in my old hamster cage!"

I'm giggling so hard I can't catch my breath and I'm starting to feel dizzy. "Put me down!"

"Put her down, man," Peter says, but he's laughing too.

Gabe runs toward somebody's pickup truck and sets me down in the back. "Get me out of here!" I yell. Gabe's already running away. All the guys start getting into their cars. "Bye, Large!" they call out. Peter jogs over to me and extends his hand so I can hop down.

"Your friends are crazy," I say, jumping onto the pavement.

"They like you," he says.

"Really?"

"Sure. They used to hate when I would bring Gen places. They don't mind if you hang out with us." Peter slings his arm around me. "Come on, Large. I'll take you home."

As we walk to his car, I let my hair fall in my face so he doesn't see me smiling. It sure is nice being part of a group, feeling like I belong.

37

I VOLUNTEERED TO BAKE SIX DOZEN CUP-
cakes for Kitty's PTA bake sale. I did it because Margot's
done it for the past two years. Margot only ever did it
because she didn't want people to think Kitty's family wasn't
involved enough in PTA. She did brownies both times, but I
signed up for cupcakes because I thought they'd be a bigger
hit. I bought a few different kinds of blue sprinkles and I
made little toothpick flags that say BLUE MOUNTAIN ACADEMY.
I thought Kitty would have fun helping me decorate.

But now I'm realizing Margot's way was better, because
with brownies, you just pour them in the pan, bake, and slice,
and there you go. Cupcakes are a lot more work. You have
to scoop the perfect amount six dozen times, and then you
have to wait for them to cool, and then you're frosting and
sprinkling.

I'm measuring out my eighth cup of flour when the
doorbell rings. "Kitty!" I scream. "Get the door!"

It rings again. "Kitty!"

From upstairs she screams back, "I'm running an important experiment!"

I run to the door and fling it open without bothering to
check who it is.

Peter. He busts up laughing.

"You have flour all over your face," he says, dusting off my cheeks with the backs of his hands.

I twist away from him and wipe my face with my apron. "What are you doing here?"

"We're going to the game. Didn't you read my note from yesterday?"

"Oh, shoot. I had a test and I forgot." Peter frowns and I add, "I can't go anyway because I have to bake seventy-two cupcakes by tomorrow."

"On a Friday night?"

"Well . . . yeah."

"Is this for the PTA bake sale?" Peter brushes past me and starts taking off his sneakers. "You guys are a no-shoes house, right?"

"Yeah," I say, surprised. "Is your mom making something too?"

"Rice Krispie treats." Another way smarter choice than seventy-two cupcakes.

"Sorry you came over here for nothing. Maybe we can go to the game next Friday," I say, expecting him to put his shoes back on.

But he doesn't, he wanders into the kitchen and sits on a stool. Huh? "Your house looks the same as I remembered," he says, looking around. He points at the framed picture of me and Margot taking a bath when we were babies. "Cute."

I can feel my cheeks burn. I go and turn the photo over. "When have you ever been to my house?"

"Back in seventh grade. Remember how we'd hang out

in your neighbor's tree house? I had to pee once and you let me use your bathroom."

"Oh, yeah," I say.

It's funny to see a boy other than Josh in our kitchen. I feel nervous for some reason. "How long's it going to take?" he asks me, his hands in his pockets.

"Hours, probably." I pick up the measuring cup again. I can't remember what cup I was on.

Peter groans. "Why can't we just go to the store and buy some?"

I start measuring the flour that's in the bowl, separating it into piles. "Because, do you think any of the other moms are buying cupcakes from Food Lion? How would that make Kitty look?"

"Well, if it's for Kitty, then Kitty should be helping." Peter hops off the stool and comes up to me and slides his hands around my waist and tries to untie my apron strings. "Where is the kid?"

I stare at him. "What . . . are you doing?"

Peter looks at me like I'm a dummy. "I need an apron too if I'm going to help. I'm not trying to get my clothes all messed up."

"We're not going to be done in time for the game," I tell him.

"Then we'll just go to the party after." Peter shoots me an incredulous look. "That was in the note I wrote you today! God, why do I even bother?"

"I was really busy today," I say meekly. I feel bad. He's

following through on his end of the deal and faithfully writing me a note a day and I can't even be bothered to read them. "I don't know if I can go to a party. I don't know if I'm allowed to go out that late."

"Is your dad home? I'll ask him."

"No, he's at the hospital. Besides I can't just leave Kitty here by herself." I pick up the measuring cup again.

"Well, what time does he get home?"

"I don't know. Maybe late." Or maybe like in the next hour. But Peter will be long gone by then. "You should just go. I don't want to hold you up."

Peter groans. "Covey. I need you. Gen hasn't said a word about us yet, which is kind of the whole point of this. And . . . she might bring that dickhole she's dating." Peter pushes out his lower lip. "Come on. I came through for you with Josh, didn't I?"

"Yes," I admit. "But, Peter, I have to make these cupcakes for the bake sale—"

Peter stretches his arms out. "Then I'll help you. Just give me an apron."

I back away from him and start rummaging around for another apron. I find one with a cupcake print and hand it to him.

He makes a face and points at mine. "I want the one you're wearing."

"But it's mine!" It's red-and-white gingham with little brown bears; my grandma got it for me in Korea. "I always bake in this. Just wear that one."

Slowly Peter shakes his head and holds out his hand. "Give me yours. You owe me for not reading any of my notes."

I untie the apron and hand it over. I turn around and go back to my measuring. "You're a bigger baby than Kitty."

"Just hurry up and give me a task."

"Are you qualified, though? Because I only have exactly enough ingredients for six dozen cupcakes. I don't want to have to start over—"

"I know how to bake!"

"Okay, then. Dump those sticks of butter into the mixing bowl."

"And then?"

"And then when you're done, I'll give you your next task."

Peter rolls his eyes but he does as he's told. "So this is what you do on Friday nights? Stay home and bake in your pj's?"

"I do other stuff too," I say, tying my hair into a tighter ponytail.

"Like?"

I'm still so flustered from Peter's sudden appearance that I can't think. "Um, I go out."

"Where?"

"God, I don't know! Quit interrogating me, Peter." I blow my bangs out of my eyes. It's getting really warm in here. I might as well just turn off the oven, because Peter's arrival has slowed down this whole process. At this rate I'll be up all night. "You made me lose my count on the flour. I'm going to have to start over from scratch!"

"Here, let me do it," Peter says, coming up close behind me.

I jerk away from him. "No no, I'll do it," I say, and he shakes his head and tries to take the measuring cup from me, but I won't let go, and flour poufs out of the cup and into the air. It dusts us both. Peter starts cracking up and I let out an outraged shriek. "Peter!"

He's laughing too hard to speak.

I cross my arms. "I'd better still have enough flour."

"You look like a grandma," he says, still laughing.

"Well, you look like a grandpa," I counter. I dump the flour in my mixing bowl back into the flour canister.

"Actually, you're really a lot like my granny," Peter says. "You hate cussing. You like to bake. You stay at home on Friday nights. Wow, I'm dating my granny. Gross."

I start measuring again. One, two. "I don't stay home every Friday night." Three.

"I've never seen you out. You don't go to parties. We used to hang out back in the day. Why'd you stop hanging out?"

Four. "I . . . I don't know. Middle school was different." What does he want me to say? That Genevieve decided I wasn't cool enough so I got left behind? Why is he so clueless?

"I always wondered why you stopped hanging out with us."

Was I on five or six? "Peter! You made me lose my count again!"

"I have that effect on women."

I roll my eyes at him and he grins back at me, but before he can say anything else, I yell, "Kitty! Get down here!"

"I'm working—"

"Peter's here!" I know that will get her.

In five seconds flat, Kitty's running into the kitchen. She skids to a stop, all of a sudden shy. "Why are you here?" she asks him.

"To pick up Lara Jean. Why aren't you helping?"

"I was running an experiment. Wanna help me?"

I answer for him. "Sure, he'll help you." To Peter I say, "You're distracting me. Go help Kitty."

"I don't know if you want my help, Katherine. See, I'm really distracting to women. I make them lose their count." Peter winks at her and I make a gagging sound. "Why don't you stay down here and help us bake?"

"Bo-ring!" Kitty turns tail and runs back up the stairs.

"Don't you dare try to sprinkle or frost when it's all over!" I yell. "You haven't earned the right!"

I'm creaming the butter and Peter's cracking eggs into a chipped salad bowl when my dad gets home. "Whose car is that out front?" Daddy asks as he walks into the kitchen. He stops short. "Hello," he says, surprised. He has a Chan's Chinese Bistro bag in his hands.

"Hey, Daddy," I say, like it's perfectly normal that Peter Kavinsky is cooking in our kitchen. "You look tired."

Peter stands up straighter. "Hi, Dr. Covey."

My dad sets the bag down on the kitchen table. "Oh, hello," he says, clearing his throat. "Nice to see you. You're Peter K., right?"

"Right."

"One of the old gang," my dad says jovially, and I cringe. "What are you kids up to tonight?"

"I'm baking cupcakes for Kitty's PTA bake sale and Peter's helping," I say.

My dad nods. "Are you hungry, Peter? I have plenty." He lifts the bag. "Shrimp lo mein, kung pao chicken."

"Actually, Lara Jean and I were going to stop by our friend's party," Peter says. "If that would be okay? I'll bring her back early."

Before my dad can answer, I say to Peter, "I told you I have to finish these cupcakes."

"Kitty and I will finish them," my dad interjects. "You two go to that birthday party."

My stomach flips. "It's really okay, Daddy. I have to be the one to do them; I'm decorating them specially."

"Kitty and I will figure it out. You can go get changed. We'll keep working on these cupcakes."

I open and close my mouth like a trout. "All right, then." And I don't make a move, I just stand there, because I'm afraid to leave the two of them alone together.

Peter smiles at me broadly. "You heard the man. We've got this covered."

I think, *Don't act too confident, because then my dad will think you're arrogant.*

There are certain outfits you have that make you feel good every time you wear them, and then there are outfits where you wore them too many times in a row because you liked them so much, and now they just feel like garbage. I'm looking at my closet now and everything looks like garbage. My anxiety is only compounded by the fact that I know Gen will be wearing the exact right thing, because she always wears the exact right thing. And I have to be wearing the right thing too. Peter wouldn't have come by and made such a point of going to this party if it weren't important to him.

I pull on my jeans and try on different tops—a frilly peach one that suddenly looks prissy in my eyes, a long fuzzy sweater with a penguin on it that looks too kiddish. I'm stepping into a pair of gray shorts with black suspenders when someone knocks at my door. I freeze and grab a sweater to cover myself up.

"Lara Jean?" It's Peter.

"Yes?"

"Are you almost ready?"

"Almost! Just—just go downstairs. I'll be down soon."

He lets out an audible sigh. "Okay. I'm gonna see what the kid's doing."

When I hear his footsteps walking away, I scramble and try a cream polka-dot blouse with the shorts-suspenders ensemble. It's cute, but is it too cute? Too much? And should I do black tights or black knee socks? Margot said I look Parisian in this outfit. Parisian is a good thing. It's sophisticated, romantic. I try on a beret, just to see the effect, and I immediately throw it off. Definitely too much.

I wish Peter hadn't snuck up on me with this. I need time to plan, to prepare. Though truthfully, if he'd asked me ahead of time, I would have come up with an excuse not to go. It's one thing to go to Tart and Tangy after school, but a party with all of Peter's friends, not to mention Genevieve?

I hop around my room, searching for my over-the-knee socks, then searching for my strawberry lip pot that looks like a strawberry. Gosh, I really need to clean my room. It's hard to find anything in this mess.

I run to Margot's room for her big grandpa cardigan, and I pass Kitty's open door, where I see Peter and Kitty lying on the floor, working with her lab set. I root through Margot's sweater drawer, which is now T-shirts and shorts because she's taken most of her sweaters. No grandpa cardigan. But at the bottom of the drawer there is an envelope. A letter, from Josh.

I want to open it so badly. I know I shouldn't.

Carefully, ever so carefully, I take out the letter and unfold it.

Dear Margot,

You say we had to break up because you don't want to go to college with a boyfriend, and you want your freedom, and you don't want to be held back. But you know and I know that's not the real reason. You broke up with me because we had sex and you were scared of getting close to me.

I stop reading.

I can't believe it. Chris was right and I was wrong. Margot

and Josh did have sex. It's like everything I thought I knew is the opposite. I thought I knew exactly who my sister was, but it turns out I don't know anything.

I hear Peter calling my name. "Lara Jean! Are you ready yet?"

Hastily I fold the letter up and put it back in the envelope. I put it back in the drawer and slam the drawer shut. "Coming!"

38

WE'RE STANDING AT THE FRONT DOOR OF
Steve Bledell's mansion. Steve's on the football team; he's
mostly known for having a rich stepdad with his own plane.

"Ready?" Peter asks me.

I wipe my palms on my shorts. I wish I'd had time to do
something better to my hair. "Not really."

"Then let's talk strategy for a second. All you have to do is
act like you're in love with me. That shouldn't be too hard."

I roll my eyes. "You're the vainest boy I've ever met."

Peter grins and shrugs. He's got his hand on the door-
knob, but then he stops. "Hold on," he says, and he pulls the
hair tie out of my hair and tosses it into the yard.

"Hey!"

"It looks better down. Just trust me." Peter runs his fingers
through my hair and fluffs it up, and I swat his hand away.
Then he takes his phone out of his back pocket and he snaps
a picture of me.

I give him a puzzled look, and he explains, "In case Gen
checks my phone." I watch as he sets the picture as his wallpaper.

"Can we do another one?" I don't like the way my hair
looks.

"Nah, I like it. You look pretty." He probably only said it so we could hurry up and go inside, but it makes me feel good.

Walking into this party with Peter Kavinsky, I can't help but feel a sudden rush of pride. He's here with me. Or is it that I'm here with him?

I see her as soon as we walk in—she's on the couch with her girls; they're all drinking from red Solo cups. No boyfriend in sight. She raises her eyebrows at me and whispers something to Emily Nussbaum. "Heyyy, Lara Jean," Emily calls out, crooking her finger at me. "Come sit by us."

I start to walk toward them, thinking Peter is next to me, but he's not. He's stopped to say hi to someone. I look at him with panicky eyes and he just gestures at me to keep going. He mouths, *You're up.*

Crossing the room alone feels like crossing a continent, with Gen and her friends watching me. "Hi, guys," I say, and my voice comes out high-pitched and little-girlish. There's no room for me on the couch, so I perch on an armrest like a bird on a telephone wire. I keep my eyes trained on Peter's back; he is across the room with some guys from the lacrosse team. It must be nice to be him. So at ease, so comfortable with himself, knowing that people are waiting for him, like *Peter's here, now the party can really get started.* I look around the room, just to have something to do, and see Gabe and Darrell, and they wave at me very nicely, but they don't come over. It feels like everyone is waiting and watching, waiting and watching to see what Genevieve will do.

I wish I hadn't come.

Emily leans forward. "We're all dying to know . . . what's the story with you and Kavinsky?"

I know she's been commissioned by Gen to ask. Gen's sipping her drink, casual as can be, but she's waiting for my answer. Is she drunk yet? I wonder. From everything I've heard and know about Gen, she is a mean drunk. Not that I've ever personally experienced it, but I've heard things. There are stories.

I wet my lips. "Whatever Peter said . . . I guess that's the story."

Emily waves this off like whatever Peter says doesn't really count. "We want to hear it from you. I mean, it's just so surprising. How did this even happen?" She leans closer, like we are girlfriends.

When I hesitate, when my eyes dart toward Genevieve, she smiles and rolls her eyes. "It's okay, you can say, Lara Jean. Peter and I are over. I don't know if he told you this, but I'm actually the one who broke up with him, so."

I nod. "That's what he said." That is *not* what he said, but it's what I already knew.

"So when did you guys get together?" She tries to sound offhand, but I know my answer is important to her. She's trying to catch me in something.

"Pretty recently," I say.

"How recently?" she presses.

I swallow. "Right before school started," I tell her. Isn't that what Peter and I decided the story was going to be?

Genevieve's eyes go bright and my heart sinks. I've

said the wrong thing, but it's too late. It's hard not to get caught up in her spell. She's the kind of person you want to like you. You know she can be cruel; you've seen her be cruel. But when her eyes are on you, and she's paying attention to you, you want it to last. Her beauty is part of it, but there's something more—something that draws you in. I think it's her transparency—everything she thinks or feels is written all over her face, and even if it wasn't, she'd say it anyway, because she says what she thinks, without thinking first.

I can see why Peter has loved her for so long.

"I think it's adorable," Genevieve says, and then the girls start talking about some concert they're trying to get tickets for and I just sit there, glad I don't have to talk anymore, wondering how it's going with the cupcakes back at home. I hope Daddy isn't overbaking them. There's nothing worse than a dry cupcake.

The girls move on to talking about Halloween costumes, so I get up and go to the bathroom. I come back to find Peter sitting in a wingback leather armchair, drinking a beer and talking to Gabe. There's nowhere for me to sit; my spot on the couch has been taken. Now what?

I stand there for a second and then I go for it: I do what a girl in love with Peter would do. I do what Genevieve would do. I march right in and plop down in his lap like it's my rightful place.

Peter yelps in surprise. "Hey," he says, coughing on his beer.

"Hey," I say. Then I tweak him once on the nose like I saw a girl do in a black-and-white movie.

Peter shifts in his seat and gives me a look like he's trying not to laugh, and I get nervous—tweaking a boy on the nose is romantic, right? Then, out of the corner of my eye, I see Genevieve glaring at us. She whispers something to Emily and stalks out of the room.

Success!

Later I am pouring myself Cherry Coke and I see Genevieve and Peter, talking in the kitchen. She's speaking to him in a low, urgent voice, and she reaches out and touches his arm. He tries to brush her hand away, but she doesn't let go.

I'm so mesmerized I don't even notice when Lucas Krapf comes up to me, popping the cap off a bottle of Bud Light. "Hey, Lara Jean."

"Hi!" I'm relieved to see a familiar face.

He stands next to me, our backs against the dining room wall. "What are they fighting about?"

"Who even knows?" I say. I smile a secret smile. Hopefully, it's about me, and Peter will be happy our plan is finally working.

Lucas crooks his finger at me so I'll come closer. He whispers, "Fighting isn't a good sign, Lara Jean. It means you still care." His breath smells like beer.

Hmm. Genevieve obviously still cares. Peter must too.

Lucas pats me on the head fondly. "Just be careful."

"Thank you," I say.

Peter stalks out of the kitchen and says, "Are you ready to go?" He doesn't wait for me to answer him; he just starts walking, his shoulders stiff.

I give Lucas a shrug. "See you on Monday, Lucas!" Then I scurry after Peter.

He's still mad; I can tell by the way he jerks the keys into the ignition. "God, she makes me crazy!" He's so keyed up energy is vibrating off him in waves. "What did you say to her?"

I shift uncomfortably in my seat. "She asked me when we got together. I told her just before school started."

Peter does a full-body groan. "We hooked up that first weekend."

"But . . . you guys were broken up already."

"Yeah, well." Peter shrugs. "Whatever. What's done is done."

Relieved, I click on my seat belt and kick my shoes off. "What were you two fighting about tonight, anyway?"

"Don't worry about it. You did a good job, by the way. She's so jealous it's killing her."

"Yay," I say. Just as long as she doesn't kill me.

We drive through the night in silence. Then I ask, "Peter . . . how did you know you loved Genevieve?"

"God, Lara Jean. Why do you have to ask those kind of questions?"

"Because I'm a naturally curious person." I flip down

his mirror and start braiding the top of my hair. "And maybe the question you should be asking yourself is, why are you so afraid to answer those kinds of questions?"

"I'm not afraid!"

"Then why won't you answer the question?"

Peter goes silent, and I'm pretty sure he's not going to answer, but then, after a long pause where my question just hangs in the air, he says, "I don't know if I ever loved Genevieve. How would I even know what that felt like? I'm seventeen, for God's sake."

"Seventeen's not so young. A hundred years ago people got married when they were practically our age."

"Yeah, that was before electricity and the Internet. A hundred years ago eighteen-year-old guys were out there fighting wars with bayonets and holding a man's life in their hands! They lived a lot of life by the time they were our age. What do kids our age know about love and life?" I've never heard him talk like this before—like he actually cares about something. I think he's still all worked up from his fight with Genevieve.

I wind my hair into a honey bun and secure it with a ponytail holder. "You know who you sound like? You sound like my grandpa," I say. "Also I think you're stalling because you don't want to answer the question."

"I answered it, you just didn't like my answer."

We pull up in front of my house. Peter turns off the engine, which is what he does when he wants to talk a little while longer. So I don't jump out right away, I put my bag in my lap and search for my keys even though the lights are on upstairs. Gosh. To be sitting in the passenger seat of Peter Kavinsky's black Audi. Isn't that what every girl has ever wanted, in the history of boys and girls? Not Peter Kavinsky specifically, or yes, maybe Peter Kavinsky specifically.

Peter leans his head back against the headrest and closes his eyes.

I say, "Did you know that when people fight with each other, that means they still really care about each other?" When Peter doesn't answer, I say, "Genevieve must really have a hold on you."

I expect him to deny it, but he doesn't. Instead he says, "She does, but I wish she didn't. I don't want to be owned by anyone. Or belong to anyone."

Margot would say she belongs to herself. Kitty would say she belongs to no one. And I guess I would say I belong to my sisters and my dad, but that won't always be true. To belong to someone—I didn't know it, but now that I think about, it seems like that's all I've ever wanted. To really be somebody's, and to have them be mine.

"So that's why you're doing this," I tell him—I'm partly asking but I'm mostly telling. "To prove you don't belong to her. Or with her." I stop. "Do you think there's a difference? Between belonging *with* and belonging *to*, I mean?"

"Sure. One implies choice; the other doesn't."

JENNY HAN

"You must really love her to go to all this trouble."

Peter makes a dismissive sound. "You're too dreamy-eyed."

"Thank you," I say, even though I know he doesn't mean it as a compliment. I say it just to bug him.

I know I've succeeded when he says, his face sour, "What would you know about love, Lara Jean? You've never even had a boyfriend before."

I'm tempted to make up someone, a boy from camp, from another town, from anywhere. *His name is Clint* is on the tip of my tongue. But it would be too humiliating, because he'd know I was lying; I already told him I never dated anybody before. And even if I hadn't, it is far more pathetic to make up a boyfriend than to just admit the truth. "No, I've never had a boyfriend. But plenty of people I know have had boyfriends but they've never once been in love. I've been in love." That's why *I'm* doing this.

Peter snorts. "With who? Josh Sanderson? That tool?"

"He's not a tool," I say, frowning at him. "You don't even know him to say that."

"Anybody with one eye and half a brain could tell what a tool that guy is."

"Are you saying my sister's blind and brainless?" I demand. If he says one bad word about my sister, that's it. This whole thing is off. I don't need him that badly.

Peter laughs. "No. I'm saying you are!"

"You know what? I changed my mind. You've obviously

never loved anyone but yourself." I try to jerk the passenger door open, but it's locked.

"Lara Jean, I was just kidding. Come on."

"See you on Monday."

"Wait, wait. First tell me something." Peter leans back in his seat. "How come you never dated anybody?"

I shrug. "I don't know . . . because nobody ever asked?"

"Bullshit. I know for a fact that Martinez asked you to homecoming and you said no."

I'm surprised he knows about that. "What is it with you guys all calling each other by your last name?" I ask him. "It's so—" I struggle to find the right word. "Effected? Affected?"

"Don't change the subject."

"I guess I said no because I was scared." I stare out the window and run my finger along the glass, making an *M* for Martinez.

"Of *Tommy*?"

"No. I like Tommy. It's not that. It's scary when it's real. When it's not just thinking about a person, but, like, having a real live person in front of you, with, like, expectations. And wants." I finally look at Peter, and I'm surprised by how hard he's paying attention; his eyes are intent and focused on me like he's actually interested in what I'm saying. "Even when I liked a boy so much, loved him even, I would always rather be with my sisters, because that's where I belong."

"Wait. What about right now?"

"Right now? Well, I don't like you that way so . . ."

"Good," Peter says. "Don't go falling for me again, okay? I can't have any more girls in love with me. It's exhausting."

I laugh out loud. "You're so full of yourself."

"I'm kidding," he protests, but he's not. "What did you ever see in me anyway?" He grins at me then, cocky again and so sure of his charm.

"Honestly? I really couldn't tell you."

The grin falters and then rights itself, but now it's not so certain. "You said it was because I make people feel special. You . . . you said it was because I was a good dancer and I was science partners with Jeffrey Suttleman!"

"Wow, you really memorized every single word of that letter, huh?" I tease. It gives me a small, mean surge of satisfaction to see Peter's grin fade completely. That surge is immediately followed by remorse, because now I've hurt his feelings for no good reason. What is it in me that wants to hurt Peter Kavinsky's feelings? To make it better, I quickly add, "No, it's true—you really did have something about you then."

I guess I made it worse, because he flinches.

I don't know what else to say, so I open the car door and climb out. "Thanks for the ride, Peter."

When I get inside the house, I go look in the kitchen first to check on the cupcakes. They're packed away in Tupperware and my cupcake carrier. The frosting's a little messy and the sprinkles are haphazard, but overall they look pretty good. That's a relief. Kitty won't be shamed at the PTA bake sale on my account, at least!

From: Margot Covey mcovey@st-andrews.ac.uk
To: Lara Jean Covey larajeansong@gmail.com

How's school going so far? Have you joined any new clubs? I think you should consider Lit Mag or Model UN. Also don't forget it's Korean Thanksgiving this week and you have to call Grandma or she'll be mad! Miss you guys.

PS Please send Oreos! I miss our dunk contests.

Love, M

From: Lara Jean Covey larajeansong@gmail.com
To: Margot Covey mcovey@st-andrews.ac.uk

School is good. No new clubs yet, but we'll see. I already have it down in my planner to call Grandma. Don't worry about a thing, I've got everything under control here!

xx

39

PETER'S MOM OWNS AN ANTIQUE STORE
called Linden & White in the cobblestoney part of downtown. She sells furniture mostly, but she has jewelry cases
too, arranged by decades. My favorite decade is the aughts,
which means the 1900s. There's this one gold heart locket
with a tiny diamond chip in the center; it looks like a star-
burst. It costs four hundred dollars. The store is right next to
McCalls bookstore, so I go in sometimes and visit with it. I
always expect it to be gone, but then it never is.

We once bought our mom a gold clover pin from the
1940s for Mother's Day. Margot and I ran a lemonade stand
every Saturday for a month, and we were able to chip in
sixteen dollars for it. I remember how proud we were when
we presented Daddy with the money, we had it nice and
neat in a ziplock bag. At the time I thought we were paying
the lion's share and my dad was only helping out a little. I
realize now that the pin cost a lot more than sixteen dollars.
I should ask Daddy how much it really cost. But then maybe
I don't want to know. Maybe it's nicer not knowing. We bur-
ied her with it because it was her favorite.

I'm standing over the case, touching my finger to the glass,
when Peter comes out from around back. "Hey," he says,
surprised.

"Hey," I say. "What are you doing here?"

Peter gives me a look like I'm a dummy. "My mom owns the place, remember?"

"Well, duh. I've just never seen you here before," I say. "Do you work here?"

"Nah, I had to drop something off for my mom. Now she's saying I have to go pick up a set of chairs in Huntsburgh tomorrow," Peter says in a grumbly voice. "It's two hours there and back. Annoying."

I nod companionably and lean away from the case. I pretend to look at a pink-and-black globe. Actually, Margot would like this. It could be a nice Christmas present for her. I give it a little spin. "How much is this globe?"

"Whatever it says on the sticker." Peter rests his elbows on the case and leans forward. "You should come."

I look up at him. "Come where?"

"To pick up the chairs with me."

"You just complained about how annoying it's going to be."

"Yeah, alone. If you go, it might be slightly less annoying."

"Gee, thanks."

"You're welcome."

I roll my eyes. Peter says "you're welcome" to everything! It's like, *No, Peter, that was not a genuine thank-you, so you do not need to say you're welcome.*

"So are you coming or what?"

"Or what."

"Come on! I'm picking the chairs up from an estate sale.

The owner was some kind of shut-in. Stuff has just been sitting there for like fifty years. I bet there'll be stuff you can look at. You like old stuff, right?"

"Yes," I say, surprised that he knows this about me. "Actually, I've kind of always wanted to go to an estate sale. How did the owner die? Like, how long was it before someone found him?"

"God, you're morbid." He shudders. "Didn't know you had that side to you."

"I have lots of sides to me," I tell him. I lean forward. "So? How did he die?"

"He isn't dead, you weirdo. He's just old. His family's sending him to a nursing home." Peter raises an eyebrow at me. "So I'll pick you up tomorrow at seven."

"Seven? You never said anything about leaving at seven in the morning on a Saturday!"

"Sorry," he says contritely. "We have to go early before all the good stuff gets snatched up."

That night I pack lunches for Peter and me. I make roast beef sandwiches with cheese and tomato, mayonnaise for me, mustard for Peter. Peter doesn't like mayonnaise. It's funny the things you pick up in a fake relationship.

Kitty zooms into the kitchen and tries to grab a sandwich half. I smack her hand away. "That's not for you."

"Then who's it for?"

"It's for my lunch tomorrow. Mine and Peter's."

She climbs onto a stool and watches me wrap the

sandwiches in wax paper. Sandwiches look so much prettier wrapped in wax paper than encased in ziplock. Any chance I get, I use wax paper. "I like Peter," Kitty says. "He's a lot different than Josh, but I like him."

I look up. "What do you mean?"

"I don't know. He's really funny. He jokes around a lot. You must really be in love if you're making sandwiches for him. When Margot and Josh first became a couple, she made three-cheese macaroni and cheese all the time because that's his favorite. What's Peter's favorite?"

"I—I don't know. I mean, he likes everything."

Kitty gives me the side eye. "If you're his girlfriend, you should know what his favorite food is."

"I know he doesn't like mayonnaise," I offer.

"That's because mayonnaise is gross. Josh hates mayonnaise too."

I feel a pang. Josh does hate mayonnaise. "Kitty, do you miss Josh?"

She nods. "I wish he still came over." A wistful look crosses over her face, and I'm about to give her a hug when she puts her hands on her hips. "Just don't use all the roast beef, because I need it for my lunch next week."

"If we run out, I'll make tuna salad. Sheesh."

"See that you do," Kitty says, and zooms off again.

"See that you do"? Where does she get this stuff?

At seven thirty I'm sitting by the window, waiting for Peter to pull up. I've got a brown paper bag with our sandwiches and my camera, in case there's anything spooky or cool I can take a picture of. I'm picturing a crumbling, gray old mansion like you see in horror movies, with a gate and a murky pond or a maze in the backyard.

Peter's mom's minivan pulls up at seven forty-five, which is annoying. I could've slept a whole hour longer. I run out to the car and hop inside, and before I can say a word, he says, "I'm sorry, I'm sorry. But look what I brought you." He passes me a donut in a napkin, still warm. "I stopped and got it special, right when they opened at seven thirty. It's mocha sugar."

I break off a piece and pop it into my mouth. "Yum!"

He gives me a sidelong glance as he pulls out of my driveway. "So I did the right thing being late, right?"

I nod, taking a big bite. "You did the exact right thing," I say, my mouth full. "Hey, do you have any water?"

Peter hands me a half-full water bottle and I gulp it down. "This is the best donut I ever had," I tell him.

"Good," he says. Then he takes one look at me and laughs. "You have sugar all over your face."

I wipe my mouth off with the other side of the napkin.

"Cheeks, too," he says.

"All right, all right." Then it's quiet, which makes me nervous. "Can I put some music on?" I start pulling out my phone.

"Actually, do you mind if we just drive in quiet for a while? I can't have music blaring in my face before my caffeine kicks in."

"Uh . . . sure." I'm not sure if that means he wants me to

be quiet too. I wouldn't have agreed to come on this little outing if I'd known I would have to be silent.

Peter has a serene look on his face, like he is a fishing-boat captain and we are floating placidly along in the middle of the sea. Except he isn't driving slowly; he is driving really fast.

I stay quiet for all of ten seconds and then say, "Wait, were you wanting me to be quiet too?"

"No, I just didn't want music. You can talk as much as you want."

"Okay." And then I'm quiet, because it's awkward when someone tells you you can talk as much as you want. "Hey, so what's your favorite food?"

"I like everything."

"But what's your *favorite?* Like, your *favorite* favorite. Is it macaroni and cheese, or um, fried chicken, or steak, or pizza?"

"I like all that stuff. Equally."

I let out an aggrieved sigh. Why does Peter not get the concept of picking a favorite thing?

Peter mimics my sigh and laughs. "Fine. I like cinnamon toast. That's my favorite thing."

"Cinnamon toast?" I repeat. "You like cinnamon toast better than crab legs? Better than a cheeseburger?"

"Yes."

"Better than *barbecue?*"

Peter hesitates. Then he says, "Yes! Now quit picking my choice apart. I stand by my choice."

I shrug. "Okay." I wait, give him a chance to ask me what

my favorite food is, but he doesn't. So I say, "My favorite food is cake."

"What kind of cake?"

"It doesn't matter. All cake."

"You just gave me so much shit for not picking," he begins.

"But it's so hard to pick one kind!" I burst out. "I mean, there's coconut cake, the kind with white frosting that looks like a snowball—I like that a lot. But then I also like cheese-cake, and lemon cake, and carrot cake. Also red velvet cake with cream cheese frosting, and chocolate cake with choco-late ganache frosting." I pause. "Have you ever had olive-oil cake?"

"No. That sounds weird."

"It's really, really good. Really moist and delicious. I'll make it for you."

Peter groans. "You're making me hungry. I should have gotten a whole bag of those donuts."

I open up my brown paper bag and pull out his sandwich. I wrote a *P* on his in Sharpie so I'd know whose was whose. "Do you want a sandwich?"

"You made that for me?"

"I mean, I was making one for myself, too. It would have been rude to just bring one sandwich and eat it in front of you."

Peter accepts the sandwich and eats it with the bottom half still wrapped. "This is good," he says, nodding. "What kind of mustard is this?"

Pleased, I say, "It's beer mustard. My dad orders it from

some fancy food catalog. My dad's really into cooking."

"Aren't you going to eat yours, too?"

"I'm saving it for later," I say.

Halfway into the ride, Peter starts weaving in and out of traffic, and he keeps looking at the clock on the dashboard.

"Why are we in such a hurry?" I ask him.

"The Epsteins," he says, rapping his fingers on the steering wheel.

"Who are the Epsteins?"

"They're an old married couple with an antiques store in Charlottesville. Last time, Phil got there five minutes before me and cleared the whole place out. That's not gonna happen today."

Impressed, I say, "Wow, I had no idea this business was so cutthroat."

Like a know-it-all Peter smirks and goes, "Isn't all business?"

I roll my eyes at the window. Peter's so Peter.

We're at a stoplight when Peter suddenly sits up straight and says, "Oh, shit! The Epsteins!"

I was halfway asleep. My eyes fly open and I yell, "Where? Where?"

"Red SUV! Two cars ahead on the right." I crane my neck to look. They are a gray-haired couple, maybe in their sixties or seventies. It's hard to tell from this far away.

As soon as the light turns green, Peter guns it and drives up on the shoulder. I scream out, "Go go go!" and then we're flying past the Epsteins. My heart is racing out of control,

I can't help but lean my head out the window and scream because it's such a thrill. My hair whips in the wind and I know it's going to be a tangled mess, but I couldn't care less. "Yahhh!" I scream.

"You're crazy," Peter says, pulling me back in by the hem of my shirt. He's looking at me like he did that day I kissed him in the hallway. Like I'm different than he thought.

We pull up to the house and there are already a few cars parked in front. I'm craning my head trying to get a good look. I was expecting a mansion with a wrought iron gate and maybe a gargoyle or two, but this just looks like a normal house. I must look disappointed, because as he puts the car in park, Peter says to me, "Don't judge an estate sale by the house. I've seen all kinds of treasures at regular houses and junk at fancy houses."

I hop out and bend down to tie my shoelace. "Hurry, Lara Jean! The Epsteins will be here any second!" Peter grabs my hand and we run up the driveway; I am breathing hard trying to keep up with him. His legs are so much longer than mine.

As soon as we are inside, Peter goes right up to a man in a suit and I bend over and try to catch my breath. A few people are milling around looking at the furniture. There's a long dining room table in the center of the room with china and milk glass and porcelain knickknacks. I go up to it and take a closer look. I like a little white creamer with pink rosebuds but I'm not sure if I'm allowed to touch it and see how much it costs. It could be really expensive.

There's a big basket with olden-day Christmas memorabilia in it, plastic Santas and Rudolphs and glass ornaments. I'm sifting through it when Peter comes up to me, a huge grin on his face. "Mission accomplished," he says. He nods at an older couple who are looking at a wooden sideboard. "The Epsteins," he whispers to me.

"Did you get the chairs?" Mr. Epstein calls out. He's trying to sound casual and not annoyed, but his hands are on his hips and he's standing very rigidly.

"You know it," Peter calls back. "Better luck next time." To me he says, "Do you see anything cool?"

"Lots of stuff." I hold up a hot pink reindeer. It's glass, with an electric blue nose. "This would look great on my vanity. Will you ask the man how much it costs?"

"No, but you can. It'll be good for you to learn how to negotiate." Peter grabs my hand and leads me over to the man in the suit. He's filling out some paperwork on a clipboard. He looks very busy and important. I'm not even sure if I'm supposed to be here. I'm thinking I don't *really* need this reindeer.

But Peter's looking at me expectantly, so I clear my throat and say, "Excuse me, sir, but how much is this reindeer?"

"Oh, that's part of a lot," he says.

"Oh. Um, I'm sorry but what's a lot?"

"It means it's part of a set," he explains. "You have to buy the whole set of ornaments. Seventy-five dollars. They're vintage, you see."

I start to back away. "Thank you anyway," I say.

Peter pulls me back and gives him a winning smile and

says, "Can't you just throw it in with the chairs? A gift with purchase?"

The man sighs. "I don't want to separate them." He turns away to flip through his clipboard.

Peter throws me a look, like *You're the one who wants the reindeer; you should step up*. I give him back a look that says *I don't want it that bad*, and Peter shakes his head firmly and pushes me toward the man. I say, "Please, sir? I'll give you ten dollars for it. No one will know they're missing a reindeer. And look, his paw is a little chipped on the bottom, see?" I hold it up.

"All right, all right. Just take it," the man says begrudgingly, and I beam at him and start to pull my wallet out of my purse, but he waves me off.

"Thank you! Thank you so much." I clutch the reindeer to my chest. Maybe haggling isn't as hard as I thought.

Peter winks at me, and then he says to the man, "I'll bring my van closer so we can load up the chairs."

They go out the back, and I hang around, looking at the framed pictures on the wall. I wonder if they're for sale too. Some of them look really old: black-and-white pictures of men in suits and hats. There's one picture of a girl in a confirmation dress, it's white and lacy like a wedding gown. The girl isn't smiling, but she has a mischievous glint in her eye that reminds me of Kitty.

"That's my daughter, Patricia."

I turn around. It's an old man in a navy blue sweater and stiff jeans. He's leaning against the staircase watching me. He looks very frail; his skin is paper white and thin.

"She lives in Ohio. She's an accountant." He's still gazing at me, like *I* remind *him* of someone.

"Your house is lovely," I say, even though it isn't. It's old; it could use a good cleaning. But the things inside it are lovely.

"It's empty now. All my things sold up. Can't take it with you, you know."

"You mean when you die?" I whisper.

He glares at me. "No. I mean to the nursing home."

Whoops. "Right," I say, and I giggle the way I do when I feel awkward.

"What do you have there in your hand?"

I lift it up. "This. He—the man in the suit gave it to me. Do you want it back? I didn't pay for it. It's part of a lot."

He smiles, and the wrinkles in his paper skin deepen. "That was Patty's favorite."

I hold it out to him. "Maybe she'd like to keep it?"

"No, you have it. It's yours. She couldn't even be bothered to help me move, so." He gives a spiteful nod. "Is there anything else you want to take? I've got a trunk full of her old clothes."

Yikes. Family drama. Best not to get involved in that. But vintage clothes! That's tempting.

When Peter finds me, I'm sitting cross-legged on the floor in the music room, looking through an old trunk. Mr. Clarke is snoozing on the couch next to me. I found a mod minidress the color of cotton candy pink that I'm crazy about, and a sleeveless button-down with little daisies on it that I can tie at the waist. "Look, Peter!" I lift up the dress. "Mr. Clarke said I could have it."

"Who's Mr. Clarke?" Peter asks, and his voice fills the room.

I point at him and put my finger to my lips.

"Well, we'd better get out of here fast before the guy in charge of the sale sees him giving stuff away for free."

I get up in a hurry. "Bye, Mr. Clarke," I say, not too loud. Probably better to let him sleep. He was very down earlier, when he was telling me about his divorce.

Mr. Clarke's eyes flutter open. "Is this your feller?"

"No, not really," I say, and Peter throws his arm around my shoulder and says, "Yes, sir. I'm her feller."

I don't like the way he says it, like he's making fun. Of both me and Mr. Clarke. "Thank you for the clothes, Mr. Clarke," I say, and he sits up straight and reaches for my hand. I give it to him and he kisses it, and his lips feel like dry moth's wings.

"You're welcome, Patty."

I give him a good-bye wave and grab my new things. As we walk out the front door, Peter says, "Who's Patty?" and I pretend I don't hear.

I must fall asleep in about two seconds from the excitement of the day, because the next thing I know, we're parked in my driveway, and Peter's shaking my shoulder, saying, "We're here, Lara Jean."

I open my eyes. I'm clutching my dress and shirt to my chest like a security blanket, and my reindeer is in my lap.

My new treasures. I feel like I just robbed a bank and got away with it. "Thanks for today, Peter."

"Thanks for coming with me." Then, abruptly, he says, "Oh yeah. I forgot to ask you something. My mom wants you to come over to dinner tomorrow night."

My mouth drops. "You told your mom about us?"

Peter gives me a dirty look. "Kitty knows about us! Besides, my mom and I are close. It's just her and me and my brother, Owen. If you don't want to come, then don't come. But just know that my mom will think you're rude if you don't."

"I'm just saying . . . the more people that know, the harder it is to manage. You have to keep lies restricted to as few people as possible."

"How do you know so much about lying?"

"Oh, I used to lie all the time as a kid." I didn't think of it as lying, though. I thought of it as playing make-believe. I told Kitty she was adopted and her real family was in a traveling circus. It's why she took up gymnastics.

40

I'M NOT SURE HOW DRESSED UP I SHOULD get for dinner at Peter's house. At the store his mom seems so fancy. I just don't want to meet her and have her be thinking of all the ways that I'm lacking compared to Genevieve. I don't see why I have to meet her at all.

But I do want her to like me.

I go through my closet, and then Margot's closet. I finally pick a cream-colored sweater and a blouse with a Peter Pan collar, with a corduroy mustard circle skirt. Plus tights and flats. Then I put on some makeup, which I hardly ever wear. I put on peach blush and I try to do some eye makeup, but I end up washing everything off and starting over again, this time with just mascara and lip gloss.

I go show Kitty and she says, "Looks like a uniform."

"Like in a good way?"

Kitty nods. "Like you work at a nice store."

Before Peter arrives at my house, I go on the computer and look up what fork to use with what, just in case.

It's strange. Sitting at Peter's kitchen table, I feel like I'm living someone else's life. It turns out Peter's mom has made pizzas, so I didn't even need to worry about forks. And their house isn't fancy on the inside; it's just normal and nice. There's a real butter churner on display in the kitchen, pictures of Peter and his brother hanging on the walls in wooden frames, and red-and-white gingham everything.

There are a bunch of pizza toppings on the breakfast bar—not just pepperoni and sausage and mushroom and pepper, but also artichoke hearts and greasy kalamata olives and fresh mozzarella and whole cloves of garlic.

Peter's mom is nice. She keeps putting more salad on my plate all throughout dinner, and I keep eating it even though I'm full. Once, I catch her looking at me, and she has a soft smile on her face. When she smiles, she looks like Peter.

Peter's younger brother is named Owen. He's twelve. He's like a miniature Peter, but he doesn't talk as much. He doesn't have Peter's easy way. Owen grabs a slice of pizza and shoves it into his mouth even though it's too hot. He puffs out hot air and he almost spits a piece back out into his napkin, and their mom says, "Don't you dare, Owen. We have company."

"Leave me alone," Owen mumbles.

"Peter says you have two sisters," Mrs. Kavinsky says with a bright smile. She cuts a piece of lettuce into bite-sized bits. "Your mother must love having three girls."

I open my mouth to answer her, but before I can, Peter does. He says, "Lara Jean's mom passed away when she was little." He says it like she should already know, and embarrassment crosses her face.

"I'm so sorry. I remember that now."

Quickly I say, "She did love having three girls. They

thought for sure my little sister Kitty was going to be a boy, and my mom said she was so used to girls she was nervous about what she was going to do with a boy. So she was really relieved when Kitty turned out to be a girl. My sister Margot and I were too; we would pray every night we'd get a sister and not a brother."

"Hey, what's wrong with boys?" Peter objects.

Mrs. Kavinsky's smiling now. She puts another piece of pizza on Owen's plate and says, "You're heathens. Wild animals. I bet Lara Jean and her sisters are angels."

Peter snorts.

"Well . . . Kitty might be part heathen," I admit. "But my older sister Margot and I are pretty good."

Mrs. Kavinsky takes her napkin and tries to wipe tomato sauce off Owen's face, and he swats her hand away. "Mom!"

When she gets up to take another pizza out of the oven, Peter says to me, "See how my mom babies him?"

"She babies you way more," Owen counters. To me he mumbles, "Peter doesn't even know how to cook ramen."

I laugh. "Can you?"

"Hell yeah, I've been cooking for myself for years," he says.

"I like to cook too," I say, taking a sip of iced tea. "We should give Peter a cooking lesson."

He eyes me and then says, "You wear more makeup than Genevieve did."

I shrink back like he slapped me. All I'm wearing is mascara! And a little lip gloss! I know for a fact that Genevieve wears bronzer and eye shadow and concealer every day. Plus mascara and eyeliner and lipstick!

Swiftly Peter says, "Shut up, Owen."

Owen's snickering. I narrow my eyes. This kid is only a few years older than Kitty! I lean forward and wave my hand in front of my face. "*This* is all natural. But thank you for the compliment, Owen."

"You're welcome," he says, just like his big brother.

On the drive home, I say, "Hey, Peter?"

"What?"

"Never mind."

"What? Just ask."

"Well . . . your parents are divorced, right?"

"Yup."

"So how often do you see your dad?"

"Not often."

"Oh, okay. I was just wondering."

Peter looks over at me with expectant eyes.

"What?" I say.

"I'm just waiting for the next question. You never just have one question."

"Well, do you miss him?"

"Who?"

"Your dad!"

"Oh. I don't know. I think it's more that I miss how it used to be with us. Him and my mom and me and Owen. We were like a team. He used to come to every lacrosse game." Peter gets quiet. "He just . . . took care of things."

"I guess that's what dads do."

"That's what he's doing for his new family." Peter says it matter-of-factly, without bitterness. "What about you? You miss your mom?"

"Sometimes, when I think about it." Suddenly I say, "You know what I miss? I miss bath time. I miss when she would wash my hair. Don't you think getting your hair washed is just the best feeling? Like, warm water and bubbles and fingers in your hair. It's so nice."

"Yeah, it is."

"Sometimes I don't think about her at all, and then . . . and then sometimes I'll have a thought like, I wonder what she would think of me now? She only knew me as a little girl, and now I'm a teenager, and I wonder, if she saw me on the street, would she recognize me?"

"Of course she would. She's your mom."

"I know, but I've changed a lot." An uncomfortable look has crossed his face, and I can tell he's regretting complaining about his dad, because at least his dad is still alive. And then, because Peter's looking at me like he feels sorry for me, I straighten up and say in a haughty voice, "I'm very mature, you know."

He's grinning now. "Oh yeah?"

"Oh, yes, I'm very refined, Peter."

When Peter drops me off, right before I get out of the car, he says, "I can tell my mom liked you." This makes me feel good inside. It's always been really important to me that other people's moms like me.

It was my favorite part of going over to Genevieve's house—hanging out with her mom. Wendy was so stylish. She used to wear a silky blouse and nice pants and a statement necklace, just for sitting around the house. Perfect hair, always smooth and flat. Genevieve has that same good hair, but she doesn't have her mom's perfect straight nose. Hers has a little bump on the bridge that I think only adds to her appeal.

"By the way, you definitely don't wear more makeup than Gen. She was always getting bronzer on my white shirts."

For someone who's over Genevieve, he sure does talk about her a lot. Though it's not just him. I was thinking about her too. Even when she's not here, she's here. That girl has some kind of reach.

41

DURING CHEMISTRY, PETER WRITES ME A note that says, *Can I come over tonight to study for the test?*

I write back, *I don't remember study sessions being in the contract.* After he reads it, he turns around and gives me a wounded look. I mouth, *I'm kidding!*

At dinner I announce that Peter's coming over to study and we're going to need the kitchen, and my dad raises his eyebrows. "Leave the door open," he jokes. We don't even have a door to the kitchen.

"Daddy," I groan, and Kitty groans with me.

Casually he asks, "Is Peter your boyfriend?"

"Um . . . something like that," I say.

After we eat and Kitty and I do the dishes, I set up the kitchen like a study room. My textbook and notes are stacked up in the center of the table, with a row of highlighters in blue, yellow, and pink, a bowl of microwave kettle corn, and a plate of peanut-butter brownies I baked this afternoon. I let Kitty have two but that's it.

He said he'd be over around eight. At first I think he's just late as usual, but the minutes tick by and I realize he's not coming. I text him once but he doesn't text back.

Kitty comes down between commercial breaks, sniffing

around for another brownie, which I give her. "Is Peter not coming?" she asks. I pretend I'm so absorbed in my studying I don't hear.

Around ten he sends a text that says, Sorry something came up. I can't come over tonight. He doesn't say where he is or what he's doing, but I already know. He's with Genevieve. At lunch he was distracted; he kept texting on his phone. And then, later in the day, I saw them outside the girls' locker room. They didn't see me, but I saw them. They were just talking, but with Genevieve it's never *just* anything. She put her hand on his arm; he brushed her hair out of her eyes. I may only be a fake girlfriend, but that's not nothing.

I keep studying, but it's hard to concentrate when your feelings are hurt. I tell myself it's just because I went to the trouble of baking brownies and cleaning up the downstairs. I mean, it's rude to just not show up somewhere. Does he not have manners? How would he like it if I did that? And really, what's the whole point of this charade if he's just going to keep going back to her anyway? What's even in it for me anymore? Things are better with Josh and me, practically normal. If I wanted to I could just call the whole thing off.

The next morning, I wake up still mad. I call Josh to ask him for a ride to school. For a second I worry he might not pick up; it's been so long since we hung out. But he does, and he says no problem.

Let's see how Peter likes it when he comes to my house to pick me up and I'm not there.

Halfway to school I start to feel uneasy. Maybe Peter had a legitimate reason for not coming over. Maybe he wasn't with Genevieve and now I've just done a very petty thing out of spite.

Josh is looking at me with suspicious eyes. "What's wrong?"

"Nothing."

He doesn't believe me, I can tell. "Did you and Kavinsky have a fight?"

"No."

Josh sighs and says, "Just be careful." He says it in a patronizing older-brother kind of way that makes me want to scream. "I don't want to see you hurt by that guy."

"Josh! He won't hurt me. Geez."

"He's a douche. I'm sorry, but he is. All the guys on the lacrosse team are. Guys like Kavinsky, they only care about one thing. As soon as they get what they want, they're bored."

"Not Peter. He dated Genevieve for almost four years!"

"Just trust me. You haven't had much experience with guys, Lara Jean."

Quietly I ask, "How would you know?"

Josh gives me an *Oh, come on* look. "Because I know you."

"Not as well as you think."

We're quiet the rest of the way.

It won't be that big of a deal. Peter will stop by my house, see that I'm not there, and then he'll leave. Big deal, so he had to go five minutes out of his way. I waited for him last night for two friggin' hours.

When we get to school, Josh heads for the senior hall and I go straight to the junior hall. I keep sneaking peeks down the hallway at Peter's locker, but he doesn't arrive. I wait at my locker until the bell rings, and he still doesn't come. I run off to first period, my backpack banging against my back as I go.

Mr. Schuller is taking attendance, when I look up and see Peter standing in the doorway glaring at me. He gestures at me to come out. I gulp and quickly look down at my notebook and pretend like I didn't see him. But then he hisses my name, and I know I have to talk to him.

Shakily I raise my hand. "Mr. Schuller, can I go the bathroom?"

"You should have gone before class," he grumbles, but he waves me on.

I hurry out to the hallway and pull Peter away from the door so Mr. Schuller can't see.

"Where were you this morning?" Peter demands.

I cross my arms and try to stand tall. It's hard, because I'm so short and he really is tall. "You're one to talk."

Peter huffs, "At least I texted you! I've called you like seventeen times. Why is your phone off?"

"You know we're not allowed to have our phones on at school!"

He huffs, "Lara Jean, I waited in front of your house for twenty minutes."

Yikes. "Well, I'm sorry."

"How'd you get to school? Sanderson?"

"Yes."

Peter exhales. "Listen, if you were pissed I couldn't come over last night, you should've just called and said so instead of the shit you pulled this morning."

In a small voice I say, "Well, what about that shit *you* pulled last night?"

A smile tugs at the corners of his mouth. "Did you just say 'shit'? It sounds really funny coming out of your mouth."

I ignore that. "So . . . where were you? Were you with Genevieve?" I don't ask what I really want to know, which is, *Did you guys get back together?*

He hesitates and then he says, "She needed me."

I can't even look at him. Why is he such a dummy? Why does she have such a hold on him? Is it just the amount of time they've been together? Is it the sex? I don't understand. It's disappointing, how little self-control boys have. "Peter, if you're just going to go running every time she beckons, I don't see a point to any of this."

"Covey, come on! I said I was sorry. Don't be pissed."

"You never said you were sorry," I say. "When did you say you were sorry?"

Chastened, he says, "Sorry."

"I don't want you to go to Genevieve's anymore. How do you think that makes me look to her?"

Peter looks at me steadily. "I can't not be there for Gen, so don't ask me to."

"But Peter, what does she even need you for when she has a new boyfriend?"

He flinches, and right away I'm sorry I said it. "I'm sorry," I whisper.

"It's fine. I don't expect you to understand it. Gen and I . . . we just get each other."

He doesn't know it, but when Peter talks about Genevieve, he gets a certain softness in his face. It's tenderness mixed with impatience. And something else. Love. Peter can protest all he wants, but I know he still loves her.

Sighing, I ask, "Did you at least study for the test?"

Peter shakes his head, and I sigh again.

"You can look at my notes during lunch," I say, and I head back to my class.

It's starting to make sense to me. Why he'd go along with a scheme like this, why he'd spend his time with someone like me. It's not so he can move on from Gen. It's so he can't. I'm just his excuse. I'm holding Genevieve's place for her. When that piece makes sense, everything else starts to.

42

JOSH'S PARENTS FIGHT A LOT. I DON'T KNOW if it's a normal amount of fighting because I only have one parent, but I don't remember my parents fighting that much when I had two. Our houses are close enough that I can hear them sometimes, if my window is open. The fights usually start out with something small, like Mrs. Sanderson accidentally leaving the car door open and the battery going dead, and end with something big, like how Mr. Sanderson works too much and is inherently selfish and not cut out for a family.

When they fight bad, Josh comes over. When we were younger, he'd sneak out sometimes in his pajamas with his pillow, and he'd stay until his mom came looking for him. It's not something we talk about. Maybe him and Margot, but not me and him. The most he ever said about it was that sometimes he wished they'd just get divorced so it could finally be over. They never did, though.

I can hear them tonight. I've heard them other nights since Margot left, but tonight sounds particularly bad. So bad I close my window. I gather up my homework and go downstairs and turn on the living room light so Josh knows he can come over if he wants.

Half an hour later there's a knock at the door. I wrap myself in my pale blue baby blanket and open it.

It's Josh. He smiles at me sheepishly. "Hey. Can I hang out here for a bit?"

"Course you can." I leave the door open and trudge back to the living room. I call back, "Lock it behind you."

Josh watches TV and I do my homework. I'm highlighting my way through US history when Josh asks me, "Are you going to try out for *Arcadia*?" That's the spring play. They just announced it yesterday.

"No," I say, switching highlighter colors. "Why would I?" I hate public speaking and getting up in front of people, and Josh knows it.

"Duh, because it's your favorite play." Josh changes the channel. "I think you'd be a really good Thomasina."

I smile. "Thanks but no thanks."

"Why not? It could be something good to put on your college apps."

"It's not like I'm going to be a theater major or anything."

"It wouldn't kill you to get out of your comfort zone a little bit," he says, stretching his arms out behind his head. "Take a risk. Look at Margot. She's all the way over in Scotland."

"I'm not Margot."

"I'm not saying you should move to the other side of the world. I know you'd never do that. Hey, what about Honor Council? You love judging people!"

I make a face at him.

"Or Model UN. I bet you'd like that. I'm just saying . . . your world could be bigger than just playing checkers with Kitty and riding around in Kavinsky's car."

I stop highlighting midsentence. Is he right? Is my world really that small? It's not like his world is so big! "Josh," I begin. Then I pause, because I don't know how I'm going to finish the sentence. So instead I throw my highlighter at him.

It ricochets off his forehead. "Hey! You could have hit me in the eye!"

"And you would have deserved it."

"Okay, okay. You know I didn't mean it like that. I just mean that you should give people a chance to know you." Josh points the remote control at me and says, "If people knew you, they would love you." He sounds so matter-of-fact.

Josh, you break my heart. And you're a liar. Because you know me, you know me better than almost anybody, and you don't love me.

After Josh goes back home, I tidy up the living room, lock all the doors, and turn off the lights. Then I pour myself a glass of water and head upstairs.

The light is on in my bedroom, and Chris is asleep in my bed. I roll her to the side so I can fit in too. Stirring, she mumbles, "Wanna go get hot wings?"

"It's too late to eat hot wings," I say, pulling my quilt up so it covers both of us. "You just missed Josh."

Her eyes fly open. "Joshy was here? Why?"

"No reason." I won't tell Josh's secrets, not even to Chris.

"Well, don't mention it to Kavinsky."

"He wouldn't care," I say.

Chris shakes her head. "All boys care."

"Peter's not like that. He's really confident."

"They're the ones that care the most," she says. I'm about to ask her what she means, but before I can, she says, "Let's go do something wild."

"Like what?" It's a school night; I can't go anywhere and she knows it. But I still like to hear her schemes. They're like bedtime stories.

"Like . . . I don't know. We could sneak into the nursing home and break out that grandma you're always talking about. What's her name again? Thunder?"

I giggle. "Stormy."

"Yeah, Stormy." She yawns. "She seems like she knows how to have a good time. I bet she'd buy us cocktails."

"Stormy goes to sleep at nine every night to get her beauty rest. Let's do it tomorrow." By tomorrow, Chris will have forgotten all about it, but it's still a nice thought. Her eyes are closed again. I poke her in the side. "Chris, wake up. Go brush your teeth." I keep a toothbrush in my bathroom drawer just for her. I painted a cursive *C* on it with red nail polish so it doesn't get mixed up with anybody else's toothbrush.

"Can't. I'm too tired to move."

"A second ago you wanted to break Stormy out of Belleview, and now you're too tired to wash your face and brush your teeth?"

Chris smiles but doesn't open her eyes.

I turn off my bedside lamp. "Night, Chris."

She wriggles closer to me. "G'night."

43

THERE ARE VERY LIMITED OPTIONS FOR Asian girls on Halloween. Like one year I went as Velma from *Scooby-Doo*, but people just asked me if I was a manga character. I even wore a wig! So now I'm committed to dressing up as Asian characters exclusively.

Margot never goes as a person; she is always an inanimate object or a concept of some kind. Like last year she went as a "formal apology": she wore a floor-length evening gown we found at Goodwill for ten dollars, and she had a sign around her neck, written in calligraphy, which said, *I'm sorry*. It won second prize in the school contest. First prize went to a Rastafarian alien.

Kitty's going as a ninja, which I suppose is in line with my whole Asian costume idea.

This year I'm going as Cho Chang from Harry Potter. I've got my Ravenclaw scarf and an old black choir robe I found on eBay, plus one of my dad's ties and a wand. I'm not going to win any contests, but at least people will know what I am. I wish I never have to answer a *What are you?* question ever again.

I'm waiting for Peter to pick me up for school, messing with my knee-highs. They won't stay up.

"Lara Jean!"

Automatically I call back, "Josh!" It's our version of Marco Polo.

Then I look up. There's Josh, standing in front of his car. In a full-on Harry Potter costume. Black robe, glasses, lightning mark on his forehead, wand.

We both burst out laughing. Of all the random costumes! Ruefully Josh says, "The guys from the graphic-novel club are going as different fantasy-book characters. I was going to go as Drogo from *Game of Thrones* because, you know, I've got the upper body for it, but . . ."

I giggle, trying to picture Josh with eyeliner and a long braid and no shirt. It's a funny picture. I wouldn't exactly call Josh scrawny, but . . .

"Hey, quit laughing so hard," he objects. "It wasn't *that* funny." He jingles his keys. "So do you need a ride, Cho?"

I look at my phone. Peter's five minutes late as usual. Not that I can really complain, because it's a free ride to school, and I could be taking the bus. But if I go with Josh, I won't have to rush to class, I can go by my locker, I can go pee, I can get a juice at the vending machine. But he's probably already nearly here. "Thanks, but I'm waiting for Peter."

Josh nods. "Oh, yeah . . . right." He starts to climb into his car.

I shout out, "Expelliarmus!" and Josh spins around and calls back, "Finite!" Then we grin at each other like goofs.

He drives off and I hug my knees to my chest. Josh and

I read Harry Potter around the same time, when I was in sixth and he was in seventh. Margot had already read them. Neither of us can read as fast as she does. It drove her crazy waiting for us to get to the third book so we could discuss.

The longer I sit waiting for Peter, the more prickly I feel. I take off my robe and put it back on a few times. It's polyester, and polyester doesn't breathe or feel nice against your skin. When he drives up, I run to his car and get in without saying hello. I spread my robe over my lap like a blanket, because my kilt is short.

His eyes are big. "You look hot," he says, sounding surprised. "What are you? An anime character?"

"No," I say, or more like snap. "I'm Cho Chang." Peter still has a blank look on his face, so I add, "From Harry Potter."

"Oh yeah. Cool."

I look over at him. He's wearing a regular button-down and jeans. "Where's your costume?"

"Me and my boys are going to change right before the assembly. It's a better effect if we unveil at the same time."

I know he wants me to ask what his costume is, but I don't feel like talking to him, so I sit there, not saying anything and looking out the window. I keep waiting for him to ask me what's wrong, but he doesn't. He's so oblivious; I don't even think he notices I'm mad.

Abruptly I say, "I wish you weren't always late."

Peter frowns. "Geez, sorry. I was trying to get my costume together."

"Today you were trying to get your costume together. But you're late all the time."

"I'm not late all the time!"

"You were late today, and yesterday, and last Thursday." I stare out the window. The autumn leaves are already falling. "If you're not going to be on time, I don't want you giving me rides anymore."

I don't have to look; I can feel him glaring at me. "Fine. That means I get five extra minutes of sleep, so, works for me."

"Good."

During the judging, Chris and I are sitting in the balcony of the theater. Chris is dressed up as Courtney Love. She's wearing a pink slip and holey knee socks and lots of smudgy eye makeup. "You should go down there too," I say. "I bet you'd win something."

"People at this school wouldn't even know who she is," Chris sneers. But I can tell she kind of wants to.

The guys in Peter's group are all superheroes. There's Batman, Superman, Iron Man, the Incredible Hulk, all to varying degrees of effort. Peter went all out. He is, of course, Peter Parker. Who else would Kavinsky go as? His Spider-Man costume is super authentic, with yellow Mylar eyes and gloved hands and bootied feet. He is a total ham up onstage. All the guys run around, capes flapping, pretend fighting each other. Peter tries to climb up a column, but Mr. Yelznik stops him before he can get far. I cheer when his group wins for best group costume.

Genevieve is Catwoman. She's wearing pleather leggings and a bustier and black cat ears. I wonder if she was in on the superhero theme, if Peter told her, or if she came up with that on her own. Every guy in the auditorium goes wild when she goes onstage for best junior costume. "What a ho," Chris says. She sounds almost wistful.

Genevieve wins, of course. I sneak a look at Peter, and he's whistling and stomping his feet with all his friends.

After the assembly I'm getting my chem book out of my locker when Peter comes over and leans his back against the locker next to mine. Through his mask he says, "Hey."

"Hey," I say. And then he doesn't say anything else; he just stands there. I close my locker door and spin the combination lock. "Congratulations on winning best group costume."

"That's it? That's all you're going to say?"

Huh? "What else am I supposed to say?"

Just then Josh walks by with Jersey Mike, who's dressed up as a hobbit, hairy feet and all. Walking backward, Josh points his wand at me and says, "Expelliarmus!"

Automatically I point my wand back at him and say, "Avada Kedavra!"

Josh clutches his chest like I've shot him. "Way harsh!" he calls out, and he disappears down the hallway.

"Uh . . . don't you think it's weird for my supposed girlfriend to wear a couples costume with another guy?" Peter asks me.

I roll my eyes. I'm still mad at him from this morning. "I'm sorry, I can't talk to you when you look like this. How am I supposed to have a conversation with a person in head-to-toe latex?"

Peter pushes his mask up. "I'm serious! How do you think it makes me look?"

"First of all, it wasn't planned. Second of all, nobody cares what my costume is! Who would even notice something like that?"

"People notice," Peter huffs. "I noticed."

"Well, I'm sorry. I'm very sorry that a coincidence like this would ever occur."

"I really doubt it was a coincidence," Peter mutters.

"What do you want me to do? Do you want me to pop over to the Halloween store during lunch and buy a red wig and be Mary Jane?"

Smoothly Peter says, "Could you? That'd be great."

"No, I could not. You know why? Because I'm *Asian*, and *people* will just think I'm in a manga costume." I hand him my wand. "Hold this." I lean down and lift the hem of my robe so I can adjust my knee socks.

Frowning, he says, "I could have been someone from the book if you'd told me in advance."

"Yes, well, today you'd make a really great Moaning Myrtle."

Peter gives me a blank look, and disbelieving, I say, "Wait a minute . . . have you never read Harry Potter?"

"I've read the first two."

"Then you should know who Moaning Myrtle is!"

"It was a really long time ago," Peter says. "Was she one of those people in the paintings?"

"No! And how could you stop after *Chamber of Secrets*? The third one's the best out of the whole series. I mean, that's literally crazy to me." I peer at his face. "Do you not have a soul?"

"Sorry if I haven't read every single Harry Potter book! Sorry I have a life and I'm not in the Final Fantasy club or whatever that geek club is called—"

I snatch my wand back from him and wave it in his face. "Silencio!"

Peter crosses his arms. Smirking, he says, "Whatever spell you just tried to cast on me, it didn't work, so I think you need to go back to Hogwarts." He's so proud of himself for the Hogwarts reference, it's kind of endearing.

Quick like a cat I pull down his mask, and then I put one hand over his mouth. With my other hand I wave my wand again. "Silencio!" Peter tries to say something, but I press my hand harder. "What? What was that? I can't hear you, Peter Parker."

Peter reaches out and tickles me, and I laugh so hard I almost drop my wand. I dart away from him but he pounces after me, pretend shooting webs at my feet. Giggling, I run away from him, further down the hall, dodging groups of people. He gives chase all the way to chem class. A teacher screams at us to slow down, and we do, but as soon as we're around the corner, I'm running again and so is he.

I'm breathless by the time I'm in my seat. He turns around and shoots a web in my direction, and I explode into giggles again and Mr. Meyers glares at me. "Settle down," he says, and

I nod obediently. As soon as his back is turned, I giggle into my robe. I want to still be mad at Peter, but it's just no use.

Halfway through class he sends me a note. He's drawn spiderwebs around the edges. It says, *I'll be on time tomorrow*. I smile as I read it. Then I put it in my backpack, in my French textbook so the page won't crease or crumble. I want to keep it so when this is over, I can have something to look at and remember what it was like to be Peter Kavinsky's girl-friend. Even if it was all just pretend.

44

WHEN WE PULL UP IN MY DRIVEWAY,
Kitty runs out of the house and over to the car. "Spider-Man!"
she shrieks. She's still in her ninja costume, though she's taken
the mask off. "Are you coming inside?"

I glance at Peter. "He can't. He has to go condition." Peter
spends an hour a day conditioning for lacrosse. He's very
dedicated to it.

"Condition?" Kitty repeats, and I know she's imagining
Peter washing his hair.

"I can hang out for a little bit," Peter says, turning the
engine off.

"Let's show him the dance!"

"Kitty, no." The dance is something Margot and I made
up when we were bored one night a few summers ago at
the beach. Let's just say neither of us is particularly talented
at choreography.

Peter's eyes light up. He'll take any opportunity for a
laugh, especially at my expense. "I wanna see the dance!"

"Forget about it," I tell him. We're in the living room;
each of us has our own couch or armchair. I poured us
iced teas and put out a bowl of potato chips, which we've
already finished.

"Come on," he pouts. "Show me the dance. Please, please show me the dance."

"That's not going to work on me, Peter."

"What's not going to work?"

I wave my hand in his Handsome Boy face. "*That*. I'm immune to your charms, remember?"

Peter lifts his eyebrows like I've dared him. "Is that a challenge? 'Cause I'm warning you, you do not want to step into the ring with me. I'll crush you, Covey." He doesn't take his eyes off mine for several long seconds, and I can feel my smile fade and my cheeks heat up.

"Come on, Lara Jean!"

I blink. Kitty. I'd forgotten she was still in the room. I scramble to my feet. "Cue up the music. Peter just challenged us to a dance-off."

Kitty squeals and runs to turn on the speakers. I push back the coffee table. We take our places in front of the fireplace, backs turned, heads down, hands clasped behind our backs.

When the bass kicks in, we jump and turn around. Hip thrust, swivel, then move into our knee slides. Then the running man, then this move Margot made up called the treadmill. The music stops, and Kitty and I freeze in our crunking positions—and then it starts up again, and we're doing the butterfly, then back into the knee slides. I forget what the next move is so I sneak a peek at Kitty, who's shimmying and clapping her hands. Oh yeah.

Our big finish is splits, with our arms crossed for emphasis. Peter's bowled over, laughing his head off. He claps and claps and stomps his feet.

When it's over, I try to catch my breath and manage to say, "Okay, you're up, Kavinsky."

"I can't," Peter gasps. "How do I follow a performance like that? Kitty, will you teach me that pop-and-lock move?"

Kitty gets shy all of a sudden. She sits on her hands and looks at him through her lashes and shakes her head.

"Please, please?" he asks.

Kitty finally caves in—I think she just wanted to make him work for it. I watch them dance all afternoon, my little sister the ninja and my pretend boyfriend Spider-Man. First I laugh, but then a worrying thought comes out of nowhere—I can't let Kitty get too attached to Peter. This is temporary. The way Kitty looks at him, so adoringly, like he's her hero. . . .

When Peter has to leave, I walk him out to his car. Before he gets in, I say, "I don't think you should come over anymore. It's confusing to Kitty."

Frowning, he says, "How is it confusing to Kitty?"

"Because . . . because when our . . . our *thing* is over, she's going to miss you."

"I'll still see the kid around." Peter pokes me in the stomach. "I want joint custody."

All I can think of is how patient he was with her, how sweet. Impulsively I get up on my tiptoes and kiss him on the cheek, and he jerks back in surprise.

"What was that for?"

My cheeks feel scalded. I say, "For being so nice to Kitty." Then I wave good-bye and I run into the house.

45

IF I DON'T BUY GROCERIES TODAY, IT'S scrambled eggs for dinner tonight. Again.

Margot's car is fixed and sitting in the driveway, where it's been sitting for the past few weeks. I could go to the store if I wanted to. I do want to. But I don't want to drive. If I was a nervous driver before, the accident has only made me worse. What business do I have behind the wheel of a car? What if I hurt someone? What if I hurt Kitty? They shouldn't just give out driver's licenses so easily. I mean, a car is a really dangerous thing. It's practically a weapon.

But the store is less than ten minutes away. It's not like I'd be getting on the highway. And I really really don't want to eat scrambled eggs for dinner tonight. Besides . . . if Peter and Genevieve are getting back together, he won't be giving me rides anymore. I've got to learn how to do for myself. I can't depend on other people to help me.

"We're going to the store, Kitty," I say.

She's lying down in front of the TV, propped up on her elbows. Her body looks so long; it's getting longer every day. Pretty soon she'll be taller than me. Kitty doesn't look away from the TV. "I don't want to come. I want to watch my shows."

"If you come, I'll let you pick out an ice cream."

Kitty gets to her feet.

On the drive there, I'm going so slow that Kitty keeps telling me the speed limit. "They give tickets for going under the limit too, you know."

"Who told you that?"

"No one. I just know it. I bet I'm going to be a better driver than you, Lara Jean."

I grip the steering wheel tighter. "I bet you are." *Brat.* I bet when Kitty starts driving, she's going to be a speed demon without the slightest concern for those around her. But she'll still probably be better at it than me. A reckless driver is better than a scared one; ask anybody.

"I'm not scared of things like you are."

I adjust my rearview mirror. "You sure are proud of yourself."

"I'm just *saying.*"

"Is there a car coming? Can I switch lanes?"

Kitty turns her head. "You can go, but hurry."

"Like how much time do I have?"

"It's already too late. Wait . . . now you can go. Go!"

I jerk into the left lane and look in my rearview. "Good job, Kitty. You just keep being my second pair of eyes."

As we push the cart around the store, I'm thinking about the drive home and having to get behind the wheel again. My heart still races even as I'm trying to decide if we should have zucchini or green beans with dinner. By the time we're in the dairy aisle, Kitty's whining. "Can you hurry? I don't want to miss my next show!"

To appease her, I say, "Go pick out an ice cream," and Kitty heads off toward the frozen-food aisle.

The way home, I stay in the right lane for blocks and blocks so I don't have to switch lanes. The car in front of me is an old lady, and she's moving at a snail's pace, which suits me just fine. Kitty begs me to switch lanes, but I just ignore her and keep doing what I'm doing, nice and easy. My hands are gripping the steering wheel so tightly my knuckles are white.

"The ice cream's going to be all melted by the time we get home," Kitty gripes. "And I've missed every single one of my shows. Can you please go to the fast lane?"

"Kitty!" I screech. "Will you just let me drive?"

"Then drive already!"

I lean across the console to cuff her upside the head, and she scoots closer to the window so I can't reach her. "Can't touch me," she says gleefully.

"Quit playing around and be my eyes," I say.

A car is coming up on my right, zooming off a highway exit. He's going to have to merge into my lane soon. Lightning fast I look over my shoulder for my blind spot, to see if I can switch lanes. Every time I have to take my eyes away from the road, even for a second, I feel so much panic in my chest. But I don't have a choice, I just hold my breath and I switch over to the left lane. Nothing bad happens. I exhale.

My heart races the whole way home. But we make it, no accidents and nobody honking their horn at me, and that's the important thing. And the ice cream is fine, only a little melted on top. It will get easier each time, I think. I hope. I just have to keep trying.

I can't stand the thought of Kitty being scornful of me. I'm her big sister. I have to be someone she looks up to, the way I look up to Margot. How can Kitty look up to me if I'm weak?

That night I pack Kitty's and my lunches. I make what Mommy used to make us sometimes when we went on picnics at the winery in Keswick. I dice up a carrot and an onion and fry it with sesame oil and a little vinegar; then I mix in sushi rice. When it's cooked, I scoop pats of rice into tofu skins. They're like rice balls in little purses. I don't have an exact recipe to follow, but it tastes right enough. When I'm finished, I get on a ladder and search for the bento boxes Mommy used to put them in. I finally find them in the back of the Tupperware cabinet.

I don't know if Kitty will remember eating these rice balls, but I hope that her heart will.

46

AT THE LUNCH TABLE PETER AND HIS
friends can't get enough of the rice balls. I only get to eat
three. "These are so good," Peter keeps saying. When he
reaches for the last one, he stops short and quickly looks up
at me to see if I noticed.

"You can have it," I say. I know what he's thinking of. The
last piece of pizza.

"No, it's all right, I'm good."

"Have it."

"I don't want it!"

I pick up the rice ball with my fingers and put it in his
face. "Say 'ah.'"

Stubbornly he says, "No. I'm not going to give you the
satisfaction of being right."

Darrell hoots with laughter. "I'm jealous of you, Kavinsky. I
wish I had a girl to feed me my lunch. Lara Jean, if he doesn't
take it, I will." He leans forward and opens his mouth for me.

Peter shoves him to the side and says, "Step off, it's mine!"
He opens his mouth and I pop it in like he's a seal at Sea
World. With his mouth full of rice and his eyes closed, he
says, "Yum yum yum."

I smile, because it's so cute. And for a second, just for a
second, I forget. I forget that this isn't real.

Peter swallows the food in his mouth and says, "What's wrong? Why do you look sad?"

"I'm not sad. I'm hungry because you guys ate my lunch." I cross my eyes at him to show him I'm joking.

Immediately Peter pushes out his chair and stands up. "I'm gonna get you a sandwich."

I grab his sleeve. "Don't. I'm just kidding."

"Are you sure?" I nod, and he sits back down. "If you're hungry later, we can stop somewhere on the way home."

"About that," I say. "My car's fixed now, so I won't be needing you to give me rides anymore."

"Oh, really?" Peter leans back in his chair. "I don't mind picking you up, though. I know you hate to drive."

"The only way I'll get better is if I practice," I say, feeling like Margot. Margot the Good. "Besides, now you'll get back your extra five minutes of sleep."

Peter grins. "True."

47

VIRTUAL SUNDAY NIGHT DINNER WAS AN idea I thought up.

I've got my laptop propped up on a stack of books in the center of the table. Daddy and Kitty and I are all sitting in front of it with our slices of pizza. It's our lunchtime and Margot's dinnertime. Margot's sitting at her desk with a salad. She's already in her flannel pj's.

"You guys are eating pizza again?" Margot gives me and Daddy a disapproving look. "Kitty's going to stay tiny if you don't feed her any green food."

"Relax, Gogo, there's peppers on this pizza," I say, holding up my slice, and everybody laughs.

"There'll be spinach salad with dinner tonight," Daddy offers.

"Can you make my spinach portion into a green juice instead?" Kitty asks. "That's the healthiest way to eat spinach."

"How do you know that?" Margot asks.

"From Peter."

The pizza slice that was halfway to my mouth freezes in midair.

"Peter who?"

"Lara Jean's boyfriend."

"Wait a minute . . . Lara Jean's dating who?" On the computer screen Margot's eyes are huge and incredulous.

"Peter Kavinsky," Kitty chirps.

I whip my head around and give her a dirty look. With my eyes I say, *Thanks for spilling the beans, Kitty.* With her eyes she says, *What? You should have told her yourself ages ago.*

Margot looks from Kitty to me. "What in the world? How did that happen?"

Lamely I say, "It just sort of . . . happened."

"Are you serious? Why would you ever be interested in someone like Peter Kavinsky? He's such a . . ." Margot shakes her head in disbelief. "I mean, did you know Josh caught him cheating on a test once?"

"Peter cheats at school?" Daddy repeats, alarmed.

I quickly look at him and say, "Once, in seventh grade! Seventh grade doesn't even count anymore it's so long ago. And it wasn't a test, it was a quiz."

"I definitely don't think he's a good guy for you. All of those lacrosse guys are so douchey."

"Well, Peter's not like those other guys." I don't understand why Margot can't just be happy for me. I was at least pretend happy for her when she started dating Josh. She could be pretend happy for me too. And it makes me mad, the way she's saying all of this stuff in front of Daddy and Kitty. "If you talk to him, if you just give him a chance, you'll see, Margot." I don't know why I'm bothering trying to convince her of Peter when it will be over soon anyway. But I want her to know that he is a good guy, because he is.

Margot makes a face like *Yeah, okay, sure* and I know she doesn't believe me. "What about Genevieve?"

"They broke up months ago."

Daddy looks confused and says, "Peter and Genevieve were an item?"

"Never mind, Daddy," I say.

Margot is quiet, chewing on her salad, so I think she's done, but then she says, "He's not very smart, though, is he? I mean, at school?"

"Not everybody can be a National Merit Scholar! And there are different kinds of intelligence, you know. He has a high emotional IQ." Margot's disapproval makes me feel prickly all over. More than prickly. Mad. What right does she have to weigh in when she doesn't even live here anymore? Kitty has more of a right than she does. "Kitty, do you like Peter?" I ask her. I know she'll say yes.

Kitty perks up, and I can tell she is pleased to be included in the big-girl talk. "Yes."

Surprised, Margot says, "Kitty, you've hung out with him too?"

"Sure. He comes over all the time. He gives us rides."

"In his two-seater?" Margot shoots a look at me.

Kitty pipes up. "No, in his mom's van!" With innocent eyes she says, "I want to go for a ride in his convertible. I've never been in a convertible."

"So he doesn't drive around his Audi anymore?" Margot asks me.

"Not when Kitty's riding with us," I say.

"Hmm" is all Margot says, and the skeptical look on her face makes me want to x her right off the screen.

48

AFTER SCHOOL I GET A TEXT FROM JOSH.

You, me, and the diner like old times.

Except old times would have included Margot. Now it's new times, I suppose. Maybe that's not altogether a bad thing. New can be good.

OK but I'm getting my own grilled cheese
because you always hog more than your fair
share.

Deal.

We're sitting in our booth by the jukebox.

I wonder what Margot's doing right now. It's nighttime in Scotland. Maybe she's getting ready to go out to the pub with her hallmates. Margot says pubs are really big over there; they have what they call pub crawls, where they go from pub to pub and drink and drink. Margot's not some big drinker, I've never even seen her drunk. I hope she's learned how to by now.

I hold my hand out for quarters. Another Lara

Jean–and-Josh tradition. Josh always gives me quarters for the jukebox. It's because he keeps mounds of them in his car for the tollbooth, and I never have quarters because I hate change.

I can't decide if I want doo-wop or folksy guitar, but then at the last second I put in "Video Killed the Radio Star," for Margot. So in a way it's like she *is* here.

Josh smiles when it comes on. "I knew you'd pick that."

"No you didn't, because I didn't know I was going to until I did." I pick up my menu and study it like I haven't seen it a million times.

Josh is still smiling. "Why bother looking at the menu when we already know what you're going to get?"

"I could change my mind at the last second," I say. "There's a chance I could order a tuna melt or a turkey burger or a chef salad. I can be adventurous too, you know."

"Sure," Josh agrees, and I know he's just humoring me.

The server comes over to take our order and Josh says, "I'll have a grilled cheese and a tomato soup and a chocolate milkshake." He looks at me expectantly. There's a smile coming up on the corners of his lips.

"Ah . . . um . . ." I scan the menu as fast as I can, but I don't actually want a tuna melt or a turkey burger or a chef salad. I give up. I like what I like. "A grilled cheese, please. And a black-cherry soda." As soon as the server is gone, I say, "Don't say a word."

"Oh, I wasn't going to."

And then, because there's a silence, we both speak at the same time. I say, "Have you talked to Margot lately?" and he says, "How are things going with Kavinsky?"

Josh's easy smile fades and he looks away. "Yeah, we chat online sometimes. I think . . . I think she's kind of homesick."

I give him a funny look. "I just talked to her last night and she didn't seem homesick at all. She seemed like the same old Margot. She was telling us about Raisin Weekend. It makes me want to go to Saint Andrews too."

"What's Raisin Weekend?"

"I'm not a hundred percent sure . . . it sounds like it was a mix between drinking a lot and Latin. I guess it's a Scottish thing."

"Would you do that?" Josh asks. "Would you go somewhere far away?"

I sigh. "No, probably not. That's Margot, not me. It'd be nice to visit, though. Maybe my dad will let me go during spring break."

"I think she'd like that a lot. I guess our Paris trip isn't happening anymore, huh?" He laughs awkwardly, and then he clears his throat. "So wait, how are things going with Kavinsky?"

Before I can answer, the server comes back with our food. Josh pushes the bowl of soup so it's in the middle of the table. "First sip?" he asks, holding up the milkshake.

Eagerly I nod and lean across the table. Josh holds the glass and I take a long sip. "Ahhh," I say, sitting back down.

"That was a pretty big sip," he says. "How come you never get your own?"

"Why should I when I know you'll share?" I break off a piece of grilled cheese and dip it into the soup.

"So you were saying?" Josh prods. When I stare at him blankly, he says, "You were about to talk about Kavinsky . . ."

I was hoping this wouldn't come up. I'm not in the mood to tell more lies to Josh. "Things are good." Because Josh is looking at me like he's expecting something more, I add, "He's really sweet."

Josh snorts.

"He's not what you'd think. People are so quick to judge him, but he's different." I'm surprised to find I'm telling the truth. Peter *isn't* what you'd think. He is cocky and he can be obnoxious and he's always late, true, but there are other good and surprising things about him too. "He's . . . not what you think."

Josh gives me a dubious look. Then he dunks half his sandwich into the soup and says, "You already said that."

"That's because it's true." He shrugs at this like he doesn't believe me. So I say, "You should see the way Kitty acts around Peter. She's crazy about him." I don't realize it until the words are actually out of my mouth, but I say it to hurt him.

Josh tears off a hunk of grilled cheese. "Well, I hope she doesn't get too attached." Even though I've had that exact same thought for different reasons, it still hurts to hear.

Suddenly the easy Josh-and–Lara Jean feeling is lost. Josh is withdrawn and closed off, and I'm stinging from what he said about Peter, and it feels like playacting to sit across from each other and pretend it's the same as the old days. How could it be, when Margot isn't here? She is the point of our little triangle.

"Hey," Josh says suddenly. I look up. "I didn't mean that. That was a shitty thing to say." He ducks his head. "I guess . . . I don't know, maybe I'm just jealous. I'm not used to sharing the Song girls."

I go soft inside. Now that he's said this nice thing, I am feeling warm and generous toward him again. I don't say what I'm thinking, which is, *You may not be used to sharing us, but we're very used to sharing you.* "You know Kitty still loves you best," I say, which makes him smile.

"I mean, I did teach her how to hock a loogie," Josh says. "You don't forget the person who teaches you something like that." He takes a long sip of his milkshake. "Hey, they're doing a Lord of the Rings marathon at the Bess this weekend. Wanna go?"

"That's like . . . nine hours!"

"Yeah, nine hours of awesome."

"True," I agree. "I wanna go; I just have to check with Peter first. He said something about going to a movie this weekend, and—"

Josh cuts me off before I can finish. "It's fine. I can just go with Mike. Or maybe I'll take Kitty. It's about time I introduced her to the genius that is Tolkien."

I'm quiet. Are Kitty and I interchangeable in his mind? Are Margot and I?

We're sharing a waffle when Genevieve walks into the diner with a little kid who I guess must be her little brother. Not her actual little brother; Gen is an only child. She's the president of the Little Sib program. It's where a high school student is paired up with an elementary school kid and you tutor them and take them out for fun days.

I slump down in my seat, but of course Gen still sees me. She looks from me to Josh, and then she gives me a little wave. I don't know what to do so I just wave back. Something about the way she's smiling at me is unsettling. It's how genuinely happy she looks.

If Genevieve is happy, that's not good for me.

At dinner I get a text from Peter. It says, If you're going to hang out with Sanderson, can you at least not do it in public?

Under the table I read it over and over. Could it be that Peter's the teensiest bit jealous? Or is he really just worried about how it looks to Genevieve?

"What do you keep looking at?" Kitty wants to know.

I put my phone down, facedown. "Nothing."

Kitty turns to Daddy and says, "I bet it was a text from Peter."

Buttering a roll, my dad says, "I like Peter."

"You do?" I say.

Daddy nods. "He's a good kid. He's really taken with you, Lara Jean."

"Taken with me?" I repeat.

To me Kitty says, "You sound like a parrot." To Daddy

she says, "What does that mean? Taken by her?"

"It means he's charmed by her," Daddy explains. "He's smitten."

"Well, what's smitten?"

He chuckles and stuffs the roll in Kitty's open, perplexed mouth. "It means he likes her."

"He definitely likes her," Kitty agrees, her mouth full. "He . . . he looks at you a lot, Lara Jean. When you're not paying attention. He looks at you, to see if you're having a good time."

"He does?" My chest feels warm and glowy, and I can feel myself start to smile.

"I'm just happy to see you so happy. I used to worry about Margot taking on so many responsibilities at home and helping out the way she did. I didn't want her to miss out on her high school experience. But you know Margot. She's so driven." Daddy reaches over and squeezes my shoulder. "To see you now, going out and doing things and making new friends . . . it makes your old man very happy. Very, very happy."

I feel a lump grow in my throat. If only it wasn't all a lie.

"Don't cry, Daddy," Kitty orders, and Daddy nods and pulls her into his arms for a hug.

"Can you do me a favor, Kitty?" he says.

"What?"

"Can you stay this age forever?"

Automatically Kitty replies, "I can if you give me a puppy."

My dad roars with laughter, and Kitty laughs too.

I really admire my little sister sometimes. She knows exactly what she wants, and she'll do whatever it takes to get it. She's shameless that way.

I'm going to talk to Daddy and help her cause. The two of us will wear him down. There'll be a puppy under our tree Christmas morning. I'd bet money on it.

49

THE NEXT NIGHT PETER AND I STUDY AT Starbucks for a few hours—well, I study, and he keeps getting up and talking to people from school. On the way home he asks, "Did you sign up for the ski trip?"

"No. I'm a terrible skier." Only cool people like Peter and his friends go on the ski trip. I could try to twist Chris's arm into going, but she'd probably laugh in my face. She's not going on any school trip.

"You don't have to ski. You can snowboard. That's what I'm doing."

I give him a look. "Can you picture me snowboarding?"

"I'll teach you. Come on, it'll be fun." Peter grabs my hand and says, "Please please please, Lara Jean? Come on, be a sport. It'll be fun, I promise."

He catches me by surprise with this. The ski trip isn't until winter break. So he wants to keep this, us, up until then. For some reason I feel relieved.

"If you don't want to snowboard," he continues, "the lodge has a big stone fireplace and big comfy chairs. You can sit and read for hours. And they sell the best hot chocolate. I'll buy you one." He squeezes my hand.

My heart does a little zing, and I say, "All right, I'll go. But the hot chocolate had better be as good as you say."

"I'll buy you as many as you want."

"Then you better bring a lot of singles," I say, and Peter snorts. "What?"

"Nothing."

When we get to my house, I climb out and he drives away before it occurs to me I left my bag on the floor of his car, and Daddy and Kitty aren't home. They're at Kitty's school for parent-teacher conferences.

I fumble around blindly under the deck, feeling around in the dark for the spare keys we keep hidden under the wheelbarrow. Then I remember that the spare keys are in the junk drawer, in the house, because I forgot to put them back the last time I got locked out. I have no keys, no phone, no way of getting into the house.

Josh! Josh has a spare key. He's watered my dad's plants for him a few times when we went away on vacation.

I find a rock in the driveway and I cross the lawn and stand underneath Josh's window. I throw the rock at it and I miss. I find another one, and it pings off the glass, barely making a sound. I try again, with a bigger rock. This one hits.

Josh opens the window and leans his head out. "Hey. Did Kavinsky leave already?"

Surprised, I say, "Yeah. I left my bag in his car. Can you throw down the spare keys?"

Josh sighs, like I'm asking for something huge. "Hold on." Then he disappears.

I stand there and wait for him to come back to the window, but he doesn't. He comes outside the front door instead.

He's wearing a hoodie and sweatpants. It's Margot's favorite hoodie. When they first got together, she used to wear it all the time, like it was a letterman's jacket or something.

I hold my hand out for the keys and Josh drops them in my hand. "Thanks, Joshy."

I turn to leave, but he says, "Wait. I'm worried about you."

"What? Why?"

He sighs heavily and adjusts his glasses. He only wears his glasses at night. "This thing with Kavinsky . . ."

"Not that again. Josh—"

"He's a player. He's not good enough for you. You're . . . innocent. You're not like other girls. He's a typical guy. You can't trust him."

"I think I know him a lot better than you do."

"I'm just looking out for you." Josh clears his throat. "You're like my little sister."

I want to hit him for saying that. "No I'm not," I say.

An uneasy look crosses over Josh's face. I know what he's thinking, because we're both thinking it.

Then, headlights are beaming down our street. It's Peter's car. He's come back. I hand Josh his set of keys and run over to my driveway. Over my shoulder I call out, "Thanks, Joshy!"

I come around the front to the driver's side. Peter's window is down. "You forgot your bag," he says, glancing over toward Josh's house.

"I know," I say breathlessly. "Thanks for coming back."

"Is he out there?"

"I don't know. He was a minute ago."

"Then just in case," Peter says, and he leans his head out and kisses me on the lips, open-mouthed and sure.

I'm stunned.

When he pulls away, Peter's smiling. "Night, Lara Jean."

He drives off into the night and I'm still standing there with my fingers to my lips. Peter Kavinsky just kissed me. He kissed me, and I liked it. I'm pretty sure I liked it. I'm pretty sure I like him.

The next morning I'm at my locker, putting my books away, when I see Peter walking down the hallway. My heart thumps in my chest so loud I can hear it echo in my ears. He hasn't seen me yet. I duck my head into my locker and start arranging my books into a pile.

From behind the locker door he says, "Hey."

"Hey," I say back.

"I just want to set your mind at ease, Covey. I'm not going to kiss you again, so don't worry about it."

Oh.

So that's that. It doesn't matter if I like him or not, because he doesn't like me back. It's kind of silly to feel so disappointed about something you only just realized you wanted, isn't it?

Don't let him see that you're disappointed.

I face him. "I wasn't worrying about it."

"Yes you were. Look at you: your face is all pinched together like a clam." Peter laughs, and I try to unpinch my face, to look serene. "It's not going to happen again. It was all for Sanderson's benefit."

"Good."

"Good," he says, and he takes my hand, and he closes my locker door, and he walks me to class like a real boyfriend, like we're really in love.

How was I supposed to know what's real and what's not? It feels like I'm the only one who doesn't know the difference.

50

MY DAD'S THRILLED WHEN I ASK HIM TO
sign the permission slip. "Oh, Lara Jean, this is great. Did
Peter convince you? You've been scared of skiing ever
since you were ten and you did the splits and you couldn't
get back up!"

"Yeah, I remember." My boots froze onto the skis, and I
lay there in the splits for what felt like days.

Signing the paper, my dad says, "Hey, maybe we can all of
us go to Wintergreen over Christmas. Peter too."

So that's where I get it from. My dad. He lives in a fantasy world. Handing me the slip, he says cheerfully, "You can
wear Margot's ski pants. Her gloves, too."

I don't tell him that I won't need them, because I'll be
cozy in the lodge reading and sipping hot cocoa by the fire.
I should bring my knitting stuff with me too.

When I talk to Margot on the phone that night, I tell
her I'm going on the ski trip, and she's surprised. "But you
hate skiing."

"I'm going to try out snowboarding."

"Just . . . be careful," she says.

I'm thinking she means on the slopes, but when Chris
comes over the next night to borrow a dress, I learn other-

wise. "You know everybody hooks up on the ski trip, right? It's like a school-sanctioned booty call."

"*What?*"

"That's where I lost my V freshman year."

"I thought you lost it in the woods near your house."

"Oh yeah. Whatever, the point is, I had sex on the ski trip."

"There are chaperones," I say worriedly. "How can people just have sex with chaperones around?"

"Chaperones go to sleep early because they're old," Chris says. "People just sneak out. Plus there's a hot tub. Did you know that there's a hot tub?"

"No . . . Peter never mentioned that." Well, that's that, I just won't pack a bathing suit. It's not like they can make you go in a hot tub if you don't want to.

"The year I went, people were skinny-dipping."

My eyes bug out. Skinny-dipping! "People were nude?"

"Well, the girls took their tops off. Just be prepared." Chris chews on her fingernail. "Last year I heard Mr. Dunham got in the hot tub with students and it was weird."

"This sounds like the Wild West," I mutter.

"More like Girls Gone Wild."

It's not that I'm worried Peter will try something with me. I know he won't, because he doesn't see me that way. But are people going to expect it? Am I going to have to sneak into his room in the middle of the night so people think we're doing something? I don't want to get in trouble on a school trip, but Peter has a way of convincing me to do stuff I don't want to do.

I grab Chris's hands. "Will you please come? Please, please!"

She shakes her head. "You know better than that. I don't do school trips."

"You have before!"

"Yeah, freshman year. Not anymore."

"But I need you!" Desperately I squeeze her hands and say, "Remember how I covered for you last year when you went to Coachella? I spent the whole weekend sneaking in and out of your house so your mom would think you were at home! Don't forget the things I've done for you, Chris! I need you now!"

Unmoved, Chris plucks her hands away from mine and goes to the mirror and starts examining her skin. "Kavinsky's not going to pressure you to have sex if you don't want to. If you minus the fact that he dated the devil, he's not a total dummy. He's kind of decent, actually."

"What do you mean by decent? Decent like he doesn't care that much about sex?"

"Oh, God, no. He and Gen were in constant heat for each other. She's been on the pill longer than I have. Too bad everyone in my family thinks she's this angel." Chris pokes at a zit on her chin. "What a fake. I should send an anonymous letter to our grandma . . . Not that I really would. I'm no rat, unlike her. Remember that time she told our grandma I was going to school drunk?" She doesn't wait for me to answer. When Chris gets going on a Genevieve rant, she is single-minded. "My grandma wanted to use the money she saved for my college for rehab! They had a family meeting about me! I'm so glad you stole Kavinsky from her."

"I didn't steal him. They were already broken up!"

Chris snorts. "Sure, keep telling that to yourself. Gen's going on the ski trip, you know. She's class president, so she's basically organizing it. So just beware. Don't ever ski alone."

I let out a gasp. "Chris, I'm begging you. Please come." In a burst of inspiration I say, "If you come, it'll make Genevieve really mad! She's organizing this whole thing; it's her trip. She won't want you there!"

Chris purses her lips into a smile. "You know how to play me." She juts her chin at me. "Do you think this zit is ready to pop?"

51

THANKSGIVING DAY, DADDY CLEANS OUT
the turkey for me and then leaves to go pick up our Korean
grandma, who lives an hour away in a retirement community with a lot of other Korean grandmas. Daddy's mom,
Nana, is spending Thanksgiving with her boyfriend's family,
which is fine by me, because I know she wouldn't have anything nice to say about the food.

I make up a green-bean dish with orange peel and dill, in
an earnest effort to be jazzy and inventive. I nominate Kitty
to be my taste tester and she takes a bite of green bean and
says it tastes like an orange pickle. "Why can't we just have
green-bean casserole with the fried onion rings that come in
the can?" Kitty ponders. She's cutting out different-colored
feathers for her turkey place mats.

"Because I'm trying to be jazzy and inventive," I say,
dumping a can of gravy into the saucepan.

Doubtfully Kitty says, "Well, are we still having broccoli
casserole? People will eat that."

"Do you see any broccoli anywhere in this kitchen?" I
ask. "No, the green in this meal is the green bean."

"What about mashed potatoes? We're still having mashed
potatoes, right?"

Mashed potatoes. I jump up and check the pantry. I forgot

to buy the potatoes. I got the whole milk and the butter and even the chives to put on top like Margot always does. But I forgot the actual potatoes. "Call Daddy and ask him to pick up Yukon gold potatoes on the way home," I say, closing the pantry door.

"I can't believe you forgot the potatoes," Kitty says with a shake of her head.

I glare at her. "Just focus on your place mats."

"No, because if I didn't just ask about the mashed potatoes, the meal would have been ruined, so you should be thanking me."

Kitty gets up to call Daddy, and I yell out, "By the way, those turkeys look more like the NBC peacock logo than actual turkeys, so!"

Kitty is unfazed, and I take another bite of the green beans. They do taste like an orange pickle.

It turns out I have cooked the turkey upside down. Also, Kitty kept hounding me about salmonella because she watched a video on it in science, so I wind up leaving the bird in too long. The mashed potatoes are fine, but there are some crunchy bits here and there because I rushed to boil them.

We are seated around the dining room table, and Kitty's place mats really do add a certain something.

Grandma is eating a whole pile of green beans, and I shoot Kitty a triumphant look. *See? Someone likes them.*

There was a minute or two, after Mommy died, when

Grandma moved in to help take care of us. There was even talk of her staying. She didn't think Daddy could manage on his own.

"So, Danny," Grandma begins. Kitty and I exchange a look across the table, because we know what's coming. "Are you seeing anyone these days? Going on dates?"

My dad reddens. "Er . . . not so much. My work keeps me so busy . . ."

Grandma clucks. "It's not good for a man to be alone, Danny."

"I've got my girls to keep me company," my dad says, trying to sound jovial and not tense.

Grandma fixes him with a cold stare. "That's not what I mean."

When we're doing the dishes, Grandma asks me, "Lara Jean, would you mind if your daddy had a girlfriend?"

It's something Margot and I have discussed at length over the years, most often in the dark, late at night. If Daddy absolutely had to date, what kind of woman would we like to see him with? Someone with a good sense of humor, kind-hearted, all of the usual things. Someone who'd be firm with Kitty but not rein her in so much that it would squash all the special things about her. But also someone who wouldn't try to be our mother; that's what Margot is fiercest about. Kitty needs a mom, but we're old enough to not need mothering, she says.

Of the three of us, Margot would be the most critical. She's incredibly loyal to Mommy's memory. Not that I'm not, but there have been times, over the years, where I've thought how it would be nice to have someone. Someone older, a lady, who knows about certain things, like the right way to put on blush, or how to flirt to get out of a speeding ticket. Things to know for the future. But then it never happened. Daddy's been on some dates, but he hasn't had a steady girlfriend he's brought around. Which has always been sort of a relief, but now that I'm getting older, I keep thinking about what it will be like when I'm gone and it's just Kitty and Daddy, and then before long it will just be Daddy. I don't want him to be alone.

"No," I say. "I wouldn't mind at all."

Grandma gives me an approving look. "Good girl," she says, and I feel warm and cozy inside, like how I used to feel after a cup of the Night-Night tea Mommy used to make me when I couldn't fall asleep at night. Daddy's made it for me a few times since, but it never tasted the same, and I never had the heart to tell him.

52

THE CHRISTMAS COOKIE BONANZA STARTS
December first. We drag out all of Mommy's old cookbooks
and cooking magazines and we spread them out on the
living room floor and turn on the *Charlie Brown Christmas*
album. No Christmas music is allowed in our house until
December first. I don't remember whose rule this is, but we
abide by it. Kitty keeps a list of which cookies we're definitely doing and which ones we're maybe doing. There are
a few perennials. My dad loves pecan crescents, so those are
a must. Sugar cookies, because those are a given. Snicker-
doodles for Kitty, molasses cookies for Margot, cowgirl
cookies for me. White-chocolate cranberry are Josh's favorite. I think this year, though, we should mix things up and do
different cookies. Not entirely, but at least a few new ones.

Peter's here; he stopped by after school to work on chem,
and now it's hours later and he's still here. He and Kitty and
I are in the living room going through the cookbooks. My
dad's in the kitchen listening to NPR and making tomorrow's lunches.

"Please no more turkey sandwiches," I call out.

Peter nudges my sock and mouths *spoiled*, and he points at
me and Kitty, shaking his finger at us. "Whatever. Your mom
makes your lunches every day, so shut it," I whisper.

My dad calls back, "Hey, I'm sick of leftovers too, but what are we going to do? Throw it away?"

Kitty and I look at each other. "Pretty much exactly," I say. My dad has a thing about wasting food. I wonder if I snuck down to the kitchen tonight and threw it out, if he'd notice. He probably would.

"If we had a dog," Kitty pipes up loudly, "there wouldn't be any more leftovers." She winks at me.

"What kind of dog do you want?" Peter asks her.

"Don't get her hopes up," I tell him, but he waves me off.

Immediately Kitty says, "An Akita. Red fur with a cinnamon-bun tail. Or a German shepherd I can train to be a seeing-eye dog."

"But you're not blind," Peter says.

"But I could be one day."

Grinning, Peter shakes his head. He nudges me again and in an admiring voice he says, "Can't argue with the kid."

"It's pretty much futile," I agree. I hold up a magazine to show Kitty. "What do you think? Creamsicle cookies?" Kitty writes them down as a maybe.

"Hey, what about these?" Peter pushes a cookbook in my lap. It's opened up to a fruitcake cookie recipe.

I gag. "Are you kidding? You're kidding, right? Fruitcake cookies? That's disgusting."

"When done right, fruitcake can be really good," Peter defends. "My great-aunt Trish used to make fruitcake, and she'd put ice cream on top and it was awesome."

"If you put ice cream on anything, it's good," Kitty says.

"Can't argue with the kid," I say, and Peter and I exchange smiles over Kitty's head.

"Point taken, but this isn't your average fruitcake. It's not, like, a wet loaf of neon jujubes. It's got pecans and dried cherries and blueberries and good stuff. I think she called it Christmas Memory fruitcake."

"I love that story!" I exclaim. "That's my favorite. It's so good but so sad."

Peter looks puzzled and so does Kitty so I explain. "'A Christmas Memory' is a short story by Truman Capote. It's about a boy named Buddy and his older lady cousin who took care of him when he was little. They'd save up all year to buy ingredients for fruitcake and then they'd send them as presents to friends, but also to, like, the president."

"Why is it so sad?" Kitty wants to know.

"Because they're best friends and they love each other more than anybody, but they get separated in the end, because the family thinks she doesn't take good enough care of him. And maybe she doesn't, but maybe it doesn't matter, because she was still his soul mate. In the end she dies, and Buddy doesn't even get to say good-bye to her. And, it's a true story."

"That's depressing," Peter says. "Forget the fruitcake cookies."

Kitty crosses out fruitcake cookies on her pad.

I'm thumbing through an old *Good Housekeeping* magazine when the doorbell rings. Kitty scrambles up and runs for the door. "Check who it is before you open it," I call after her. She's always forgetting to check first.

"Josh!" I hear her squeal.

Peter's head jerks up.

"He's here to see Kitty," I tell him.

"Yeah, right."

Josh walks into the living room with Kitty hanging around his neck like a monkey. "Hey," he says, eyes flickering in Peter's direction.

"What's up, man," Peter says, friendly as can be. "Have a seat."

I give him a strange look. Just a second ago he was grousing, and now he's happy as a clam. I don't get boys.

Josh holds up a plastic bag. "I brought back your casserole dish."

"Is that Josh?" my dad calls from the kitchen. "Josh, do you want a snack? Turkey sandwich?"

I'm positive he's going to say no, because I'm sure he's had as many leftover turkey sandwiches over at his house as we've been eating over here, but then he goes, "Sure!" Josh disentangles himself from Kitty and plops down on the couch. To me he says, "Christmas Cookie Bonanza?"

"Christmas Cookie Bonanza," I confirm.

"You're making my favorite, right?" Josh gives me puppy-dog eyes, which always makes me laugh, because it's so un-Josh.

"You're such a dork," I say, shaking my head.

"What's your favorite?" Peter asks him. "Because I think the list is pretty set."

"I'm pretty sure it's already on the list," Josh says.

I look from Josh to Peter. I can't tell if they're kidding or not.

Peter reaches out and tickles Kitty's feet. "Read us the list, Katherine."

Kitty giggles and rolls over to her notepad. Then she stands up and grandly says, "M&M cookies are a yes, cappuccino cookies are a maybe, Creamsicle cookies are a maybe, fruit-cake cookies are a *no way*—"

"Wait a minute, I'm a part of this council too," Peter objects, "and you guys just turned down my fruitcake cookies without a second thought."

"You said to forget the fruitcake cookies, like, five seconds ago!" I say.

"Well, now I want them back under consideration," he says.

"I'm sorry, but you don't have the votes," I tell him. "Kitty and I both vote no, so that's two against one."

My dad pops his head into the living room. "Put me down as a yes vote for the fruitcake cookies." His head disappears back into the kitchen.

"Thank you, Dr. Covey," Peter crows. He drags me closer to him. "See, I knew your dad was on my side."

I laugh. "You're such a suck-up!"

And then I look over at Josh, and he is staring at us with a funny, left-out look on his face. It makes me feel bad, that look. I scoot away from Peter and start flipping through my books again. I tell him, "The list is still a work in progress.

The cookie council will strongly consider your white-chocolate cranberry cookies."

"Greatly appreciated," Josh says. "Christmas isn't Christmas without your white-chocolate cranberry cookies."

Kitty pipes up, "Hey, Josh, you're a suck-up too." Josh grabs her and tickles her until she's laughing so hard she has tears in her eyes.

After Josh leaves and Kitty goes upstairs to watch TV, I'm tidying up the living room and Peter's sprawled out on the couch watching me. I keep thinking he's about to leave, but then he keeps lingering.

Out of nowhere he says, "Remember back at Halloween how you were Cho Chang and Sanderson was Harry Potter? I bet you that wasn't a coincidence. I bet you a million bucks he got Kitty to find out what your costume was and then he ran out and bought a Harry Potter costume. The kid is into you."

I freeze. "No, he isn't. He loves my sister. He always has and he always will."

Peter waves this off. "Just you wait. As soon as you and I are done, he's gonna pull some cheesy-ass move and, like, profess his love for you with a boom box. I'm telling you, I know how guys think."

I yank away the pillow he's got cushioning his back and put it on the recliner. "My sister will be home for winter break soon. I bet *you* a million dollars they get back together."

Peter holds his hand out for me to shake on it, and when I take it, he pulls me onto the couch next to him. Our legs touch. He has a mischievous glint in his eye, and I think maybe he's going to kiss me, and I'm scared, but I'm excited, too. But then I hear Kitty's footsteps coming down the stairs, and the moment's over.

53

"CAN WE PUT UP THE TREE THIS WEEKEND?"
Kitty asks at breakfast.

My dad looks up from his bowl of oatmeal. Oatmeal, ugh.
"I don't see why not."

Halfheartedly I say, "Margot might be mad if we do it
without her." Truth be told, I want to put up the tree too.
It's so cozy to do Christmas Cookie Bonanza and have the
lights twinkling on the tree and Christmas music and the
whole house smelling like sugar and butter.

"Brielle's family put their tree up the day after
Thanksgiving," Kitty says.

"Let's just do it, then," I say. "Can we, Daddy?"

"Well, if Brielle's family is doing it," Daddy says.

We drive out to the Christmas tree farm an hour away,
because that's where the really nice ones are. Kitty insists on
seeing each and every tree to make sure ours is the best one.
I vote for a plump balsam fir because it smells the best, but
Kitty doesn't think it's tall enough. We go for a Douglas fir
instead, and the whole drive home the air smells like Christmas morning.

Josh runs out of his house when he sees us struggling
to get the tree inside. He and my dad heft it up and take it

inside the house. He holds the tree up straight as my dad screws the Christmas tree stand around it tight. I have a feeling like he's going to want to stay and help decorate the tree. I can't stop thinking about what Peter said. How Josh could maybe like me.

"A little to the left," Kitty directs. "It's not straight enough."

I bring down the box with the twinkle lights and the ornaments and start sorting through them. My favorite is the painted blue star I made in kindergarten out of dough. It's my favorite because there's a bite taken out of it—I told Kitty it was a cookie and she chomped right into it like the Cookie Monster. And then she cried, and I got in trouble, but it was worth it. "Should we do colored lights or white lights this year?" I ask.

"White," Kitty says. "It's classier."

"But colored lights are whimsical," Josh argues. "I mean, they're nostalgic."

I roll my eyes. "Whimsical, Josh?" And then Josh proceeds to make a case for colored lights, and he and I argue back and forth until Daddy intercedes and says we should just do half and half. This is when things finally feel really and truly normal between us, now that we are bickering again like old times. Peter was wrong about Josh.

The tree is so tall it nearly touches the ceiling. We run out of lights, so Daddy goes to buy more at the store. Josh puts Kitty on his shoulders so she can put the star on the tippy top.

"I'm glad we got a big tree this year," I say with a happy

sigh, falling back onto the sofa and looking up at the top. There's nothing cozier than a Christmas tree all lit up.

A little later, Daddy has to go in to the hospital, and Kitty goes over to our neighbor's house because they're making s'mores in the fireplace, so it's just Josh and me cleaning up. I'm putting ornament hooks back into their different ziplock bags and Josh is loading up a cardboard box with the ornaments we didn't have room for. He hoists the box in his arms and bumps into a branch on the tree, and a glass ornament slips off and breaks.

Josh groans.

"Jo-osh," I say. "I made that in home ec."

"Sorry."

"It's okay. It wasn't my best work anyway. I put in too many feathers." It's a clear glass ball with white feathers and white sequins inside.

I go get a broom, and when I come back, he says, "You act different around Kavinsky. Did you know that?"

I look up from sweeping the broken ornament. "No I don't."

"You don't act like you. You act like . . . like how all girls act around him. That's not you, Lara Jean."

Annoyed, I say, "I act the same as I always do. What would you know about it, Josh? You've barely ever even been around us." I crouch down and pick up a shard of glass.

"Be careful," Josh says. "Here, I'll do it." He stoops down next to me and reaches for another shard. "Ow!"

"*You* be careful!" I lean close to him and try to get a closer look at his finger. "Are you bleeding?"

He shakes his head. "I'm fine." And then he says, "You know what I don't get?"

"What?"

Josh stares at me, his cheeks a dull red. "Why you never said anything. If all that time you felt like that about me, why didn't you say anything?"

My whole body goes stiff. I wasn't expecting that. I'm not prepared. I swallow hard and say, "You were with Margot."

"I wasn't always with Margot. The stuff you wrote—you liked me before I ever liked her. Why didn't you just tell me?"

I let out a breath. "What does that even matter now?"

"It matters. You should have told me. You should have at least given me a chance."

"It wouldn't have made a difference, Josh!"

"And I'm telling you it would have!" He steps toward me.

Jerkily I rise to my feet. Why is he bringing this up now, just when things are back to normal again? "You're so full of it. You've never thought of me that way, not ever, so don't go trying to reinvent history now when I have somebody."

"Don't tell me what I think," he snaps. "You don't know my every thought, Lara Jean."

"Yes I do. I know you better than anyone. You know why? You're predictable. Everything you do. It's so predictable. The only reason you're even saying this now is because you're jealous. And it's not even because of me. You don't care about who I'm with. You're just jealous that Peter took your spot. Kitty likes him better than you now too."

His face darkens. He glares at me and I glare back. "Fine!" he yells. "I'm jealous! Are you happy now?"

And then he jerks his head toward mine, and he kisses me. On the lips. His eyes are closed, mine are wide open. And then mine close too, and for a second, just for a second, I kiss him back. Then I break away. I push him off.

Triumphantly he says, "Did you predict that, Lara Jean?"

My mouth opens and closes, but no words come out. I drop the broom and run up the stairs, as fast as I can. I run all the way to my room and lock my door behind me. Josh just kissed me. In my living room. My sister is coming back in a few weeks. And I have a fake boyfriend I just cheated on.

54

AFTER THIRD PERIOD, LUCAS IS WAITING for me.

He's wearing a skinny tie today with a V-neck and he has a full-size bag of Cheetos in his hand. He stuffs a handful of Cheetos into his mouth, and orange dust floats onto his white V-neck. The corners of his mouth look slightly orange too. With his mouth full he says, "Look, there's something I need to tell you."

I laugh. "I can't believe I ever thought you were so refined," I say, blowing Cheetos powder off his shirt. "What do you need to tell me?" I ask. I steal a few Cheetos out of the bag. When he hesitates, I say, "Lucas, I hate when people say that they have something to tell you and they don't just say it. It's like when people say they have a funny story—like, just hurry up and tell the story and I'll decide for myself if I think it's funny or not."

Lucas licks cheese off his lips. "Well, you know I live in the same neighborhood as Genevieve, right?" I nod. "Last night I saw Kavinsky leaving her house."

"Oh." That's all I say. Just "oh."

"Normally I wouldn't think it was that big of a deal, but there's one other thing." Lucas wipes his mouth off with the back of his hand. "Genevieve and her college guy broke up over the weekend. You know what that means, right?"

I'm nodding but I'm numb inside. "Yes. . . . Wait, what?"

Lucas gives me a look that's half pitying, half impatient. "She's going to try to get Peter back, Lara Jean!"

"Right," I say, and I feel a pang even as I'm saying it. "Of course she will."

"Don't let her," he warns.

"I won't," I say, and the words come out soft like jelly, without any conviction at all.

I didn't know it until now but I think maybe I've been counting down to this moment all along. For Genevieve to want Peter back. For Peter to figure out this whole thing has been a zany little detour and now it's time for him to go back where he belongs. To the person he belongs to.

I wasn't planning on telling Peter a thing about Josh kissing me. I really wasn't. But then, as Lucas and I are walking together, I see him and Genevieve walking down the hallway. Lucas gives me a meaningful look, which I pretend not to see.

In chemistry class I write Peter a note.

You were right about Josh.

I tap him on the back and slip the note in his hand. When he reads it, he sits up straight and immediately scrawls something back.

Be more specific.

He kissed me.

When Peter stiffens, I am ashamed to say that I feel a little bit vindicated. I wait for him to write back, but he doesn't.

As soon as the bell rings, he turns around and says, "What the hell? How did that even happen?"

"He came over to help us trim the tree."

"And then what? He kissed you in front of Kitty?"

"No! It was just the two of us at the house."

Peter looks really irritated, and I'm starting to regret mentioning it. "What the hell is he thinking, kissing my girlfriend? It's fucking ridiculous. I'm gonna say something to him."

"Wait, what? No!"

"I have to, Lara Jean. He can't just get away with it."

I stand up and start packing up my bag. "You'd better not say anything to him, Peter. I mean it."

Peter watches me silently. And then he asks, "Did you kiss him back?"

"What does it matter?"

He looks taken aback. "Are you mad at me for something?"

"No," I say. "But I will be if you say anything to Josh."

"Fine," he says.

"Fine," I say back.

55

I HAVEN'T SEEN JOSH SINCE HE KISSED ME,
but when I get home that night from studying at the library,
he is sitting on the front porch in his navy parka, waiting for
me. The lights are on in the house; my dad is home. Kitty's
bedroom light is on. I'd rather go on avoiding Josh, but here
he is, at my house.

"Hey," he says. "Can I talk to you?"

I sit down next to him and look straight ahead, across the
street. Ms. Rothschild's put her Christmas tree up too. She
always puts it by the window near the door so people can
see it from the outside.

"We have to figure out what we're going to do before
Margot gets here. It was my fault what happened. I should
be the one to tell her."

I stare at him in disbelief. "Tell her? Are you nuts? We're
never telling Margot because there's nothing to tell."

He juts his chin out. "I don't want to keep a secret from her."

"You should have thought of that before you kissed me!"
I hiss. "And for the record, if anybody was going to tell her,
it would be me. I'm her sister. You were just her boyfriend.
And you're not even that anymore, so . . ."

Hurt flashes across his face and it stays there. "I was never
just Margot's boyfriend. This is weird for me, too, you know.

It's like, ever since I got that letter . . ." He hesitates. "Forget it."

"Just say it," I say.

"Ever since I got that letter, things have been messed up between us. It's not fair. You got to say everything you wanted to say, and I'm the one who has to rearrange the way I think about you; I have to make sense of it in my head. You totally blindsided me, and then you just shut me out. You start dating Kavinsky, you stop being my friend." He exhales. "Ever since I got your letter . . . I haven't been able to stop thinking about you."

Whatever I was expecting him to say, it wasn't that. It definitely wasn't that. "Josh . . ."

"I know you don't want to hear it, but just let me say what I need to say, okay?"

I nod.

"I hate that you're with Kavinsky. I hate it. He's not good enough for you. I'm sorry to say it, but he's just not. In my opinion, no guy will ever be good enough for you. Least of all me." Josh ducks his head, and then suddenly he looks up at me and says, "There was this one time, I guess it was a couple of summers ago. We were walking home from some-body's house—I think it was Mike's."

It was hot, around dusk. I was mad because Mike's older brother Jimmy had said he'd give us a ride home, and then he went somewhere and didn't come back, so we had to walk. I was wearing espadrilles and my feet were hurting something terrible. Josh kept telling me to keep up with him.

Quietly he says, "It was just me and you. You had on that

tan suede fringy shirt you used to wear, with the straps, and it showed your belly button."

"My Pocahontas-meets-seventies-Cher-style shirt." Oh, how I loved that shirt.

"I almost kissed you that day. I thought about it. It was this weird impulse I had. I just wanted to see what it would be like."

My heart stops. "And then?"

"And then I don't know. I guess I forgot about it."

I let out a sigh. "I'm sorry you got that letter. You were never supposed to see that. It wasn't meant for you to ever read. It was just for me."

"Maybe it was fate. Maybe this was all supposed to happen just like this, because . . . because it was always gonna be you and me."

I say the first thing that comes to mind. "No, it wasn't." And I realize it's true.

This is the moment I realize I don't love him, that I haven't for a while. That maybe I never did. Because he's right there for the taking: I could kiss him again; I could make him mine. But I don't want him. I want someone else. It feels strange to have spent so much time wishing for something, for someone, and then one day, suddenly, to just stop.

I tuck my fingers inside my jacket sleeves. "You can't tell Margot. You have to promise me, Josh."

Reluctantly he nods.

"Has Margot been in touch with you recently?" I ask him.

"Yeah. She called the other night. She said she wants to

hang out while she's home. She wants to go to DC for the day. Go to the Smithsonian, get dinner in Chinatown."

"Great. Then that's what you'll do." I pat him on the knee and then quickly take my hand back. "Josh, we just have to act like before. Like always. If we do that, everything will be fine." I repeat it to myself in my head. *Everything will be fine.* We'll all go back to our proper places now. Josh and Margot. Me. Peter.

56

AFTER SCHOOL LETS OUT THE NEXT DAY, I go look for Peter in the weight room. He's sitting at the bench press. I think it's better to talk here and not in his car. I'm going to miss riding around in his car. It was starting to feel like home. I'm going to miss being somebody's pretend girlfriend. Not just somebody's—Peter's. I've gotten to really like Darrell and Gabe and the other lax guys. They aren't as douchey as people say. They're good people.

The weight room is empty except for Peter. He's at the bench press, lifting weights. When he sees me, he smiles. "Are you here to spot me?" He sits up and wipes sweat off his face with the collar of his T-shirt.

My heart squeezes painfully. "I'm here to break up. To fake break up, I mean."

Peter does a double take. "Wait. What?"

"There's no need to keep it going. You got what you wanted, right? You saved face, and so did I. I talked to Josh, and everything's back to normal with us again. And my sister will be home soon. So . . . mission accomplished."

Slowly he nods. "Yeah, I guess."

My heart is breaking even as I smile. "So okay, then." With a flourish I whip our contract out of my bag. "Null and void. Both parties have hereby fulfilled their obligations to each other in perpetuity." I'm just rattling off lawyer words.

"You carry that around with you?"

"Of course! Kitty's such a snoop. She'd find it in two seconds."

I hold up the piece of paper, poised to rip it in half, but Peter grabs it from me. "Wait! What about the ski trip?"

"What about it?"

"You're still coming, right?"

I hadn't thought of that. The only reason I was going to go was for Peter. I can't go now. I can't be a witness to Peter and Genevieve's reunion, I just can't. I want them to come back from the trip magically together again, and it will be like this whole thing was just something I dreamed up. "I'm not going to go."

His eyes widen. "Come on, Covey! Don't bail on me now. We already signed up and gave the deposits and everything. Let's just go, and have that be our final hurrah." When I start to protest, Peter shakes his head. "You're going, so take this contract back." Peter refolds it and carefully puts it back in my bag.

Why is it so hard to say no to him? Is this what it's like to be in love with somebody?

57

I GET THE IDEA DURING THE MORNING announcements, when they announce that our school's hosting a Model UN scrimmage this weekend. John Ambrose McClaren was the middle school Model UN president. I wonder if he's on his school's team.

I bring it up to Peter at lunch, before any of the guys sit down. "Do you know if John McClaren still does Model UN?"

He gives me a funny look. "How should I know?"

"I don't know. I was just wondering."

"Why?"

"I think maybe I'm going to go to the Model UN scrimmage this weekend. I have a feeling that he'll be there."

"For real?" Peter hoots. "If he is, what are you going to do?"

"I haven't figured that part out yet. Maybe I'll go up to him, maybe I won't. I just want to see how he turned out."

"We can look him up online right now and I'll show you."

I shake my head. "No, that would be cheating. I want to see him with my own eyes. I want to be surprised."

"Well, don't bother asking me to go and keep you company. I'm not going to waste a whole Saturday on Model UN."

"I wasn't planning on asking you to go."

Peter throws me a hurt look. "What? Why not?"

"It's just something I want to do by myself."

Peter lets out a low whistle. "Wow. The body ain't even cold yet."

"Huh?"

"You're a little player, Covey. We aren't even broken up yet and you're already trying to talk to other guys. I would be hurt if I wasn't impressed."

This makes me smile.

In eighth grade I kissed John McClaren at a party. It wasn't a romantic kiss. It was a barely anything kiss. We were playing spin the bottle, and when it was his turn, I held my breath and prayed the bottle would land on me. And it did! It almost landed on Angie Powell, but luck was on my side that day, and he was mine by half an inch. I tried to keep my face very still and robotic so I wouldn't smile. John and I crawled into the center and we did this very quick chicken peck, and everybody groaned, and his face was red. I was disappointed; I think maybe I'd expected something more, a kiss with more weight to it. More va-va-va-voom. More zsa zsa zsu. But that was it. Maybe I'll get a second chance. Maybe it'll make me forget Peter.

58

AS I WALK INTO SCHOOL ON SATURDAY morning, I go over what I'm going to say. Maybe just, *Hey, John, how are you? It's Lara Jean.* I haven't seen him since the eighth grade. What if he doesn't recognize me? What if he doesn't even remember me?

I scan the sandwich boards in the lobby and I find John's name under General Assembly. He's representing the People's Republic of China.

The General Assembly is meeting in the auditorium. There are desks set up for each delegate, and onstage there is a podium where a girl in a black suit is making a speech about nuclear nonproliferation. I'm thinking I'll just slip in the back and sit and watch but there's nowhere to sit, so I just stand at the back of the room with my arms crossed and look for John. There are so many people here, and everybody's facing the front, so it's hard to tell what's what.

A kid in a navy suit turns around and looks at me and whispers, "Are you a page?" He's holding up a folded piece of paper.

"Um . . ." I'm not sure what a page is, and then I see a girl hustling around the room delivering notes to people.

The boy thrusts the piece of paper at me and turns back around and scribbles in his notebook. The note is addressed to Brazil, from France. So I guess I'm a page.

The tables aren't in alphabetical order, so I just start wandering around trying to find Brazil. I finally find Brazil, a guy in a bow tie, and other people are raising their hands with notes for me to deliver. Before long I'm hustling too.

From behind I see a boy's hand raised for me to pick up his note, so I hurry forward, and then he turns his head just slightly. And oh my God, it's John Ambrose McClaren, delegate from the People's Republic of China, a few feet away from me.

He has sandy hair, clean-cut. His cheeks are rosy, just the way I remember. They still have that fresh-scrubbed wholesomeness that makes him look young. He's wearing khakis and a light blue button-down with a navy crew-neck sweater. He looks serious, focused, like he's a real delegate and this isn't pretend.

Honestly, he looks just the way I imagined he'd grow up to look.

John's holding the piece of paper out for me as he takes notes with his head down. I reach for it; my fingers close around the paper, and then he looks up and does a double take.

"Hi," I whisper. We're both still holding on to the note.

"Hi," he says back. He blinks, and then he lets go of the paper, and I hurry away, my heart pounding in my ears. I hear him call out my name in a loud whisper, but I don't slow down.

I look down at the paper. His handwriting is neat, precise.

I go deliver his note to the USA, and then I ignore Great Britain, who is waving a note at me, and I walk right out the auditorium double doors and into the afternoon light.

I just saw John McClaren. After all these years, I finally saw him. And he knew me. Right away he knew who I was.

I get a text from Peter around lunchtime.

Did you see McClaren?

I type back yes, but then I delete it before I hit send. I write back no instead. I'm not sure why I do it. I think maybe I just want to keep it for myself, and be happy just knowing that John remembered me, and have that be enough.

59

WE ALL GO TO PICK UP MARGOT FROM THE airport. Kitty's made a sign that says *Welcome Home Gogo*. I keep my eyes peeled for her, and when she comes out I almost don't recognize her for a second—her hair is short! It's cut in a bob! When Margot sees us, she waves, and Kitty drops her sign and runs toward her. Then we're all hugging and Daddy has tears in his eyes. "What do you think?" Margot says to me, and I know she means her hair.

"It makes you look older," I lie, and Margot beams. If anything it makes her look younger, but I knew she wouldn't want to hear that.

On the way home, Margot makes Daddy pull over at Clouds for a cheeseburger, even though she says she isn't hungry. "I've missed this so much," she says, but she only has a few bites and Kitty has the rest.

I'm excited to show Margot all the cookies we made, but when I take her into the dining room and show her all the tins, she frowns. "You guys did the Christmas Cookie Bonanza without me?"

I feel a little bit guilty, but I honestly didn't think Margot would mind. I mean, she was in Scotland, doing way more fun stuff than baking cookies, for Pete's sake. "Well, yeah. We kind of had to. School ends tomorrow. If we'd waited for you, we wouldn't have had time. We saved half the dough in the freezer, though, so you can still help us bake the rest for the neighbors." I open the big blue tin so she can see the cookies layered and lined up in rows. I'm proud of how they are the same size and height. "We did some new cookies this year. Try an orange Creamsicle; it's really good."

Margot picks through the tin and frowns. "You didn't do molasses cookies?"

"Not this year . . . We decided to do orange Creamsicle cookies in their place." She picks one up and I watch her bite into it. "Good, right?"

She nods. "Mm-hmm."

"Those were Kitty's pick."

Margot glances toward the living room. "When did you guys do the tree?"

"Kitty couldn't wait," I say, and it sounds like an excuse, but it's true. I try not to sound defensive as I add, "I think it'll be nice to enjoy the tree for as long as we can."

"So when did you put it up?"

Slowly I say, "A couple of weeks ago . . ." Why is she in such a bad mood?

"That's so long ago. It'll probably be dried out by Christmas Day." Margot walks over to the tree and moves the wooden owl ornament to a different branch.

"I've been watering it every day and putting in Sprite like Grandma taught us."

Somehow this feels like a fight, and we never fight.

But then Margot yawns and says, "I'm really jet-lagged. I think I'm going to take a nap."

When someone's been gone a long time, at first you save up all the things you want to tell them. You try to keep track of everything in your head. But it's like trying to hold on to a fistful of sand: all the little bits slip out of your hands, and then you're just clutching air and grit. That's why you can't save it all up like that.

Because by the time you finally see each other, you're catching up only on the big things, because it's too much bother to tell about the little things. But the little things are what make up life. Like a month ago when Daddy slipped on a banana peel, a literal banana peel that Kitty had dropped on the kitchen floor. Kitty and I laughed for ages. I should have e-mailed Margot about it right away; I should have taken a picture of the banana peel. Now everything feels like *you had to be there* and *oh never mind, I guess it's not that funny.*

Is this how people lose touch? I didn't think that could happen with sisters. Maybe with other people, but never us. Before Margot left, I knew what she was thinking without having to ask; I knew everything about her. Not anymore. I don't know what the view looks like outside her window, or if she still wakes up early every morning to have a real breakfast or if maybe now that she's at college she likes to go out late and sleep in late. I don't know if she prefers Scottish boys to American boys now, or if her roommate snores. All I know is she likes her classes and she's been to visit London once. So basically I know nothing.

And so does she. There are big things I haven't told her—how my letters got sent out. The truth about me and Peter. The truth about me and Josh.

I wonder if Margot feels it too. The distance between us. If she even notices.

Daddy makes spaghetti bolognese for dinner. Kitty has hers with a big pickle and a glass of milk, which sounds terrible, but then I take a bite, and actually pickle and spaghetti taste good together. Milk, too.

Kitty's dumping more noodles on her plate when she says, "Lara Jean, what are you going to get Peter for Christmas?"

I glance at Margot, who is looking at me. "I don't know. I hadn't thought about it."

"Can I go with you to pick it out?"

"Sure, if I get him something."

"You have to get him something; he's your boyfriend."

"I still can't believe you're dating Peter Kavinsky," Margot says.

She doesn't say it in a nice way, like it's a good thing. "Can you just . . . not?" I say.

"I'm sorry, I just don't like the guy."

"Well, you don't have to like him. I do," I say, and Margot shrugs.

Daddy stands up and claps his hands together. "We have three different kinds of ice cream for dessert! Pralines and cream, Chunky Monkey, and strawberry. All your favorites,

Margot. Help me get the bowls, Kitty." They gather up the dirty dishes and go into the kitchen.

Margot looks out the window, toward Josh's house. "Josh wants to see me later. I hope he finally gets that we're broken up and he doesn't try to come over every day while I'm home. He needs to move on."

What a mean thing to say. She's the one who's been calling Josh, not the other way around. "He hasn't been pining for you, if that's what you're imagining," I say. "He gets that it's over."

Margot stares at me in surprise. "Well, I hope that's true."

60

"*I THINK WE SHOULD DO RECITAL PARTY* this year," Margot says from her spot on the couch.

When my mom was alive, every Christmas we'd have what she called a recital party. She'd make tons of food and invite people over one night in December, and Margot and I would wear matching dresses and play Christmas carols on the piano all night. People would drift in and out of the piano room and sing along, and Margot and I would take turns playing. I hated real piano recitals because I was the worst in my age group and Margot was the best. It was humiliating to have to play some easy "Für Elise" while the other kids had already moved on to Liszt. I always hated recital party. I used to beg and beg not to have to play.

The last Christmas, Mommy bought us matching red velvet dresses to wear, and I threw a fit and said I didn't want to wear it, even though I did, even though I loved it. I just didn't want to have to play the piano in it next to Margot. I screamed at her and I ran to my room and slammed the door and I wouldn't come out. Mommy came up and tried to get me to open the door, but I wouldn't, and she didn't come back. People started arriving, and Margot started playing the piano, and I stayed upstairs. I sat in my room, crying and thinking about all the dips and little canapés Mommy and Daddy had made and how there would be none left for me and how Mommy probably didn't even want me down there anyway after the way I'd behaved.

After Mommy died, we never had another recital party.

"Are you serious?" I ask her.

"Why not?" Margot shrugs. "It'll be fun. I'll plan it all, you won't have to do anything."

"You know I hate piano."

"Then don't play."

Kitty's looking from me to Margot with worried eyes. Biting her lip, she offers, "I'll do some tae kwon do moves."

Margot reaches out and cuddles Kitty to her and says, "That's a great idea. I'll play the piano and you'll do tae kwon do, and Lara Jean will just—"

"Watch," I finish.

"I was going to say hostess, but suit yourself."

I don't answer her.

Later, we're watching TV and Kitty's asleep, curled up on the couch like she's a real cat. Margot wants to wake her up and make her go to her bed, but I say just let her sleep, and I put a quilt over her.

"Will you help me work on Daddy about a puppy for Christmas?" I ask.

Margot groans. "Puppies are so much work. You have to let them out to pee like a million times a day. And they shed like crazy. You'll never be able to wear black pants again. Also who's going to walk it, and feed it, and take care of it?"

"Kitty will. And I'll help."

"Kitty is so not ready for the responsibility." Her eyes say, *And neither are you.*

"Kitty's matured a lot since you've been gone." *And so have I.* "Did you know that Kitty packs her own lunch now? *And* she helps with the laundry? I don't have to nag her to do her homework, either. She just does it on her own."

"Really? Then I'm impressed."

Why can't she just say, *Good job, Lara Jean?* That's it. If she could just acknowledge that I've been doing my part to keep the family going since she's been gone. But no.

61

AT SIX THIRTY IN THE MORNING THE DAY OF the ski trip, Daddy drops me off at school. It's not even light out yet. It seems like every day the sun takes longer and longer to come up. Before I hop out of the car, my dad pulls a hat out of his coat pocket. It's light pink yarn with a pom-pom on top. He fits it on my head so it covers my ears. "I found this in the hall closet. I think it was one of your mom's. She was such a great skier."

"I know. I remember."

"Promise me you'll go out on the slopes at least once."

"I promise."

"I'm so glad you're doing this. It's good for you to try new things."

I smile weakly. If he only knew what went down at the ski trip, he wouldn't be so glad then. Then I spot Peter and his friends messing around outside by the charter bus. "Thanks for the ride, Daddy. See you tomorrow night." I give him a peck on the cheek and grab my duffel bag.

"Zip up your coat," he calls out as I shut the car door.

I zip up my coat and watch his car drive off. Across the parking lot, Peter's talking to Genevieve. He says something that makes her laugh. Then he sees me and gestures at me to come over. Genevieve walks away, looking down at her clipboard. When I get there, he takes my duffel bag off my shoulder and puts it next to his. "I'll put this on the bus."

"It's freezing," I say, my teeth chattering.

Peter pulls me in front of him and puts his arms around me. "I'll keep you warm." I look up at him like *so cheesy*, but his attention is somewhere else. He's watching Genevieve. He snuggles against my neck, and I squirm away from him. "What's with you?" he asks.

"Nothing," I say.

Ms. Davenport and Coach White are looking through kids' bags—Ms. Davenport's doing the girls and Coach White is doing the boys. "What are they looking for?" I ask Peter.

"Alcohol."

I whip out my phone and text Chris.

Don't bring alcohol! They are checking!

No response.

Are you awake??

Wake up!

But then her mom's SUV pulls into the parking lot and she stumbles out of the passenger seat. She looks like she just woke up.

What a relief! Peter can talk to Genevieve all he wants; I'll be sharing a seat with Chris and eating the snacks I packed. I have strawberry gummies and the wasabi peas that Chris loves, and Pocky sticks.

Peter groans. "Chris is coming?"

I ignore him and wave at her.

Genevieve's standing by the bus with her clipboard when she spots Chris too. She has a big frown on her face. She marches right up to Chris and says, "You didn't sign up."

I run over to them and hover next to Chris. In a small voice I say, "In the announcements last week they said there were still spots left."

"Yeah, that you had to sign up for." Genevieve shakes her head. "I'm sorry, but Chrissy can't come if she didn't sign up or give a deposit."

I wince. Chris hates being called "Chrissy." She always has. She started going by Chris as soon as we got to high school, and the only people who still call her that are Genevieve and their grandma.

Peter shows up beside me out of nowhere. "What's going on?" he asks.

Folding her arms, Genevieve says, "Chrissy didn't sign up for the ski trip, so I'm sorry, but she can't come."

I'm panicking, but all the while Chris is smirking and saying nothing.

Peter rolls his eyes and says, "Gen, just let her come. Who gives a shit if she didn't sign up?"

Her cheeks flush with anger. "I didn't make the rules,

Peter! Should she just get to come for free? How is that fair to everybody else?"

Chris finally speaks. "Oh, I already talked to Davenport and she said it was cool." Chris makes a kissy face at Genevieve. "Too bad, Gen."

"Fine, whatever, I don't care." Genevieve turns on her heel and spins off in Ms. Davenport's direction.

Chris watches her go, grinning. I tug on her coat sleeve. "Why didn't you say so from the beginning?" I whisper.

"Obvi because it was more fun that way." She slings her arm around my shoulder. "It's going to be an interesting weekend, Covey."

Worried, I whisper, "You didn't bring any alcohol, did you? They're checking bags."

"Don't worry about me. I'm covered."

When I give her a dubious look, she whispers back, "Shampoo bottle filled with tequila at the bottom of my bag."

"I hope you washed it out really well! You could get sick!" I'm envisioning Chris and company trying to take shots of bubbly tequila and then having to go to the hospital to get their stomachs pumped.

Chris ruffles my hair. "Oh, Lara Jean."

We file onto the bus and Peter slides into a seat in the middle and I shuffle forward. "Hey," he says, surprised. "You're not going to sit with me?"

"I'm sitting with Chris." I try to keep walking down the aisle, but Peter grabs my arm.

"Lara Jean! Are you kidding me? You have to sit with me." He looks around to see if anybody's listening. "You're my *girlfriend*."

I shake him off. "We're breaking up soon, aren't we? We might as well make it look more realistic."

When I slide into the seat next to her, Chris is shaking her head at me.

"What? I couldn't just let you sit alone. You came here for me, after all." I open up my backpack and show her the snacks. "See? I brought your favorite things. What do you want to eat first? Gummies or Pocky?"

"It's barely even morning," she grouses. Then: "Hand me the gummies."

Smiling, I rip open the bag for her. "Have as much as you want."

I stop smiling when I see Genevieve get on the bus and sit down in the seat next to Peter.

"You did that," Chris says.

"For you!" Which isn't true, not really. I think maybe I'm just tired of all this. This in-betweenness of being somebody's girlfriend but not really.

Chris stretches. "I know you're all about hos before bros, but if I were you, I'd be careful. My cousin's a barracuda."

I stuff a gummy into my mouth and chew. It's hard to swallow. I watch Genevieve whisper something in Peter's ear, and Chris falls asleep right away just like she said, her head on my shoulder.

★ ★ ★

The lodge is exactly the way Peter described—there's a big fireplace and bearskin rugs and lots of little nooks. It's snowing outside, tiny little whisper flakes. Chris is in good spirits—halfway through the bus ride she woke up and started flirting with Charlie Blanchard, who's going to take her out on the black diamond slopes. We even lucked out with a double room instead of a triple, because all the other girls had signed up for triples together.

Chris went off to snowboard with Charlie. She invited me to come along, but I said no thanks. I tried to ski next to Margot when she snowboarded once, and it ended up with us coming down the slopes at different times and waiting for each other and then losing each other all day.

If Peter were to invite me to go snowboarding with him, I think I'd go. But he doesn't, and I'm hungry anyway, so I go to the lodge to eat lunch.

Ms. Davenport is there looking at her cell phone and eating a bowl of soup. Ms. Davenport is young, but she presents herself old. I think it's her heavy foundation and her severe part down the middle. She isn't married. Chris told me she saw her having an argument with some guy outside the Waffle House once, so I guess she has a boyfriend.

When she spots me sitting alone, eating a sandwich by the fireplace, she waves me over. I carry my plate to her table and sit down across from her. I'd rather eat alone and read my book, but it's not like I have much of a choice in the matter. I ask her, "Do you have to stay here in the lodge all weekend, or can you go ski too?"

"I'm officially home base," she says, wiping the corners of her mouth. "Coach White's on slope duty."

"That doesn't seem very fair."

"I don't mind. I actually like sitting in the lodge. It's peaceful. Besides, somebody has to be here for emergencies." She takes another bite of soup. "What about you, Lara Jean? Why aren't you out on the slopes with everybody else?"

"I'm not the best skier," I say, feeling embarrassed.

"Oh, really? I hear Kavinsky's a very good snowboarder. You should get him to teach you. Aren't you two dating?"

Ms. Davenport loves being in on student drama. She calls it having her finger on the pulse, but really she's just a gossip. If you give her an opening, she'll burrow in for as much dirt as she can. I know she and Genevieve are close.

I have a quick flash of Genevieve and Peter on the bus with their heads close together, and the picture makes my heart squeeze. Our contract isn't over yet. Why should I let her have him back even one second early? "Yes," I say. "We're together." Then I stand up. "You know what? I think I will go check out the slopes."

62

I'M BUNDLED UP IN MARGOT'S PINK SKI BIB
and the pom-pom hat and my parka and I feel like an Easter
treat—a strawberry-flavored marshmallow. As I try to click
into my skis, a group of girls from school walk by in cute
yoga-ish ski pants. I didn't even know those existed.

I always think I could like skiing and then I go on a ski
trip and I remember, oh yeah, I hate it. All the other kids
are on the black diamond slopes and I'm on green circle,
aka the bunny slope. I pizza wedge down the whole way,
and little kids keep zooming by me, which makes me lose
my concentration because I'm terrified they're going to
run into me. They whoosh back and forth like Olympic
skiers. Some of them aren't even using poles. They're like
Kitty. She can go down black diamond slopes. She and
my dad love it. Margot, too, though Margot prefers snowboarding to skiing now.

I've been keeping my eyes peeled for Peter but I haven't
seen him yet, and it's starting to feel a bit bleak out here all
alone.

I'm considering giving the intermediate slope a try, just
for kicks, when I spot Peter and all his friends carrying their
snowboards. No Genevieve in sight. "Peter!" I call out, feeling very relieved.

He turns his head and I think he sees me, but he keeps walking.

Huh.

He saw me. I know he saw me.

After dinner, Chris goes back to the slopes to snowboard. She says she's addicted to the rush. I'm heading back to the room when I run into Peter again, this time in swimming trunks and a hoodie. He's with Gabe and Darrell. They have towels around their necks. "Hey, Large," Gabe says, flicking me with his towel. "Where you been all day?"

"I've been around." I look over at Peter, but he won't meet my eyes. "I saw you guys on the slopes."

Darrell says, "Then why didn't you holler at us? I wanted to show off my ollies for you."

Teasingly I say, "Well, I called Peter's name, but I guess he didn't hear me."

Peter finally looks me in the eyes. "Nope. I didn't hear you." His voice is cold and indifferent and so un-Peterlike, the smile fades from my face.

Gabe and Darrell exchange looks like *oooh* and Gabe says to Peter, "We're gonna head out to the hot tub," and they trot off.

Peter and I are left standing in the lobby, neither of us saying anything. I finally ask, "Are you mad at me or something?"

"Why would I be mad?"

And then it's back to quiet again.

I say, "You know, you're the one who talked me into coming on this trip. The least you could do is talk to me."

"The least you could do was sit next to me on the bus!" he bursts out.

My mouth hangs open. "Are you really that mad that I didn't sit next to you on the *bus*?"

Peter lets out an impatient breath of air. "Lara Jean, when you're dating someone, there are just . . . certain things you do, okay? Like sit next to each other on a school trip. That's pretty much expected."

"I just don't see what the big deal is," I say. How can he be this mad over such a tiny thing?

"Forget it." He turns like he's going to leave, and I grab his sweatshirt sleeve. I don't want to be in a fight with him; I just want it to be fun and light the way it always is with us. I want him to at least still be my friend. Especially now that we're at the end.

I say, "Come on, don't be mad. I didn't realize it was that big of a deal. I swear I'll sit next to you on the way home, okay?"

He purses his lips. "But do you get why I was pissed?"

I nod back. "Mm-hmm."

"All right then, you should know that you missed out on mocha sugar donuts."

My mouth falls open. "How'd you get those? I thought the shop didn't open that early!"

"I went out and got them last night specifically for the bus ride," Peter says. "For you and me."

Aw. I'm touched. "Well, are there any left?"

"Nope. I ate them all."

He looks so smug that I reach out and swat at his hoodie strings. "You creep," I say, but I mean it affectionately.

Peter grabs my hand mid-swat and says, "Wanna hear something funny?"

"What?"

"I think I started liking you."

I go completely still. Then I pull my hand away from his, and I start to gather my hair into a ponytail, and then I remember I don't have a hair tie. My heart is thudding in my chest and it's hard to think all of a sudden. "Stop teasing."

"I'm not teasing. Why do you think I kissed you that day at McClaren's house back in seventh grade? It's why I went along with this thing in the first place. I've always thought you were cute."

My face feels hot. "In a quirky way."

Peter grins his perfect grin. "So? I guess I must like quirky, then."

Then he leans his head closer to mine, and I blurt out, "But aren't you still in love with Genevieve?"

Peter frowns.

"Why are you always bringing up Gen? I'm trying to talk about us, and all you want to do is talk about her. Yeah, Gen and I have history. I'm always going to care about her." He shrugs. "But now . . . I like you."

People are walking in and out of the lodge; a guy from school walks by and claps Peter on the shoulder. "What up,"

Peter says. When he's gone, Peter says to me, "So what do you say?" He's looking at me expectantly. He's expecting me to say yes.

I want to say yes, but I don't want to be with a boy whose heart belongs to somebody else. Just once, I want to be somebody's first choice. "You might think you like me, but you don't. If you did, you wouldn't still like her."

Peter shakes his head. "What Gen and I have is completely separate from you and me," he says.

"How can that be true when from the very first minute, this has been about Genevieve?"

"That's not fair," he objects. "When we started this thing, you liked Sanderson."

"Not anymore." I swallow hard. "But you still love Genevieve."

Frustrated, Peter backs away from me and runs his hands through his hair. "God, what makes you such an expert on love? You've liked five guys in your life. One was gay, one lives in Indiana or Montana or some place, McClaren moved away before anything could actually happen, one was dating your sister. And then there's me. Hmm, what do we all have in common? What's the common denominator?"

I feel all the blood rush to my face. "That's not fair."

Peter leans in close and says, "You only like guys you don't have a shot with, because you're scared. What are you so scared of?"

I back away from him, right into the wall. "I'm not scared of anything."

"The hell you're not. You'd rather make up a fantasy version of somebody in your head than be with a real person."

I glare at him. "You're just mad because I didn't die of happiness because the great Peter Kavinsky said he liked me. Your ego really is that enormous."

His eyes flash. "Hey, I'm sorry I didn't show up on your doorstep with flowers and profess my undying love for you, Lara Jean, but guess what, that's not real life. You need to grow up."

That's it. I don't have to listen to this. I turn on my heel and walk away. Over my shoulder I say, "Enjoy the hot tub."

"I always do," he calls back.

I'm shaking.

Is it true? Could he be right?

Back at the room, I change into my flannel nighty and put on thick socks. I don't even go wash up. I just turn out the lights and crawl into bed. I can't fall asleep, though. Every time I close my eyes, I see Peter's face.

How dare he say I need to grow up? What does he know about anything? As if he's so mature!

But . . . is he right about me? Do I only like the boys I can never have? I've always known Peter was out of my reach. I've always known he didn't belong to me. But tonight he said he liked me. The thing I've been hoping for, he said it. So why didn't I just tell him I liked him back when I had the chance? Because I do. I like him back. Of course I do. What girl wouldn't fall for Peter Kavinsky, handsomest boy of all the Handsome Boys. Now that I really know him, I know he's so much more than that.

I don't want to be afraid anymore. I want to be brave. I want . . . life to start happening. I want to fall in love and I want a boy to fall in love with me back.

Before I can talk myself out of it, I put on my puffy coat, slip my keycard in my pocket, and head off to the hot tub.

63

THE HOT TUB IS BEHIND THE MAIN LODGE, tucked in the woods on a wooden platform. On the way there, I run into kids with wet hair who are on their way back to their rooms before curfew. Curfew is at eleven, and it's already ten forty-five. There's not much time left. I hope Peter's still out there. I don't want to lose my nerve. So I quicken my pace and that's when I spot him, alone in the hot tub, his head tipped back with his eyes closed.

"Hi," I say, and my voice echoes into the woods.

His eyes fly open. Nervously, he looks over my shoulder. "Lara Jean! What are you doing out here?"

"I came to see you," I say, and my breath comes out in white puffs. I start taking off my boots and socks. My hands are shaking, and not because it's cold. I'm nervous.

"Uh . . . what are you doing?" Peter's looking at me like I'm crazy.

"I'm getting in!" Shivering, I unzip my puffy coat and set it on the bench. Steam is rising out of the water. I dip my feet in and sit down on the ledge of the hot tub. It's hotter than a bath, but it feels nice. Peter's still watching me warily. My heart is racing out of control and it's difficult to look him in the eyes. I've never been so scared in my life. "That thing you brought up earlier . . . you caught me off guard, so I didn't know what to say. But . . . well, I like you too." It comes out so fumbly and uncertain, and I wish I could start over and say it smoothly and confidently. I try again, louder. "I like you, Peter."

Peter blinks, and he looks so young all of a sudden. "I don't understand you girls. I think I have you figured out, and then . . . and then . . ."

"And then?" I hold my breath as I wait for him to speak. I'm so nervous; I keep swallowing, and it sounds loud to my ears. Even my breathing sounds loud, even my heartbeat.

His pupils are dilated he's looking at me so hard. He's staring at me like he's never seen me before. "And then I don't know."

I think I stop breathing when I hear him say "I don't know." Did I screw things up that badly that now he doesn't know? It can't be over, not when I finally found my courage. I can't let it be. My heart is pounding like a million trillion beats a minute as I scoot closer to him. I bend my head down and press my lips against his, and I feel his jolt of surprise. And then he's kissing me back, open-mouthed, soft-lipped kissing-me-back, and at first I'm nervous, but then he puts his hand on the back of my head, and he strokes my hair in a reassuring way, and I'm not so nervous anymore. It's a good thing I'm sitting down on this ledge, because I am weak in the knees.

He pulls me into the water so I'm sitting in the hot tub too, and my nightgown is soaked now but I don't care. I don't care about anything. I never knew kissing could be this good.

My arms are at my sides so the jets won't make my skirt fly up. Peter's holding my face in his hands, kissing me. "Are you okay?" he whispers. His voice is different: it's ragged and urgent and vulnerable somehow. He doesn't sound like the Peter I know; he is not smooth or bored or amused. The way he's looking at me right now, I know he would do anything I asked, and that's a strange and powerful feeling.

I wind my arms around his neck. I like the smell of chlorine on his skin. He smells like pool, and summer, and vacations. It's not like in the movies. It's better, because it's real.

"Touch my hair again," I tell him, and the corners of his mouth turn up.

I lean into him and kiss him. He starts to run his fingers through my hair, and it feels so nice I can't think straight. It's better than getting my hair washed at the salon. I move my hands down his back and along his spine, and he shivers and pulls me closer. A boy's back feels so different than a girl's back—more muscular, more solid somehow.

In between kisses he says, "It's past curfew. We should go back inside."

"I don't want to," I say. All I want is to stay and be here, with Peter, in this moment.

"Me either, but I don't want you to get in trouble," Peter says. He looks worried, which is so sweet.

Softly, I touch his cheek with the back of my hand. It's smooth. I could look at his face for hours, it's so beautiful.

Then I stand up, and immediately I'm shivering. I start wringing the water out of my nightgown, and Peter jumps out of the hot tub and gets his towel, which he wraps around my shoulders. Then he gives me his hand and I step out, teeth chattering. He starts drying me off with the towel, my arms and legs. I sit down to put on my socks and boots. He puts my coat on me last. He zips me right in.

Then we run back inside the lodge. Before he goes to the boys' side and I go to the girls' side, I kiss him one more time and I feel like I'm flying.

64

WHEN I SEE PETER AT THE BUS THE NEXT
morning, he's standing around with all his lacrosse friends,
and at first I feel shy and nervous, but then he sees me, and
his face breaks into a grin. "C'mere, Covey," he says, so I go
to him and he throws my tote over his shoulder. In my ear
he says, "You're sitting with me, right?"

I nod.

As we make our way onto the bus, somebody wolf whistles.
It seems like people are staring at us, and at first I think it's just
my imagination, but then I see Genevieve look right at me and
whisper to Emily Nussbaum. It sends a chill down my spine.

"Genevieve keeps staring at me," I whisper to Peter.

"It's because you're so adorably quirky," he says, and he
rests his hands on my shoulders and gives me a kiss on the
cheek, and I forget all about Genevieve.

Peter and I sit in the middle of the bus with Gabe and the
lacrosse guys. I wave to Chris so she'll sit with us, but she's
cozy with Charlie Blanchard. I haven't had a chance to tell
her about last night. When I got back to the room, she was
already asleep. This morning, we both overslept and there
wasn't time. I'll tell her all about it later. But, for now, it's
kind of nice that Peter and I are the only ones who know
about it.

The way down the mountain, I share my Pocky sticks with the boys and we play a heated round of Uno, which I also brought.

An hour into the trip, we stop at a rest-stop diner for breakfast. I eat a cinnamon bun, and under the table Peter and I hold hands.

I go to use the bathroom, and there is Genevieve, alone, applying lip gloss with a little brush. I step inside the stall to pee and hope she'll be gone by the time I come out, but she's still there. I wash my hands quickly, and then she says, "Did you know that when we were kids, I used to wish I was you?" I freeze. Genevieve snaps her compact shut. "I used to wish your dad was my dad and Margot and Kitty were my sisters. I loved coming over to your house. I would hope and pray that you would invite me to sleep over. I hated being at home with my dad."

Haltingly, I say, "I-I didn't know that. I used to like going to your house, because your mom was so nice to me."

"She really liked you," Genevieve says.

I screw up all my courage and I ask, "So why did you stop being friends with me?"

Genevieve narrows her eyes at me. "You really don't know?"

"No."

"You kissed Peter that day at my house in seventh grade. You knew I liked him, but you kissed him anyway." I recoil, and she continues. "I always knew your goody-goody act was fake. It's no wonder you and my cousin are BFFs now. Although at least Chris owns her sluttiness. She doesn't put on an act."

My whole body goes rigid. "What are you talking about?"

She laughs, and it's chilling how happy she sounds. That's when I know I'm already dead. I brace myself for whatever mean thing will come out of her mouth, but even still I'm not ready for what comes next.

"I'm talking about how you and Peter had full-on sex in the hot tub last night."

My mind goes completely blank. I might even black out for a second. I can feel myself sway on my feet. Somebody come quick with the smelling salts; I'm about to faint.

My head is swimming. "Who told you that?" I choke out. "Who said that?"

Genevieve tilts her head to the side. "Everybody?"

"But—but we *didn't*—"

"I'm sorry, but I think it's absolutely disgusting. I mean, sex in a hot tub—a *public* hot tub—is just . . ." She shudders. "God only knows what kind of stuff is floating around in there now. *Families* use that hot tub, Lara Jean. There could be a family in there right now."

Tears are spiking my eyes. "All we did was kiss. I don't know why people would even say that."

"Um, because Peter's telling them you did?"

My whole body goes cold. It's not true. There's no way that's true.

"All the guys think he's a god 'cause he got sweet little

Lara Jean Covey to give it up in the hot tub. Just so you know, the only reason Peter even dated you was to make me jealous. His ego couldn't take the fact that I dumped him for an older guy. He was *using* you. If he got free sex out of it, all the better. But he still came running whenever I called. That's because he loves me. He will never love another girl as much as he loves me." Whatever she sees in my face must please her, because she smiles. "Now that Blake and I are done . . . well, I guess we'll see, won't we?"

I stand there mute and numb as she fluffs her hair in the mirror.

"But don't worry. Now that you're a slut, I'm sure you'll have plenty of guys who'll want to date you. For a night."

I flee. I run out of the ladies' room and out the doors, back onto the bus, and I cry.

65

PEOPLE ARE STARTING TO FILE BACK ON THE bus. I can feel their eyes on me so I keep my head turned toward the window. I run my finger along the edge of the foggy glass. The window is cold, so it leaves a trail.

Chris slides in next to me. In a low voice she says, "Um, I just heard something cray-cray."

Dully I say, "What did you hear? That Peter and I had sex in the hot tub last night?"

"Oh my God! Yeah! Are you okay?"

My chest feels really tight. If I get in a good breath, I am going to start crying again, I know it.

I close my eyes. "We didn't have sex. Who told you that?"

"Charlie."

Peter's making his way down the aisle. He stops at our seat. "Hey, why didn't you come back to the table? Is everything okay?" Peter is looming over the seat, looking at me with concerned eyes.

In a quiet voice I say, "Everybody's saying how we had sex in the tub."

Peter groans. "People need to mind their own business." He doesn't sound surprised, not at all.

"So you already knew?"

"Some of the guys were asking me about it this morning."

"But . . . where did they even get that idea?" I feel like I'm going to be sick.

Peter shrugs. "I don't know, maybe somebody saw us. What does it even matter? It's not true."

I screw my lips together tight. I can't cry right now, because if I start, I'll never be able to stop. I will cry the whole way home, and everyone will see, and I can't have that. I fix my gaze somewhere over Peter's shoulder.

"I don't get it. Why are you mad at me?" He's still confused.

People are starting to bottleneck behind Peter. They need to get to their seats. "People are waiting behind you," I say.

Peter says, "Chris, can I have my seat?"

Chris looks at me and I shake my head.

"It's my seat now, Kavinsky," she says.

"Come on, Lara Jean," Peter says, touching my shoulder.

I jerk away from him and his mouth drops open. People are looking at us and whispering and snickering. Peter glances over his shoulder, his face red. Then he finally makes his way down the aisle.

"Are you okay?" Chris asks.

I can feel my eyes welling up. "No. Not really."

She sighs. "It's not fair for the girl. Guys have it easy. I'm sure they were all congratulating him, pounding him on the back for being such a stud."

Sniffling, I say, "Do you think he's the one who told people?"

"Who knows?"

A tear trickles down to my cheek and Chris wipes it away with her sweater sleeve. "It might not have been him. But it doesn't matter, Lara Jean, because even if he didn't encourage all the talk, I doubt he discouraged it, if you know what I'm saying."

I shake my head.

"What I'm saying is, I'm sure he denied it—with a shit-eating grin on his face. That's how guys like Peter are. They love to look like the man, have all the other guys look up to them." Bitterly she says, "They care more about their reputation than yours." She shakes her head. "But what's done is done. You've just gotta hold your head up and act like you don't give a shit."

I nod, but more tears leak out.

"I'm telling you, he isn't worth it. Let Gen have him." Chris tousles my hair. "What else can you do, kid?"

Genevieve comes on board last. I quickly straighten up and wipe my eyes and brace myself. But she doesn't go directly to her seat. She stops at Bethy Morgan's seat and whispers something in her ear. Bethy gasps and turns in her seat—and looks right at me.

Oh my God.

Chris and I watch as Genevieve goes from seat to seat.

"Bitch," Chris breathes.

Tears burn my eyes. "I'm just gonna go to sleep now," and I rest my head on Chris's shoulder, and I cry. She keeps her arm tight around me.

66

MARGOT AND KITTY PICK ME UP FROM school. They ask me how the trip was, if I stayed on the bunny slope all day. I try to be upbeat; I even make up a story about how I went down a blue circle slope. Softly Margot asks, "Is everything okay?"

I falter. Margot always knows when I'm not telling the truth.

"Yeah. I'm just tired. Chris and I stayed up late talking."

"Take a nap when we get home," Margot advises.

My phone buzzes, and I look down at it. A text from Peter.

Can we talk?

I turn off my phone. "I think maybe I'll just sleep right through Christmas break," I say. Thank God and Jesus for Christmas break. At least I have ten days before I have to go back to school and face everyone. Maybe I'll just never go back. Maybe I can convince Daddy to home school me.

When Daddy and Kitty go to bed, Margot and I wrap presents in the living room. Mid-wrap, Margot decides that we should have recital party the day after Christmas. I'd hoped she'd forgotten all about her grand idea to have recital party, but Margot's memory has always been killer. "It'll be a post-Christmas, pre–New Year's Eve party," she says, tying a bow on one of Kitty's presents from Daddy.

"It's too last-minute," I say, carefully cutting a sheet of rocking-horse wrapping paper. I'm being extra careful because I want to save a strip of it for a background page in Margot's scrapbook, which is nearly done. "No one will come."

"Yes they will! We haven't had one in ages; tons of people used to come." Margot gets up and starts pulling down Mommy's old cookbooks and stacking them on the coffee table. "Don't be a Grinch. I think this should be a tradition that we bring back for Kitty's sake."

I cut off a strip of fat green ribbon. Maybe this party will help me take my mind off things. "Find that Mediterranean chicken dish Mommy used to make. With the honey-yogurt dip."

"Yes! And remember the caviar dip? People *love* the caviar dip. We have to make that, too. Should we do cheese straws or cheese puffs?"

"Cheese puffs," I say. Margot's so excited about it that even in my current state of self-pity, I can't begrudge her.

She gets a pen and paper from the kitchen and starts writing things down. "So we said the chicken dish, caviar dip, cheese puffs, punch . . . We can bake some cookies or brownies. We'll invite all the neighbors—Josh and his parents, the Shahs, Ms. Rothschild. Who of your friends do you want to invite? Chris?"

I shake my head. "Chris is visiting her relatives in Boca Raton."

"What about Peter? He could bring his mom, and doesn't he have a younger brother?" I can tell she is trying.

"Let's leave off Peter," I say.

Her forehead creases and she looks up from her list. "Did something happen on the ski trip?"

Too quickly I say, "No. Nothing happened."

"Then why not? I want to get to know him better, Lara Jean."

"I think he might be going out of town too." I can tell Margot doesn't believe me, but she doesn't press me further.

She sends the evites out that night, and right away there are five yeses. In the comments section Aunt D. (not our real aunt, but one of Mommy's best friends) writes, *Margot, I can't wait to hear you and dad sing "Baby, It's Cold Outside!"* Another recital party tradition. Margot and Daddy sing "Baby, It's Cold Outside" and I am always commissioned to sing "Santa Baby." I used to do it lying on top of the piano with my mom's high heels on and our grandma's fox stole. Not this year. No way.

When Margot tries to get me to go with her and Kitty to deliver our cookie baskets to the neighbors the next day, I beg off and say I'm tired. I go up to my room to put the finishing touches on Margot's scrapbook and listen to only the slow songs from *Dirty Dancing*, and I keep checking my phone to see if Peter's texted again. He hasn't, but Josh has.

I heard what happened. Are you okay?

So even Josh knows? He's not even in our grade. Does the whole school know?

I write back, It isn't true, and he writes back, You don't have to tell me—I didn't believe it for a second, which makes me feel weepy.

He and Margot have hung out once since she's been home, but they haven't taken that DC trip Josh mentioned. It's probably for the best if I go ahead and take the Josh-and-Margot page out of the scrapbook.

I stay up late just in case Peter texts again. I think to myself, if Peter calls or texts me tonight, I'll know he's thinking about me too and maybe I'll forgive him. But he doesn't text or call.

Around three a.m. I throw away Peter's notes. I delete the picture of him from my phone; I delete his number. I think that if I just delete him enough, it will be like none of it ever happened and my heart won't hurt so badly.

67

CHRISTMAS MORNING, KITTY WAKES UP
everyone while it is still dark out, which is her tradition, and
Daddy makes waffles, which is his tradition. We only ever
eat waffles on Christmas, because we all agree it's too much
trouble to lug the waffle iron out and clean it and store it
back on the cabinet top shelf where we keep it. And anyway
it makes waffles more of a special occasion this way.

We take turns opening presents to make it last longer. I
give Margot her scarf, and the scrapbook, which she loves.
She pores over every page, exclaiming over my handiwork,
marveling over my font choices and paper scraps. Hugging
it to her chest, she says, "This is the perfect gift," and I feel
like all the tension and bad feelings between us evaporate
into nothingness. Margot's gift to me is a pale pink cashmere
sweater from Scotland. I try it on over my nightgown and it's
so soft and luxurious.

Kitty's present from Margot is an art set with oil pastels and
watercolors and special markers, which makes Kitty squeal
like a piglet. In return Kitty gives her socks with monkeys
on them. I give Kitty a new basket for her bike and the ant
farm she asked for months ago, and Kitty gives me a book
on knitting. "So you can get better," she says.

The three of us pitched in for Daddy's present—a thick

Scandinavian sweater that makes him look like an ice fisher-man. It's a little too big, but Daddy insists he likes it that way. He gives Margot a fancy new e-reader, Kitty a bike helmet with her name on it—Katherine, not Kitty—and me a gift certificate to Linden & White. "I wanted to get you that locket necklace you're always looking at, but it was gone," he says. "But I bet you'll find something else you like just as much." I jump up and throw my arms around him. I feel like I could cry.

Santa, aka Daddy, brings silly gifts like sacks of coal and water guns with disappearing ink inside, and also practical things like athletic socks and printer ink and my favorite kind of pens—I guess Santa shops at Costco too.

When we're done opening presents, I can tell Kitty is disappointed there is no puppy, but she doesn't say anything. I pull her into my arms and whisper to her, "There's always your birthday next month," and she nods.

Daddy goes to see if the waffle iron is hot and the doorbell rings. "Kitty, could you get that?" he calls from the kitchen.

Kitty goes to the door, and seconds later we hear her high-pitched scream. Margot and I leap up and run to the door, and right there on the welcome mat is a basket with a biscuit-colored puppy in it and a ribbon around its neck. We all start jumping up and down and screaming.

Kitty scoops the puppy up in her arms and runs into the living room with it, where Daddy stands grinning. "Daddy Daddy Daddy!" she squeals. "Thank you thank you thank you!"

According to Daddy, he picked the puppy up from the animal shelter two nights ago, and our neighbor Ms. Rothschild has been hiding him in her house. It's a boy, by the way—we figure that out pretty quick, since he pees all over the kitchen floor. He is a Wheaten Terrier mix, which Kitty declares is far better than an Akita or a German shepherd.

"I always wanted a dog with bangs," I say, cuddling him to my cheek.

"What should we name him?" Margot asks. We all look to Kitty, who chews on her bottom lip in a contemplative way.

"I don't know," she says.

"How about Sandy?" I suggest.

Kitty sneers. "Unoriginal."

So I say, "What about François? We can call him Frankie for short."

"No thanks," Kitty says. Cocking her head, she says, "What about Jamie?"

"Jamie," Daddy repeats. "I like it."

Margot nods. "It has a nice ring to it."

"What's his full name?" I ask, setting him down on the floor.

Kitty promptly says, "Jamie Fox-Pickle, but we'll only call him that when he's in trouble." She claps her hands and coos, "Come here, Jamie!" and he skitters over to her, tail wagging like mad.

I've never her seen her so happy or so patient. She spends all of Christmas Day trying to teach him tricks and taking him outside to pee. Her eyes never stop shining. It makes me wish I was little again and everything could be solved with a Christmas Day puppy.

I only check my phone once to see if Peter called. And he didn't.

68

THE MORNING OF THE PARTY I COME DOWN-
stairs after ten, and they've been working for hours. Margot's
the head chef and Daddy's her sous-chef. She has him chop-
ping onions and celery and washing pots. To us she says,
"Lara Jean, I need you to clean the downstairs bathroom and
mop and tidy. Kitty, you're overseeing decorations."

"Can we at least have some cereal first?" I ask.

"Yes, but be quick about it." She goes back to scooping
cookie dough.

To Kitty I whisper, "I didn't even want to have this party
and now she's got me scrubbing the toilet. Why do you get
the good job?"

"Because I'm the littlest," Kitty says, climbing onto a stool
at the breakfast bar.

Margot spins around and says, "Hello, the toilet needed to
be scrubbed anyway! Besides, it'll all be worth it. We haven't
done recital party in so long." She slides a cookie sheet into
the oven. "Daddy, I'm going to need you to make a run to
the store soon. We're out of sour cream and we need a big
bag of ice."

"Aye, aye, Captain," our dad says.

The only one of us Margot doesn't put to work is Jamie
Fox-Pickle, who is taking a nap under the Christmas tree.

I'm wearing a red-and-green plaid bow tie with a white button-down and a tartan skirt. I read on a fashion blog that mixing plaids is a thing. I go to Kitty's room to beg her to give me a braid crown, and she curls her lip at me and says, "That's not very sexy."

I frown. "Excuse me? I wasn't trying to look sexy! I was trying to look festive."

"Well . . . you look like you're a Scottish waiter, or maybe a bartender at a bar in Brooklyn."

"What do you know about bartenders in Brooklyn, Katherine?" I demand.

She gives me a withering look. "Duh, I watch HBO."

Hmm. We might need to put some parental controls on the TV.

Kitty goes to my closet and pulls out my red off-the-shoulder knit dress with the swishy skirt. "Wear this. It's still Christmasy but less elf-costumey."

"Fine, but I'm putting my candy-cane pin on it."

"Fine, you can wear the pin. But leave your hair down. No braid." I give her my best sad pouty face, but Kitty shakes her head. "I'll curl the ends to give it some body, but no braids of any kind."

I plug in the curling iron and sit on the floor with Jamie in my lap, and Kitty sits on the bed and sections my hair off. She wraps my hair around the barrel like a real pro. "Did Josh RSVP yes to the party?" she asks me.

"I'm not sure," I say.

"What about Peter?"

"He's not coming," I say.

"Why not?"

"He just can't," I tell her.

Margot's at the piano playing "Blue Christmas," and our old piano teacher Mr. Choi is sitting next to her singing along. Across the room, Daddy's showing off a new cactus to the Shahs from down the street, and Kitty and Josh and a few of the other little kids are trying to teach Jamie how to sit. I'm sipping cranberry-and-ginger-ale punch and talking to Aunt D. about her divorce when Peter Kavinsky walks in wearing a hunter-green sweater with a button-down shirt underneath, carrying a Christmas tin. I almost choke on my punch.

Kitty spots him when I do. "You came!" she cries. She runs right into his arms, and he puts down the cookie tin and picks her up and throws her around. When he sets her down, she takes him by the hand and over to the buffet table, where I'm busying myself rearranging the cookie plate.

"Look what Peter brought," she says, pushing him forward.

He hands me the cookie tin. "Here. Fruitcake cookies my mom made."

"What are you doing here?" I whisper accusingly.

"The kid invited me." He jerks his head toward Kitty, who has conveniently run back over to the puppy. Josh is standing up now, looking over at us with a frown on his face. "We need to talk."

So now he wants to talk. Well, too late. "We don't have anything to talk about."

Peter takes me by the elbow and I try to shake him off, but he won't let go. He steers me into the kitchen. "I want you to make up an excuse to Kitty and leave," I say. "And you can take your fruitcake cookies with you."

"First tell me why you're so pissed at me."

"Because!" I burst out. "Everyone is saying how we had sex in the hot tub and I'm a slut and you don't even care!"

"I told the guys we didn't!"

"Did you? Did you tell them that all we did was kiss and that's all we've ever done?" Peter hesitates, and I go on. "Or did you say, 'Guys, we didn't have sex in the hot tub,' wink wink, nudge nudge."

Peter glares at me. "Give me a little more credit than that, Covey."

"You're such a scumbag, Kavinsky."

I spin around. There is Josh, in the doorway, glaring at Peter.

"It's your fault people are saying that crap about Lara Jean." Josh shakes his head in disgust. "She'd never do that."

"Keep your voice down," I whisper, my eyes darting around. This is not happening right now. At recital party, with everyone I've ever known my whole entire life in the next room.

Peter's jaw twitches. "This is a private conversation, Josh, between me and my girlfriend. Why don't you go play World of Warcraft or something. Or maybe there's a Lord of the Rings marathon on TV."

"Fuck you, Kavinsky," Josh says. I gasp. To me Josh says, "Lara Jean, this is exactly what I've been trying to protect you from. He's not good enough for you. He's only bringing you down."

Beside me Peter stiffens. "Get over it! She doesn't like you anymore. It's over. Move on."

"You have no idea what you're talking about," Josh says.

"Whatever, dude. She told me you tried to kiss her. You try that again, and I'm kicking your ass."

Josh lets out a short laugh. "Go ahead."

Panic rises in my chest as Peter moves toward Josh with purpose. I pull Peter's arm back. "Stop it!"

That's when I see her. Margot, standing a few feet behind Josh, her hand to her mouth. The piano music has stopped, the world has stopped spinning, because Margot has heard everything.

"It's not true, is it? Please tell me it's not true."

I open and close my mouth. I don't have to say anything, because she already knows. Margot who knows me so well.

"How *could* you?" she asks, and her voice trembles. The hurt in her eyes makes me want to die. I've never seen that look in her eyes before.

"Margot," Josh begins, and she shakes her head and backs away.

"Get out," she says, her voice breaking. Then she looks at me. "You're my *sister*. You're the person I trust more than anybody."

"Gogo, wait—" But she's already gone. I hear her feet run up the stairs. I hear her door shut and not slam.

And then I burst into tears.

"I'm so sorry," Josh says to me. Bleakly, he says, "This is all my fault." He walks out the back door.

Peter moves to put his arms around me, but I stop him. "Can you just . . . can you just go?"

Hurt and surprise register on his face. "Sure, I can go," he says, and he walks out of the kitchen.

I go to the bathroom off the side of the kitchen and sit on the toilet and cry. Someone knocks and I stop crying and call out, "Just a minute."

Mrs. Shah's cheery voice says, "Sorry, dear!" and I hear her heels clack away.

Then I get up and splash cold water on my face. My eyes are still red and puffy. I run water over a hand towel and I wet my face with it. My mom used to do this for me when I was sick. She'd put an ice-cold washcloth over my forehead and she'd switch it out with a fresh one when it wasn't cold anymore. I wish my mom was here.

When I step back into the party, Mr. Choi is sitting at the piano playing "Have Yourself a Merry Little Christmas," and Ms. Rothschild has my dad cornered on the couch. She's throwing back champagne, and he has a mildly startled look on his face. As soon he sees me, my dad jumps off the couch and over to me. "Oh, thank God," he says. "Where's Gogo? We haven't done our number yet."

"She doesn't feel well," I say.

"Hm. I'll go check on her."

"I think she just wants to be left alone."

Daddy's forehead creases. "Did she and Josh have a fight? I just saw him leave."

I swallow. "Maybe. I'll go talk to her."

He pats me on the shoulder. "You're a good sister, honey."

I force a smile. "Thank you, Daddy."

I go upstairs and Margot's bedroom door is locked. I stand outside it and ask, "Can I come inside?"

No answer.

"Please, Margot. Please just let me explain. . . ."

Still nothing.

"I'm sorry. Margot, I'm so sorry. Please talk to me."

I sit down outside my door and start to cry. My big sister knows how to hurt me best. Silence from her, being shut out by her, is the worst punishment she could conjure up.

69

BEFORE MOMMY DIED, MARGOT AND I WERE enemies. We battled constantly, mostly because I was always messing up something of hers—some game, some toy.

Margot had a doll she loved named Rochelle. Rochelle had silky auburn hair, and she wore glasses like Margot did. Mommy and Daddy had given her to her for her seventh birthday. Rochelle was Margot's only doll. She adored her. I remember begging Margot to let me hold her, just for a second, but Margot always said no. There was this one time, I had a cold, and I stayed home from school. I crept into Margot's room and I took Rochelle, I played with her all afternoon, I pretended Rochelle and I were best friends. I got it into my head that Rochelle's face was actually kind of plain; she would look better with lipstick on. It would be a favor to Margot if I made Rochelle more beautiful. I got one of Mommy's lipsticks out of her bathroom drawer and I put some on her lips. Right away I knew it was a mistake. I'd drawn it on outside of her lip lines, she looked clownish, not sophisticated. So then I tried to clean off the lipstick with toothpaste, but it only made her look like she had a mouth disease. I hid under my blankets until Margot came home. When she found the state Rochelle was in, I heard Margot's scream.

After Mommy died, we all had to realign ourselves. Everybody had new roles. Margot and I were no longer locked in battle, because we both understood that Kitty was ours to take care of now. "Look out for your sister," Mommy was always saying. When she was alive, we did it begrudgingly. After she was gone, we did it because we wanted to.

Days go by and still nothing. She looks through me, speaks to me only when necessary. Kitty watches us with worried eyes. Daddy is bewildered and asks what's going on with us, but doesn't push me for an answer.

There is a wall between us now, and I can feel her moving farther and farther away from me. Sisters are supposed to fight and make up, because they are sisters and sisters always find their way back to each other. But the thing that scares me is that maybe we won't.

70

OUTSIDE MY WINDOW, SNOW IS FALLING IN clumps that look like cotton. The yard is starting to look like a cotton field. I hope it snows all day and all night. I hope it's a blizzard.

There's a knock at my door.

I lift my head up from my pillow. "Come in."

My dad comes in and sits down at my desk. "So," he says, scratching his chin the way he does when he's uncomfortable. "We need to talk."

My stomach drops. I sit up and wrap my arms around my knees. "Did Margot tell you?"

My dad clears his throat. "She did." I can't even look at him. "This is awkward. I never had to do this with Margot, so . . ." He clears his throat again. "You'd think I would be better at this since I'm a health professional. I'll just say that I think you're too young to be having sex, Lara Jean. I don't think you're ready yet." He sounds like he's about to cry. "Did . . . did Peter pressure you in any way?"

I can feel all the blood rush to my face. "Daddy, we didn't have sex."

He nods, but I don't think he believes me. "I'm your dad, so of course I'd rather you wait until you're fifty, but . . ." He clears his throat again. "I want you to be safe. I'm making an appointment with Dr. Hudecz on Monday."

I start to cry. "I don't need an appointment, because I'm not doing anything! I didn't have sex! Not in the hot tub or anyplace. Somebody made the whole thing up. You have to believe me."

My dad has a pained expression on his face. "Lara Jean, I know it's not easy to talk about this with a dad and not a mom. I wish your mom was here to navigate us through this."

"I wish she was too, because she'd believe me." Tears are running down my cheeks. It's bad enough for strangers to think the worst of me, but I never thought my sister and dad would believe it.

"I'm sorry." My dad puts his arms around me. "I'm sorry. I do believe you. If you tell me you're not having sex, you're not having sex. I just don't want you to grow up too fast. When I look at you, you're still as young as Kitty to me. You're my little girl, Lara Jean."

I sag against him. There's no place safer than my dad's arms. "Everything's a mess. You don't trust me anymore; Peter and I are broken up; Margot hates me."

"I trust you. Of course I trust you. And of course you and Margot will make up like you always do. She was only worried about you; that's why she came to me." No, it's not. She did it out of spite. It's her fault that Daddy thought that of me for even a second.

Daddy lifts my chin and wipes the tears off my face. "You must really like Peter, huh?"

"No," I sob. "Maybe. I don't know."

He tucks my hair behind my ears. "Everything will work out."

There is a specific kind of fight you can only have with your sister. It's the kind where you say things you can't take back. You say them because you can't help but say them, because you're so angry it's coming up your throat and out your eyes; you're so angry you can't see straight. All you see is blood.

As soon as Daddy leaves and I hear him go to his room to get ready for bed, I barge into Margot's room without knocking. Margot is at her desk on her laptop. She looks up at me in surprise.

Wiping my eyes, I say, "You can be mad at me all you want, but you had no right to go to Daddy behind my back."

Her voice is piano-string tight as she says, "I didn't do that as revenge. I did it because you clearly have no idea what you're doing, and if you're not careful, you're going to end up some sad teenage statistic." Coldly, as if she is speaking to a stranger, Margot continues. "You've changed, Lara Jean. I honestly don't even know who you are anymore."

"No, you definitely don't know me anymore, if you think for one second that I would have sex on a school trip! In a hot tub, in plain view of anybody who might happen to walk by? You must not know me at all!" And then I lay it down, the card I've been holding against her. "Just because you had sex with Josh, that doesn't mean I'm going to have sex with Peter."

Margot sucks in her breath. *"Lower your voice."*

I feel happy that I've wounded her too. I yell, "Now that Daddy's already disappointed in me, he can't be disappointed in you, too, right?"

I whirl around to go back to my room, and Margot follows close behind me.

"Come back here!" she shouts.

"No!" I try to close my door in her face, but she wedges her foot inside. "Get out!"

I lean my back against the door, but Margot is stronger than me. She pushes her way in and locks the door behind her.

She advances toward me and I back away from her. There's a dangerous light in her eyes. She's the righteous one now. I can feel myself start to shrink, to cower. "How did you know Josh and I had sex, Lara Jean? Did he tell you that himself while you two were going behind my back?"

"We never went behind your back! It wasn't like that."

"Then what was it like?" she demands.

A sob escapes my throat. "I liked him first. I liked him all that summer before ninth grade. I thought . . . thought he liked me back. But then one day you said you were dating, and so I just, I just swallowed it. I wrote him a good-bye letter."

Margot's face twists into a sneer. "Do you seriously expect me to feel sorry for you now?"

"No. I'm just trying to explain what happened. I stopped liking him, I swear I did. I didn't think of him like that again, but then, after you left, I realized that deep down I still had feelings for him. And then my letter got sent and Josh found out, so I started pretend dating Peter—"

She shakes her head. "Just stop. I don't want to hear it. I don't even know what you're talking about right now."

"Josh and I only kissed one time. *Once*. And it was a huge mistake, and I didn't even want to do it in the first place! You're the one he loves, not me."

She says, "How can I believe anything you ever say to me now?"

"Because it's the truth." Trembling, I tell her, "You have no idea the power you have over me. How much your opinion means to me. How much I look up to you."

Margot's face screws up like a fist; she is holding back tears. "You know what Mommy would always say to me?" She lifts her chin higher. "'Take care of your sisters.' So that's what I did. I've always tried to put you and Kitty first. Do you have any idea how hard it was being so far away from you guys? How lonely it was? All I wanted to do was come back home, but I couldn't, because I have to be strong. I have to be"—she struggles for a breath—"the good example. I can't be weak. I have to show you guys how to be brave. Because . . . because Mommy isn't here to do it."

Tears roll down my cheeks. "I know. You don't have to tell me, Gogo. I know how much you do for us."

"But then I left, and it's like you didn't need me as much as I thought." Her voice breaks. "You were fine without me."

"Only because you taught me everything!" I cry out.

Margot's face crumbles.

"I'm sorry," I weep. "I'm so sorry."

"I *needed* you, Lara Jean."

She takes one step toward me and I take one toward her, and we fall into each other's arms, crying, and the relief I feel is immeasurable. We are sisters, and there's nothing she or I can ever say or do to change that.

Daddy knocks on the door. "Girls? Everything okay in there?"

We look at each other and together at the same time, we say, "We're fine, Daddy."

71

IT'S NEW YEAR'S EVE. NEW YEAR'S EVE HAS
always been a stay-at-home holiday for us. We make popcorn and drink sparkling cider, and at midnight we go outside to the backyard and light up sparklers.

Some of Margot's friends from high school are having a
party at a cabin in the mountains, and she said she wasn't
going to go, that she'd rather stay with us, but Kitty and I
made her. My hope is that Josh is going too, and that they'll
talk, and who knows what will happen. It's New Year's Eve,
after all. The night for new beginnings.

We sent Daddy to a party someone from the hospital is
throwing. Kitty ironed his favorite button-down shirt and
I picked the tie and we shoved him out the door. I think
Grandma is right; it's not good to be alone.

"Why are you still sad?" Kitty asks me as I dump popcorn
into a bowl for us. We're in the kitchen; she's sitting on a
stool at the breakfast bar with her legs dangling. The puppy
is curled up like a centipede under her stool, gazing up at
Kitty with hopeful eyes. "You and Margot made up. What's
to be sad about?"

I'm about to deny being sad, but then I just sigh and say,
"I don't know."

Kitty grabs a handful of popcorn and drops a few kernels on

the floor, which Jamie gobbles up. "How can you not know?"

"Because sometimes you just feel sad and you can't explain it."

Kitty cocks her head to the side. "PMS?"

I count the days since my last period. "No. It's not PMS. Just because a girl is sad, it doesn't mean it has anything to do with PMS."

"Then why?" she presses.

"I don't know! Maybe I miss someone."

"You miss Peter? Or Josh?"

I hesitate. "Peter." Despite everything, Peter.

"So call him."

"I can't."

"Why not?"

I don't know how to answer her. It's all so embarrassing, and I want to be someone she can look up to. But she's waiting, her little brow furrowed, and I know I have to tell her the truth. "Kitty, it was all fake. The whole thing. We were never really together. He never really liked me."

Kitty wrinkles. "What do you mean it was fake?"

Sighing, I say, "It all started with those letters. Remember how my hatbox went missing?" Kitty nods. "I had letters inside, letters I wrote to the boys I loved. They were supposed to be private, they were never supposed to be sent, but then somebody did, and everything turned into a mess. Josh got one, and Peter got one, and I was just so humiliated. . . . Peter and I decided to pretend to date so I could save face in front of Josh and he could make his ex-girlfriend jealous, and the whole thing just spun out of control."

Kitty is biting her lip nervously. "Lara Jean . . . if I tell you something, you have to promise not to be mad."

"What? Just tell me."

"First promise."

"Okay, I promise I won't be mad." Prickles are going up my spine.

In a rush Kitty says, "I'm the one who sent the letters."

"What?" I scream.

"You promised you wouldn't be mad!"

"What?" I scream again, but less loud. "Kitty, how could you do that to me?"

She hangs her head. "Because I was mad at you. You were teasing me about liking Josh; you said I was going to name my dog after him. I was so mad at you. So when you were sleeping . . . I snuck into your room and stole your hatbox and I read all your letters and then I sent them. I regretted it right away, but it was too late."

"How did you even know about my letters?" I yell.

She squints at me. "Because I go through your stuff sometimes when you're not at home."

I'm about to scream at her some more, and then I remember how I read Margot's letter from Josh and I bite my tongue. As calmly as I can, I say, "Do you even know how much trouble you've caused? How could you be so spiteful to me?"

"I'm sorry," she whispers. Fat teardrops form in the corners of her eyes, and one plops down like a raindrop.

I want to hug her, to comfort her, but I'm still so mad. "It's fine," I say in a voice that is the exact opposite of fine. None of this would have happened if she hadn't sent those letters.

Kitty jumps up and runs upstairs, and I think she's going to her room to cry in private. I know what I should do. I should go comfort her, forgive her for real. It's my turn to be the good example. To be the good big sister.

I'm about to go upstairs when she comes running back into the kitchen. With my hatbox in her arms.

72

WHEN IT WAS JUST MARGOT AND ME, MY mom used to buy two of everything, blue for Margot and pink for me. The same quilt, stuffed animal, or Easter basket in two different colors. Everything had to be fair; we had to have the exact same number of carrot sticks or french fries or marbles or erasers shaped like cupcakes. Except I was always losing my erasers or eating my carrot sticks too fast, and then I'd beg for just one of Margot's. Sometimes Mommy would make her share, which even then I realized wasn't fair, that obviously, Margot shouldn't be penalized for eating her snack slowly or keeping track of her erasers. After Kitty was born, Mommy tried to do blue, pink, and yellow, but it's just a lot harder finding one thing in three different colors. Also, Kitty was enough years younger than us that we didn't want the same kinds of toys as her.

The teal hatbox might be the only gift from Mommy I got that was just for me. I didn't have to share it; this one was mine and mine alone.

When I opened it, I expected to find a hat, maybe a straw hat with a floppy brim, or maybe a newsboy—but it was empty. "This is for your special things," she said. "You can put all your most precious, most favorite, most secret things in here."

"Like what?" I said.

"Whatever fits inside. Whatever you want to keep just for you."

Kitty's pointy little chin trembles, and she says, "I really am sorry, Lara Jean."

When I see that, the chin tremble, I can't be mad anymore. I just can't, not even a little bit. So I go to her, and I hug her tight. "It's all right," I say, and she sags against me in relief. "You can keep the box. Put all your secrets in it."

Kitty shakes her head. "No, it's yours. I don't want it." She thrusts it at me. "I put something in there for you."

I open the box, and there are notes. Notes and notes and notes. Peter's notes. Peter's notes I threw away.

"I found them when I was emptying your trash," she says. Hastily she adds, "I only read a couple. And then I saved them because I could tell they were important."

I touch one that Peter folded into an airplane. "Kitty . . . you know Peter and I aren't getting back together, right?"

Kitty grabs the bowl of popcorn and says, "Just read them." Then she goes into the living room and turns on the TV.

I close the hatbox and take it with me upstairs. When I am in my room, I sit on the floor and spread them out around me.

A lot of the notes just say things like *"Meet you at your locker after school"* and *"Can I borrow your chemistry notes from yesterday?"* I find the spiderweb one from Halloween, and it makes me smile. Another one says, *"Can you take the bus home today? I want to surprise Kitty and pick her up from school so she can show me and my car off to her friends." "Thanks for coming to the estate sale with me this weekend. You made the day fun. I owe you one." "Don't forget to pack a Korean yogurt for me!" "If you make Josh's dumb white-chocolate cranberry cookies and not my fruitcake ones, it's over."* I laugh out loud. And then, the one I read over and over: *"You look pretty today. I like you in blue."*

I've never gotten a love letter before. But reading these notes like this, one after the other, it feels like I have. It's like . . . it's like there's only ever been Peter. Like everyone else that came before him, they were all to prepare me for this. I think I see the difference now, between loving someone from afar and loving someone up close. When you see them up close, you see the real them, but they also get to see the real you. And Peter does. He sees me, and I see him.

Love is scary: it changes; it can go away. That's part of the risk. I don't want to be scared anymore. I want to be brave, like Margot. It's almost a new year, after all.

Close to midnight, I gather up Kitty and the puppy and the sparklers. We put on heavy coats and I make Kitty wear a hat. "Should we put a hat on Jamie too?" she asks me.

"He doesn't need one," I tell her. "He's already got on a fur coat."

The stars are out by the dozen; they look like faraway gems. We're so lucky to live by the mountains the way we do. You just feel closer to the stars. To heaven.

I light up sparklers for each of us, and Kitty starts dancing around the snow making a ring of fire with hers. She's trying to coax Jamie to jump through but he isn't having it. All he wants to do is pee around the yard. It's lucky we have a fence, or I bet he'd pee his way down this whole block.

Josh's bedroom light is on. I see him in the window just as he opens it and calls out, "Song girls!"

Kitty hollers, "Wanna light a sparkler?"

"Maybe next year," Josh calls back. I look up at him and wave my sparkler, and he smiles, and there's just this feeling of all rightness between us. One way or another, Josh will be in our lives. And I'm certain, I'm so suddenly certain that everything is exactly the way it's supposed to be, that I don't have to be so afraid of good-bye, because good-bye doesn't have to be forever.

When I'm back in my room in my flannel nightgown, I get out my special flowy pen and my good thick stationery, and I start to write. Not a good-bye letter. Just a plain old love letter.

Dear Peter . . .

Acknowledgments

To All My Literary Loves:

To Zareen Jaffery, fairest of them all. I think you and I might just be meant to be.

To Justin Chanda, for putting a ring on it.

To everyone at S&S and especially Paul Crichton, Lydia Finn, Sooji Kim, Chrissy Noh, Lucille Rettino, Nicole Russo, Anne Zafian for being my main squeeze(s). And hello there, Katy Hershberger, we're about to get to know each other very well.

To Lucy Cummins, I lay flowers and chocolate-covered hearts at your feet for all the beauty you bring to each book.

To Adele Griffin, Julie Farkas, and Bennett Madison—readers, writers, and friends—sonnets for you all. I'm so in awe of your talent and so honored to be your friend.

To Siobhan Vivian, my dearest, if there is such a thing as literary soul mates, you are mine.

And to Emily van Beek, for everything, always.

All of my love,

Jenny